THE *Killing* GAME

M.R. Henderson

ST. MARTIN'S PRESS/NEW YORK

St. Martin's Press titles are available at quantity discounts for sales promotions, premiums or fund raising. Special books or book excerpts can also be created to fit specific needs. For information write to special sales manager, St. Martin's Press, 175 Fifth Avenue, New York, N.Y. 10010.

THE KILLING GAME

Copyright © 1989 by M. R. Henderson.

All rights reserved. No part of this book may be used or reproduced in any manner whatsoever without written permission except in the case of brief quotations embodied in critical articles or reviews. For information address St. Martin's Press, 175 Fifth Avenue, New York, N.Y. 10010.

Library of Congress Catalog Card Number: 88-29806

ISBN: 0-312-92088-1   Can. ISBN: 0-312-92090-3

Printed in the United States of America

St. Martin's Press hardcover edition published 1989
First St. Martin's Press mass market edition/February 1990

10 9 8 7 6 5 4 3 2 1

APPLAUSE FOR THE SUSPENSE NOVELS OF M.R. HENDERSON

The Killing Game
"Genuinely suspenseful...Enough red herrings to have readers pinning the rap on half the book's characters."
—*Booklist*

"Murder on the downside of Hollywood ...Henderson works it well."
—*The Anniston Star* (AL)

If I Should Die
"Hooks you on page one and doesn't let you go. M. R. Henderson is a fine suspense writer."
—Mary Higgins Clark

"A suspense novel that truly stands out from the ordinary. M. R. Henderson's characters are real people, trapped by real terrors—and every reader will be trapped with them."
—Robert Bloch, author of *Psycho*

"As exciting a page-turner as I've read in a long while."
—Phyllis A. Whitney

By Reason Of
"From the beginning, this story grips the reader with its masterful narration, and the tension carries through the last, suspenseful pages."
—*Publishers Weekly*

"Keeps the reader riveted to the page. Scarifying and believable suspense."
—Thomas Chastain, author of *Nightscape*

*This book is dedicated to
three of the people who made it possible:
Jim, Jonathon, and Big Al.*

Evil is easy, and has infinite forms.

—Blaise Pascal, *Pensées*

PROLOGUE
†

The first Santa Ana winds of the season blew across the flats of West Hollywood with the intensity of a blast furnace, sweeping hot, dry air from the desert down through the basin. Papery eucalyptus leaves and palm fronds slithered sibilantly, and although the fluttering greenery gave an illusion of motion that might cool the sun-baked streets, the air was suffocatingly hot and almost too sharp to breathe.

He let himself into the apartment with the slender metal key he'd made from a piece of scrap steel. He'd experimented on other doors—in the studio, his own apartment, the gate to the complex—and the key worked perfectly. Actually the complex was so jerry-built, the doors could be opened with a strip of plastic or a credit card. He'd seen it done dozens of times in movies and television and tried it just for the hell of it. His first clumsy attempts on his own door failed, and all he had to show for them was a badly creased Visa card. After a while he learned exactly where and how to insert the card and apply leverage. The trouble was, a card didn't work on a lock with a dead-bolt bar like the one

Gretchen had installed, so he made the key. A lock pick actually. Something else he'd learned from a movie.

The drapes were closed, but the afternoon sun beating against them made the room an airless oven dotted with shabby rental furniture. The apartment was a dreary clone of dozens of other one-bedrooms that were popular with singles: a stopping place, a halfway house with movie posters tacked to the walls by starry-eyed youths with dreams of sugarplum-stardom in their heads and hope in their hearts. A place that those who made it could eventually look back upon with nostalgia made possible by escape. Those who didn't make it were more apt to remember it as a place where dreams and hope had thrived in better times.

He crossed the room and squatted in front of the television set. Turning it on, he studied the gray screen where dots of light skittered without forming a picture. He rotated the channel selector to check the other stations, shut off the set, then moved behind it. Using a screwdriver from the small kit he'd brought with him, he unfastened the back and lifted it off. His brow furrowed while he studied the circuit layout. Sweat beaded in his sideburns and trickled down his jaw, but he showed no other effects of the stifling heat. When he decided where the problem was, he worked quickly, reaching into the bowels of the set to disconnect the tuner. Sitting back on his heels, he examined the part and cleaned the contacts carefully. After making a final adjustment, he blew away any invisible specks of dust before he replaced it and unclipped the line cord so he could plug in the set. This time when he snapped it on, a game-show host and a woman in a garish, red-print dress mouthed words on the silent screen. He tested the volume, then checked the other channels. Satisfied, he turned it off and began to replace the back.

He was still on his knees behind the set when the door opened. For a moment his pulse raced, not with fear at being discovered in the apartment, but at the sight of Gretchen.

From the first time he'd seen her, she had had that effect on him. He'd watched her for several days before he made up his mind to talk to her. Much longer before he asked her out.

Her shoulder-length hair gleamed pink-gold in the sunlight haloing it. Her delicate, perfect features were the picture of innocence and purity. She was wearing a green sundress that left her shoulders exposed and brushed her knees above bare legs and flat-heeled sandals. She was carrying a large straw purse and a grocery bag from which a loaf of French bread rose like a flagpole. She pushed the door with her hip to slam it before she headed for the tiny kitchenette. He stayed very still, and she passed within three feet of the television set without seeing him.

He listened to her unpack the groceries, open cupboards, slam the refrigerator. Remembering to finish tightening the last screw on the back of the set, he got to his feet. When the air conditioner whirred suddenly, it took him a moment to recall that the thermostat was in the hall near the bedroom. He walked toward it with steps silent on the cheap gold carpeting.

Her back was half-turned to the open door, and she was tugging at the zipper of her dress. Her arm twisted awkwardly as she maneuvered the metal tab down. When it passed hip level, she wriggled out of top of the sundress. Her bare breasts hypnotized him. He wasn't aware of his sharply drawn breath until she whirled. Her face went pale under her golden tan, and she tried to cover herself.

"What are you doing here?" she demanded. When he stepped toward her, she backed away. "Get out! I told you I'm not going out with you. You've got some nerve walking in here! Get out right now or I'll scream."

"Don't yell," he said softly. He raised his hand in a calming gesture, and her gaze darted to the screwdriver he was still holding. She went a shade paler. "I fixed your TV," he said.

"You fixed my—? How did you get in?" Her gaze skittered to the door and came back nervously.

She was clutching the sundress to her chest, and the effect was tantalizing because her breasts were pushed upward like a show girl's in a skimpy costume. He had trouble concentrating on her voice because suddenly he was feeling a lot more than friendliness. He wanted her. He wanted her with a need that was a painful knot in his guts. He wanted her more than he ever had when he believed she wanted him. The idea filled him with heat that offset the icy air blowing from the noisy air conditioner. He took another step.

Gretchen backed away. Her gray eyes were wide as she struggled with anger and fear and tried to regain control. "Thanks," she said, and her voice cracked slightly. "You shouldn't have— That was—it was very thoughtful of you. I couldn't afford to get it fixed until I get a check." She managed a nervous smile and forced her gaze away from the screwdriver. "I've been dying to watch that new sitcom on NBC. My agent is sending me out on an audition next week—"

She bumped into the bed as he came toward her. The dress slipped from her fingers, and she fell backward as his knees pressed hers. He bent over her. Seeing the expression in his eyes, she opened her mouth to scream, but his hand clamped over it before any sound escaped.

"Don't scream," he told her again.

Fighting panic, she nodded, promising, resigning herself to whatever he wanted to do as long as she stayed alive.

But in the end her efforts were wasted. At the moment of his climax he was carried away by frenzy, and he plunged the screwdriver into her golden flesh just below the perfect, pale globe of her left breast. She died quietly, with a look of surprise in her gray eyes.

RESIDENTIAL RENTALS

Furnished/Unfurnished

Los Feliz. Pleasant 2 br w/patio, small, clean, quiet, security bldg, furn or unfurn. Carpet/drapes/laundry. No pets. Sec. deposit. 213-555-8888.

CHAPTER

I

✝

JEANNE FOUGHT DISAPPOINTMENT as she glanced through the doorway. Of all the rooms, she hoped the bedroom would be bright and cheerful. It wasn't. The bed and the dresser were discount-store specials, and the nightstand showed a cigarette burn not completely covered by an ugly wicker lamp. The quilted bedspread was a washed-out gray with monstrous cabbage roses. Vertical blinds and green drapes hung over a sliding glass door that led to a tiny, redwood patio edged with ragged ice plant and a few other spiny succulents. The late-afternoon sun spotlighted the rough fencing to expose its scars and weathering. The patio *was* a bonus. It needed a good cleaning, but flowers would brighten it. She could put in a bird feeder. Glenn might enjoy watching birds, and it would help to pass the time. She could buy a field guide so he could identify California species. In a no-pet building she wondered if she would be creating a fast-food diner for neighborhood cats if she coaxed birds to the small enclosure.

"The patio would be nice for Mr. Donovan when he can get out," the building manager said. Jeanne gave a start as if her thoughts somehow had been exposed. Crenshaw was a plump man with almost colorless blue eyes and soft, fleshy fingers. His expression had been disinterested when she explained about Glenn's being invalided because of the automobile accident.

"Yes, it would," she said, smiling. She shouldn't make snap judgments, but she didn't like Crenshaw. His pale gaze made her uneasy, even though it was his job to scrutinize prospective tenants. No Los Angeles neighborhood was immune from thieves or con artists who might gain entrance to buildings by pretending to be prospective renters.

She'd been apartment hunting for a week, and she still felt lost in the maze of unfamiliar streets. Several times when she checked out what seemed like ideal ads, she found herself in areas where she was afraid to get off the bus. Finally, at the studio, Terry Faust went through the want ads with her and circled those where she wouldn't have to worry about being mugged every time she went out. This place was the best she'd seen in the price range she'd set. Some apartments were larger and more modern, but the buildings were filled with singles and young couples who clustered around the pool and attended perpetual parties in the recreation rooms. Glenn would hate that, and right now she was eager to do anything she could to keep him happy.

This neighborhood was pleasant, with tree-lined streets and a half block of apartment houses bordering an area of older, well-kept homes. It was close to the bus line, so she could get back and forth to work easily. Unlike other places she'd looked at, the building was small, with only two floors and eight apartments. No rec room or pool. Definitely not the type swinging singles favored. And quiet enough so Glenn could rest comfortably. Trying to view the rooms through her husband's eyes, Jeanne could find fault with a lot of things, but most of them could be easily corrected: new bedspread and drapes, framed colorful posters on the wall—

"The entrance doors are kept locked. No one gets in or out without a key or someone buzzes 'em on the intercom." Crenshaw jingled coins in his pocket. His attitude clearly said he didn't understand her hesitation. Why would anyone in her right mind not recognize the value he was offering? "I have another couple coming to see it at six," he added. "I can't hold it without a deposit."

His prodding made her nervous, though she wasn't sure why. She'd dealt with enough landlords and apartment managers the past few days that she should be used to their high-handed attitudes. Maybe it was the touch of desperation she couldn't shake off. She couldn't bear the weekly-rental apartment near the hospital any longer. It was so depressing and noisy, she hated to go back—she couldn't call it home—at night. It was the least-expensive place she'd been able to find, but even so, the cost was eating into their savings at an alarming rate. The traveler's checks were gone, and she was dipping into the money they'd transferred from their bank in Minneapolis. More important, Glenn would be out of the hospital soon, and she had to be settled. She didn't want to give him any ammunition for a campaign to return to Minnesota.

Make a decision, she told herself. "Do you mind if I walk through again?"

Crenshaw shuffled to the front door and stood with his hand on the knob.

Jeanne glanced into the long, narrow bathroom with an arched, curtained shower stall, a pink bathtub, and the mismatched pedestal sink and toilet in green. The bathroom was only a few steps from the bed. Glenn would be able to make it on crutches. The second bedroom was closet sized, with a studio couch that Crenshaw claimed opened to a double bed. Not without moving out the dresser and the desk that stood against the opposite wall, she thought. It didn't matter. She'd sleep there only if Glenn was restless. As soon as he was well enough to be up and around more, he could use it as an office until he gained enough strength to go back to work. If the sound studio held the job for him.

Despair washed over her again. The great adventure had gone sour. It was almost as if the seeds of doubt Glenn had sown when she first told him of the fantastic job offer from Harvest Films had germinated and were stubbornly pushing through the hard earth of her determination. The Big Move, she'd dubbed it, laughing and making plans for the good life in California. Good-bye snow, good-bye hot, humid summers, good-bye Minnesota.

Not that she didn't like Minneapolis. They were both natives. They'd met doing graduate work at the university and dated four years while they established their careers. They were young, ambitious, and determined to reach the top. When they finally set the date for their wedding, Glenn was already an assistant engineer at WTC-TV and Jeanne was an assistant director at Talent Media, a company that produced commercials and industrial films. They settled into a pleasant life—a condo near Lake Harriet, two cars, season tickets at the Guthrie and Orchestra Hall. Jeanne was astonished but pleased when the offer came from Harvest Films in Los Angeles. Terry Faust, one of her graduate teachers who'd worked briefly with Talent Media before returning to the Coast, had recommended her as first assistant director for Harvest's upcoming production. He called urging her to take it.

"It'll be years until the Mini-apple can compete with Hollywood on feature films. You're good, Jeanne, and you deserve to be in on the ground floor of an outfit that's going places. This picture's going to be even bigger than *Death Pact*. Brad Raven made a name with that one picture. The trades have dubbed him Wonder Boy, and half this town would bleed for the chance to work with him. You're crazy if you pass up the offer. And," he added, "the heart of the record industry is right here in La-La Land. Glenn won't have any trouble hooking up with one of the top studios."

California was a nice place to visit, but at first Jeanne and Glenn weren't sure they wanted to live there. But they did want to be fair, and it was a wonderful excuse for a spring vacation from the slushy mess April had become in Minnesota. They flew out to convince themselves they'd never exchange their security for the golden promise of the Coast. To her astonishment, Jeanne loved California, and the offer turned out to be everything Terry predicted. It was a chance to be doing what she really wanted to do *now,* and more than that, it was a chance to use her creative talents in a way Minneapolis couldn't offer for years. *Death Pact,* which Harvest Films had produced last year, was a low-budget film that had become a cult favorite and made huge profits at the box office. Harvest was a company on the way up. She was so excited, it had been easy to overlook the vague signs of dissatisfaction Glenn displayed. The questions he raised could have been honest probing: the high cost of living versus salary . . . commuting problems . . . smog . . .

They stayed a week, sampling the beaches, enjoying the excitement of being tourists in Hollywood and Beverly Hills. Glenn visited several sound studios, almost indifferently, to check out job possibilities. To Jeanne's delight, he was offered a challenging position by Newell Audio, a midsize company of young, ambitious music recorders. The salary was good, though not quite as big a leap as Jeanne was making. She had to fight the feeling that Glenn's hesitation stemmed from jealousy more than any concrete objections to the move. They had always talked openly, discussing the pros and cons, being fair, even bending over backward to allow each other room to grow, but now so much seemed unsaid. Glenn's job at the television station was good, but its future was limited. Los Angeles held much more promise for him as well as Jeanne.

If he hadn't really wanted to come, he should have said it then, she told herself. But he had agreed to the move, and they'd drunk champagne to celebrate the shining future.

The accident on the freeway changed everything. An elderly man in a pickup hauling a trailer swerved out of his lane without warning. The horrible crash had left her untouched except for scrapes and bruises and a cut on the temple, but it left Glenn with a concussion, a badly cut arm, a broken leg, and four cracked vertebrae. But alive, thank God! For a week she'd sat at his bedside waiting and praying. Her sister Caroline flew out to be with her and stayed until Glenn was out of danger. Then Caroline returned to her family, and Jeanne started her new job at Harvest Films.

At first Glenn was in a lot of pain and was depressed much of the time. He complained frequently and indiscriminately—about his discomfort, the nursing staff, the incompetence of the doctors, and about the god-awful Los Angeles freeway system that had created the situation for the accident in the first place. Jeanne tried to be tolerant, but the sharp edge in his voice grated on her nerves, and she began to detect strains of self-pity in much of what he said. And although she fought it, she heard his resentment, and she reacted with resentment of her own. He was angry because she was moving faster than he was, angry because she already had the opportunity they both wanted. He had agreed to the move out of a sense of obligation, she was sure, and now she suspected he was trying to sabotage her chance for success.

Unfair! her conscience screamed. Glenn wasn't used to being an invalid. Neither of them had been sick with anything more serious than a cold since they'd known each other. She'd probably be foul-tempered too if their positions were reversed. So she held her tongue and tried to cheer him up with flowers and books and as many phone calls as she could fit into her working day.

In spare minutes between work and the time she spent

at the hospital, she began exploring the city in search of an apartment. Later, when they were sure where they wanted to locate permanently, they'd invest in a house. When they could afford it, she thought. With only one salary coming in, the rent here was all they could manage right now without touching the money from the sale of their condo. *That* was their down payment on a house.

"It's ten to six," Crenshaw said, swinging the open door.

Jeanne took another hurried peek at the old-fashioned, narrow kitchen. The stove was decent, and there were plenty of cupboards. The eating space near the window was just large enough for an ice cream parlor table and two chairs.

The living room wasn't big. Its outside wall angled as the building narrowed toward the rear of the triangular lot. It gave the rooms a peculiar charm despite the fact it cut down floor space. The living room had a fake-beam ceiling, a fake fireplace, and two casement windows that were fitted with shiny brass dead bolts as well as the original painted-over latches. The furniture was practical and in decent condition. The unimaginative colors could be disguised with throws and pillows, and when she began a new collection of plants, she was sure the room would take on a cheerful atmosphere. It *was* the best apartment she'd seen for the money, she couldn't argue that.

"I'll take it," she said, making up her mind before any new qualms set in. Crenshaw nodded as though he hadn't ever doubted it. "I'll write a check for the deposit," she told him.

CHAPTER
2
✝

THE STREETLIGHTS OOZED cloudy pools in the darkness. Music and voices drifted faintly from bright squares of apartment windows. The breeze that usually swept in from the Pacific was a sluggish current stirring the heat and forcing air conditioners into twenty-four-hour duty for the third consecutive night. It was the kind of weather that kept Southern Californians on the beach long after dark and made movie theaters, shopping malls, and bars cool islands of escape.

He blanked the heat from his mind and ignored the sweat that dampened his shirt. He walked slowly, hands shoved in the pockets of his worn jeans, his fingers curling and uncurling restlessly as he touched coins, keys, and other objects. Each time he felt the knife, it sent a shiver through him like the chill of a sudden wind.

The weapon was his, conceived and crafted with the patience of a suitor winning the woman of his dreams. It was a masterpiece, unique and more beautiful than a canvas hung in a museum. No engraved silver, no mother-of-pearl inlays, no flashy colors. A plain black grip with a steel release button in the hilt and a special cap to cover the needle-sharp point.

He'd made it after he killed Gretchen, when the memory of the steel screwdriver piercing her flesh still throbbed in his mind and body like an erotic dream. Made it with loving care and with the need to prolong the ecstasy of those final moments with her.

He ran his finger lightly over the button, savoring the memory of sound imprinted on his mind: the click of the blade snapping out. It was like a spectacular special effect in a movie, a contributing bonus to what was already a magnificent production. That, and the way the light glinted on the blade that sprang out. He touched the button very gently now to assure himself of its hidden power.

With the knife in his pocket he felt the thrill of knowing the strong, case-hardened steel blade was at his fingertip. It was his equalizer on the dark streets of the city, his armor if some rotten punk tried to mug him for a few bucks to nurse a filthy drug habit. His answer to the hip-swinging whores like Gretchen who tried to entice every guy who came along, offering lush promises while one hand reached for his crotch and the other for his wallet. These days an honest citizen needed a little power on his side.

He crossed a street and glanced toward the traffic and lights on Vermont Avenue. Maybe he should take in a movie. It would be cool inside the theater. Five bucks was a lot of money to be comfortable for a few hours when he had to come back out into the staggering heat, but he was too restless to go home.

He hesitated as he saw a couple come around the corner and head toward him, weaving slightly. The woman was wearing a miniskirt and red, high-heeled sandals with straps that crisscrossed her bare ankles. Her bleached hair took on a red glow from the traffic light on the corner. Hanging from a strap over her shoulder, a small purse bounced on her hip as she walked with the unmistakable suggestive stride of a hooker. She clung to the man's arm. Her laughter was rich and throaty when he put his hand to the low-cut neckline of her blouse. She pushed him away playfully and said something in a soft murmur. The guy grabbed again, but she drew back and held him at arm's length.

"The twenty first." Her voice floated down the quiet street like the throb of perfectly tuned engine.

The man staggered back and reached into his pocket. Then as if he'd thought better of it, he lunged suddenly, bumping into her so she fell against the fender of a car parked at the curb. Cursing, she swung at him with the brick-sized purse. He let out a yelp, ducked, then clamped his hand over her mouth as he sprawled on her eagerly, tugging at her clothes in a drunken, lustful frenzy. She ducked her head and bit his arm hard enough to make him pull away swearing, but he did it without letting go of her blouse, which ripped. Cursing, she tried to shove off his weight. Over the faint noise of the traffic on Vermont, running footsteps thumped on the pavement. The woman looked up, and in that moment she was distracted, the drunk swung wildly and landed a beefy fist on the side of her head. She fell back with a stunned gasp of pain. The man sprawled over her, pawing at his fly.

The runner reached them then and grabbed the drunk by the arm, yanking him from the woman and spinning him around. In almost the same motion, he punched the cheap bastard in the gut. With a grunt, the big slob folded like the windbag he was.

Still heaving for breath, the woman tugged at the edges of her torn blouse as she struggled up from the fender. She rubbed her head and winced. Brushing back her teased hair, she smiled at her rescuer and smoothed the satiny skirt that barely brushed her thighs.

"Thanks, mister. I don't know what you hit him with, but you did me a big favor."

He didn't answer. It happened so fast, he had acted

instinctively, as if he were following a script. As in a film scene, he expected an off-stage voice to yell, "Cut!" and the actor to jump up, but the guy was out cold.

He looked at the woman. Even in the deep shadows under the trees he could see the white flesh exposed where her blouse was torn. She was holding the edges of the cloth so her naked breasts were framed rather than covered, like a stripper playing with a curtain. He forced his gaze away from the breasts when she spoke.

"I should lift fifty from his wallet, the creep. Look at this blouse! Now I gotta go home and change." She spread the ripped edges, then made a feeble pretense at covering herself again. With a sultry glance she gave him an inviting smile. "Why am I sounding off at you? I don't know what I'd of done if you hadn't come along. Thanks, I really mean it."

The smile might have looked genuine if she wasn't standing there half-naked like a slut. "That's okay," he said. "I'm glad I was here."

"Yeah, me too." Letting go of the edges of the blouse, she started to turn away very slowly.

"Hey—"

She glanced back.

"If you want, I can give you a ride home. My car's around the corner. I mean, there are a lot of creeps out there, and with your blouse . . ."

She smiled provocatively. "I'd love a ride." She slipped her arm through his and pressed her breasts against his biceps as she fell in step beside him. They turned away from the lights of the busy avenue and headed down the dark street.

CHAPTER 3
✝

JEANNE'S PINK SHIRTWAIST clung to her damp skin as she juggled the armload of packages and her purse to unlock the front door of the apartment building. Pushing it open with her hip, she eased into the foyer, relieved to have gotten home from the bus stop without dropping anything. It was ridiculous to be without a car. The check from the insurance company had come a few days ago, but Glenn insisted on waiting until he was well enough to shop for a new one. She hadn't had the energy to argue then, but now she was determined to bring up the subject again. When she was living close to the hospital it wasn't so bad, but now the bus ride home every night took an hour and a half, and shopping was a miserable chore.

She glanced at the row of mailboxes and saw a white envelope pressed behind the cut-out design of the one marked 104. The first mail since she had moved into the apartment! Readjusting her burdens, she sorted through the keys on her chain to find the small flat one that opened the mailbox. Her spirits sagged like a deflated balloon when she saw the envelope addressed to "Occupant." Not exactly a day brightener. Realistically, it was too soon to expect mail. She'd been in the apartment three days, and the only people who had the address and phone number other than Glenn and the studio were her sister and Glenn's father back home. Both had promised to pass them on, but even if someone was inspired to write immediately, there hadn't been time for mail to cross the country.

Behind her, the outside door opened and a plump, round-faced woman came in. She was middle-aged, with softly waved, champagne-colored hair and thickly applied makeup. She hugged a straw purse to the bosom of her cotton print dress as the iron-grillwork-over-glass door shut behind her.

"Oh, you startled me," she said in a chirpy voice. She blinked rapidly as she freed a hand to rattle the doorknob and make sure the latch caught.

Jeanne summoned a smile. "I'm Jeanne Donovan. I just moved into 104."

"Oh, yes. How's your poor husband?"

It was Jeanne's turn to be startled. How did the woman know about Glenn? The building manager, of course. Crenshaw probably had contact with all the tenants from time to time. She supposed it was natural for him to talk about a new tenant.

"He's coming along fine," Jeanne said.

"That's good. I'm Mrs. Saidlow. My husband and I are in 201." She pointed a plump finger toward the ceiling as she walked to the mailboxes and peered into one. Unlocking it, she pulled out a stack of letters and circulars. "Are you getting settled?"

"A little. I really haven't had time to do much." Jeanne shifted her packages.

Mrs. Saidlow moved toward the carpeted stairs that led to the upper floor. "If there's anything I can do . . ." She let the perfunctory offer drift.

13

"Thanks," Jeanne said with another polite smile. As the woman climbed the stairs, Jeanne went down the dim hall. The lights weren't on yet. Crenshaw didn't turn them on until the last daylight faded and deep shadows crowded the corridor. With dark carpeting and beige walls, the hall was perpetually dim. The foyer garnered light from the glass door and the narrow, translucent side-windows that flanked it. At the far end of the hall, a fanlight over the rear door cast a small patch of sunlight near the back stairway. The only other illumination came from two low-wattage ceiling fixtures—when they were turned on.

Apartment 104 was halfway down the hall. Jeanne had to put down her packages and finger the keys and the locks to undo the Yale and the dead bolt. Swinging the door open, she bent to retrieve her bundles, then muttered with annoyance as one of the bags ripped. When she tried to scoop it up before it gave way, a hand shot out to grab the bag as it tore again.

Jeanne straightened with a start. She hadn't seen or heard anyone, but a young man was standing beside her. In the light spilling through the doorway from the apartment, she could see that he was medium height, with a thin face and deep-set eyes, and collar-length hair that was neither blond nor brown but a muddy shade between.

"Let me help you," he said, stepping toward the open door. Jeanne retreated into the living room as he carried the torn bag carefully, and set it on the sofa. With two long strides he retrieved the other packages from the hall and brought them in. "I'm Mark Bonner, 102." He smiled, and his face, which had seemed all angles and hollows, smoothed pleasantly. He put out his hand.

Jeanne shook it. "Thank you, Mr. Bonner—"

"It's Mark, please."

"Mark. Thanks. I guess I got carried away and bought

more than I could carry. I was in trouble as soon as I got off the bus."

"You don't have a car?" He sounded astonished.

Jeanne laughed at his incredulous expression. "Not at the moment. It was totaled in an accident."

His face sobered instantly. "Oh, sure—I heard your husband was in the hospital. I should have realized about the car. How's he doing?"

"Fine. He's coming home soon." She glanced around. "That's why I'm trying to get the apartment in shape."

Mark looked around the living room. Jeanne had taken down the nondescript drapes and left the frosted-glass casement windows unadorned. She'd hung a framed Schiffert poster and two colorful prints from a small gallery on Beverly Boulevard. A bright-colored Guatemalan throw covered the drab armchair. The welded iron statue of an African warrior, which she and Glenn had laughing dubbed "Elmer," and which had miraculously survived the crash with only a bent spear, stood on the mantel above the fake fireplace.

"You've done wonders," he said in genuine admiration. "Our building manager's taste runs to Salvation Army Renaissance."

Jeanne laughed. "It did need brightening. That's why I keep loading myself down like a pack mule. Thanks again for the help."

He moved toward the door. "I have a friend who can get you a decent used car. You can always trade it in on something better when you're ready. I assume the insurance company is paying off?"

"Yes." She answered automatically, too surprised to be offended by his inquisitiveness.

"No one survives in Los Angeles without a car. You'll get sick of RTD in a hurry. Think about it."

"Thanks, I will." He was absolutely right. It was one

thing for Glenn to want to choose their new car, but she was the one enduring the inconvenience. She was already sick of rushing to catch buses and having to limit her shopping to how much she could carry.

"If there's anything I can do, don't be afraid to ask. I'm around most days. I work nights and don't leave until late. I'm not an expert with tools, but I can hammer a nail, and I'm a lot easier to pin down than the elusive Harry Crenshaw." Grinning, he flipped her a friendly salute, then shoved his hands in the pockets of his jeans and walked down the hall.

Jeanne closed and locked the door. The building wasn't air-conditioned, but the thick walls and the high ceilings kept the apartment fairly cool. The building next door, separated by a walkway, was less than ten feet away, and it cut off direct sunlight except in the late afternoon to the patio. But the apartment got stuffy shut up all day. She went through it opening windows. According to the newspapers, the second Santa Ana of the season was threatening to break records. She'd tried to buy a fan at the department stores in Beverly Center, but their stocks were exhausted because of the heat wave. Without a car it was impossible to canvass drug and discount stores.

She thought about Mark Bonner's unexpected and generous offer. Glenn always chose their cars and kept them running because he was clever with anything mechanical or electronic. But right now he wouldn't be able to drive or even shop for a car for weeks. Mark's offer might be a godsend. If he really could get them a good deal, it would make life much easier for her now, and as Mark said, Glenn could pick out something else later if he wanted to. Or maybe they could keep the car. They'd probably need two when Glenn went back to work.

Returning to the living room, she unpacked her purchases and carried the Melitta coffee maker and a pound of freshly roasted Costa Rican beans to the kitchen. The dented aluminum percolator she'd unearthed in a cupboard made such horrible brew, she'd gone without this morning, opting instead for a cup of tea made on the hot plate of the lounge at the studio. Her electric coffee grinder was among the few things that had survived the accident. Most of the boxes in the trunk and the backseat had either been smashed open and scattered or saturated with gasoline from the ruptured tank. Dry cleaning had salvaged clothes and linens, but small appliances, pictures, and glassware had been a total loss. Thank heaven they'd put their furniture in storage instead of loading it into a U-Haul and bringing it out with them. She missed the familiar pieces they had collected over four years of marriage, but at least they were not gone forever.

En route to the bedroom she collected the padded hangers and drawer lining paper she'd bought. She'd stayed at the hospital only an hour so she'd have time to get things done. Glenn pouted when she said she had to leave, and Jeanne resented it. She knew he looked forward to her visits, but he didn't realize how much time they cut from her days. Even when she promised to stay longer tomorrow, he didn't snap out of his gloom. As she gathered her purse and briefcase, his joke that he was going to call every half hour to make sure she wasn't out dancing irked her and Jeanne's voice was sharp when she countered that maybe she'd slip back to catch him chasing pretty nurses down the hall. The uncomfortable moment passed, but there was a touch of sullenness in his kiss when she left.

She sighed wearily. Glenn wasn't used to inactivity. His nerves were frazzled by pain, worry, and impatience. The weeks he'd been laid up seemed more like months. They'd both be under a lot less stress when he got home. Once he was able to go back to work, his natural enthusiasm for life would return and he'd like California as much as she did.

She dropped the hangers and lining paper on the studio

couch in the den en route to the bedroom. Pulling the cord that turned on the bare-bulb ceiling light to illuminate the narrow, tapering closet, she thought again how lucky it was they'd left some of their clothes at Caroline's to be sent on later. The closet was already crammed with things that had been rescued from the suitcases. She planned to move as many of her clothes as possible into the miniscule closet in the den, which she had scrubbed down thoroughly last night. This closet at the end of the room was too dark to see without the light, and if she turned it on, it might wake Glenn if he was resting. Determined, she gathered an armload of skirts and blouses.

As she came out of the closet, a shadow moved across the tiny patch of sunlight that brightened the patio, and she halted, hugging the armload of clothes against her body. Staring through the screen beyond the open door, she tried to control her fluttery breathing as her gaze searched the small enclosed area. The uneven bricks were filmed with dust, and the straggly border plants fluttered aimlessly in the hot wind. A cat prowling along the fence? A bird casting a larger-than-life shadow? It had seemed too big, but it had come and gone so quickly— She forced herself to walk to the door and look out. The patio gate was ajar, and she could see a slash of walkway and shrubbery beyond it. The gate was still, but somehow Jeanne had the eerie feeling it had just stopped swaying. Air pressed against her ribs as if she were holding her breath underwater. She opened the screen and crossed the small, sun-baked enclosure to shut the gate and slide the bolt. She was back inside in seconds, chiding herself for her skittishness as she closed the sliding glass door and snapped the lock before she went into the den and began to arrange the closet.

She'd line the dresser drawers next and transfer her lingerie and sweaters. She'd be done before dark. Then she'd relax with a glass of wine while she heated one of the frozen dinners she'd stocked in the freezer. By then she'd be ready to wind down with a relaxing bath before bed. She hated to admit it, but the strain of the past few weeks had drained her reserve energy. One thing for sure, she'd better restore it before Glenn came home. She was going to need it.

Then quit dawdling, she told herself, and went back to the bedroom for another armload of clothes. She couldn't help glancing nervously at the patio as she went by.

CHAPTER 4
✝

FROM THE HALL the smell might have been mistaken for garbage left too long under a sink, but when the building manager opened the apartment door, there was no mistaking the putrid stench of death. The beer-bellied manager gagged and pressed his hand over his mouth as he stepped back.

Sergeant Ignacio Lopez unbuttoned the coat of his light tan suit and breathed shallowly though his mouth to steel himself against nausea. No matter how many corpses a cop investigated, he never got used to the smell, especially when the body had been in a hot, closed room a couple of days.

"Wait here, Mr. Harris," he told the building manager. The paunchy man bobbed his head and moved quickly down the hall as Lopez and his partner entered the apartment.

"Christ," Detective Ken Parch muttered. His voice sounded as if he were holding his nose, and he patted sweat from his temples with a folded handkerchief.

The apartment was a single room with a tiny kitchenette in one corner and the type of utilitarian, unimaginative furniture that came with furnished rentals. A studio bed stood between two windows on the outside wall. Over it was tacked a colorful unframed poster of Tivoli Gardens. On it was a naked, bloated corpse. It was colorful too: carmine lipstick and nail polish, auburn hair, and pasty-gray flesh spotted with dots and slashes of blood dried to a rusty brown. If the smell wasn't proof enough, the advanced stage of decomposition indicated the body had been there awhile.

"Christ, can we open a window?" Parch asked. "There ought to be a law against murder in this kind of weather." He used the handkerchief again to wipe away beads of perspiration that had reformed along his blond hairline.

Lopez grunted. "The coroner and crime unit are on the way."

Ignacio Lopez, nicknamed Nasty by his fellow detectives at LAPD Northeast Division, was two inches shorter, forty pounds lighter, and fifteen years older than Parch. He showed no effects of the heat. He was good-looking, with dark eyes and complexion that boasted his Hispanic heritage and a relaxed air that belied his observant, probing mind. Although he took his share of kidding in the squad room for always being so calm, he was respected for his ability and success. He'd risen through the ranks without any hint of racial tokenism.

He walked to the bed and looked down at the dead woman. She was wearing a lot of makeup, and there weren't any lines etched around her eyes or mouth. She was young, probably in her early twenties. It was impossible to tell if she'd been pretty. Gases of decomposition had bloated her features so they were strained and misshapen. The bedspread and the top sheet were folded neatly across the foot of the bed. Under her, the bottom sheet was rumpled and stained with a few spatters of blood. She was lying on her back with her legs spread.

Parch indicated a miniskirt and underpants on a chair. On the floor under it was a spike-heeled, red-strapped sandal. "Looks like the killer was here by invitation."

Lopez wondered if she'd been walking around topless. He used the back of his hand to swing open the closet door. A blouse hanging on a hook swayed, and he used his finger to spread the cloth. It was torn almost in half. He examined it without touching it. The edges followed the grain of the material, which was definitely ripped, not cut. The killer? If so, why didn't he toss the blouse aside instead of hanging it up? It would have been more in keeping with the frenzied action the corpse and the bed suggested.

He glanced at the rack of shoes on the closet floor. The mate to the one under the chair wasn't visible, but he didn't search. That was the crime unit's job. Straightening, he motioned to the door.

"Let's talk to Harris."

"Anything to get out of here," Parch said.

As they went out, three men from the mobile crime lab entered the apartment. A tall, bean-pole man raised his hand in greeting. "I can smell her from here."

"We made sure we didn't air the place out too much," Parch said with a grin.

"We'll dust the windows first," the tall man countered. "We got word the coroner's on another call. He won't be here for at least a half hour."

Out in the hall the manager was as far from the open door as he could get. He was pasty white, and his hand shook as he puffed a cigarette nervously.

Lopez leaned against the railing of the back stairs. "You say you opened the door because someone complained about the smell, Mr. Harris?"

"Yeah, that's right."

"Who complained?"

"One of the neighbors."

"Which one?"

Harris's gaze shifted along the hall. "Uh, 210. Walker."

"Did you touch anything?"

"In there? Hell, no!"

"Did you get a good look at the body?"

His pallor became green tinged. "Too good."

"Can you identify her positively?"

The question worried Harris. "What's 'positive'? She's the one rented the place. That's all I know."

"What's her name?"

"I told you, White. Lily White." He dropped the cigarette and ground it with his shoe.

"How long has she lived here?"

"Four months."

"Did she fill out a renter's application or give references?"

Harris looked annoyed. "We get a lot of turnover here. I ain't got time to do all that shit if I want to keep the place filled. Rent in advance. She don't cough up, she's gone, man, out, history."

"So she always paid on time?"

"First of the month, like clockwork."

Parch refolded his handkerchief. "Did she give a previous address?"

Harris shook his head. "She said she was new in L.A. She didn't say where she come from."

Lopez wrote in a small notebook, and Harris watched him nervously. "Mr. Harris, was Miss White employed?"

"I suppose so. Everybody works, don't they?"

"Where did she work?" Parch asked.

"I told you, I dunno. Hey, look—"

"Yeah, sure, she paid her rent on time so it was none of your business," Parch shot back.

"That's right."

Lopez snapped the notebook closed. "All right, Mr. Harris, we want a list of the other tenants. You can come down to the station later to sign a statement."

Harris's gaze was wary. "I told you all I know."

"We need an offical statement for the records."

"Yeah, sure, okay," Harris said unhappily. He went down the back stairs without passing the open door of the apartment.

When he was out of sight, Parch said, "What do you think, Nasty?"

"No references, no known employment, paid the rent in advance. I think he knows she was a hooker."

"Christ, with a name like Lily White, what else could she be? You think that's all he's lying about?"

Lopez shrugged. "Who knows? Let's check the neighbors. Maybe we'll get lucky."

CHAPTER 5
✝

> **WOMAN SLAIN IN LOS FELIZ**
>
> The body of a woman was found yesterday in a Los Feliz apartment by the building manager, who entered after neighbors complained of a bad odor. The coroner estimated that the woman had been dead between forty-eight and seventy-two hours. The partially clad body had been stabbed repeatedly and strangled. Police are withholding identification until notification of next of kin.

THE NEWSPAPER RUSTLED like distant whispering voices. His hands began to shake, and he dropped the paper as if it had burned his fingers. He stared at it, head cocked, then realized the sound he still heard was inside his head—the steady, heavy beat of a pulse in his temples . . . much faster than normal. Excitement or fear?

There had been an unreal quality about the past three days. They were faintly blurred, soft-focused with diffused light. Sometimes he was convinced the whole thing had been a dream, a mirage conjured by the unrelenting heat, a scenario his mind had invented to relieve the stupifying boredom. At night, when he was alone, he closed his eyes and tried to remember details in order to test himself. The texture of the woman's skin? Smooth but without the silkiness he had imagined, or maybe hoped for. The color of her eyes? A strange mixture of blue and green and brown that was no particular color at all, as if it didn't matter any more than her body. Her name? That one always stumped him. At times he was sure she'd never told him. They really hadn't talked much. Other times he was positive she must have mentioned it. It was the natural thing to do. But then, he hadn't told her his name, not his real one. He had pulled one out of his head on the spur of the moment. He wasn't sure why then, but later he figured out that it was because he hadn't really planned any of what happened. His actions, his words, even his thoughts, had come from some distant part of him, beyond his conscious thought processes, from the dark depths of a deep pool.

Just as Gretchen had.

Gretchen. God, he hadn't even thought about her these past weeks. The first couple of days after he'd left her apartment, he broke into a sweat every time he heard a siren, afraid the police had found some way to link him to her. Gretchen's body hadn't been discovered for four days. The story in the *Times* was only one paragraph on an inside page. If he hadn't recognized her name, he never would have spotted it. He searched the paper every day for a while after that, but there was nothing else. Gretchen Peters disappeared from the news as she had from life: a bit player, unnoticed and unmourned. An unsolved murder.

Murder. It had been so easy. And it hadn't changed his life one bit. At first he felt only vast relief, but gradually that was replaced by a sense of pride and accomplishment. He had gotten away with murder. The cops didn't have a clue, not a single lead pointing to him, or they would have been around to question him. They didn't have a clue about who killed Gretchen *or* the woman three nights ago.

He hadn't planned to kill her any more than he had Gretchen. He didn't even know this woman. He happened to walk down that street when she needed help. It was a chance meeting. He could have turned the opposite direction or at a different corner. But he'd chosen that one. At that time.

It was like the opening play of a chess game. He made a move. She made a move. Then it was his turn. Each of them made only one move at a time. It was her game as much as his. Any change in his strategy was the result of what she did. She could have changed her tactics anytime, so obviously the final outcome was the result of her moves as much as his. More. He hadn't even been thinking about her kind of woman when he went out to walk. She had invited him to play the game.

Leaning forward, he read the article again without lifting the paper. Then, unable to resist, he tore it out even though it was short enough for total recall anytime he wanted to remember it. He sat holding the clipping and thought about that night.

He was pretty sure no one had seen him or noticed the car parked in front of her building. It had been stupid—and risky—to park there, but didn't that prove he wasn't planning all along to kill her? He remembered being surprised at the building and wondering if she really lived there. Cheap hookers belonged in sleazy hotel rooms down on Sunset or Hollywood boulevards, not in decent neighborhoods.

Later, when he left her apartment, he was dazed. He drove around a long time before he went home and carefully cleaned the knife to remove the blood. He'd let a steady flow of cold water run inside the handle where the blade was stored, then dried it by holding it in front of the fan before he sprayed it with lubricant to prevent the spring mechanism from rusting. After all the work he put into crafting the weapon, it deserved the utmost care.

When the knife was clean, he had wrapped it in an old T-shirt and hid it behind some boxes on the closet shelf. It was still there. He wasn't going to carry it around like some stupid street-gang kid. But he could summon an image of it at will. He could remember the feel of the casing in his fist when he walked into her apartment that night. Warm and smooth, soothing to his palm. When he took it out of his pocket, he just stood there holding it at his side, with his fingertip brushing the release button the way it might a turgid nipple. Even then he wasn't thinking about killing her. Maybe if she hadn't taken off the mangled blouse and turned so he got the full impact of her naked breasts and the smile that invited and offered and promised. Maybe if she'd just said thanks for the ride and his offer to wait and drive her wherever she wanted to go after she changed clothes. Maybe if she had come right out and propositioned him instead of pretending and playing a game that way. Maybe he would have put the knife away without using it.

It was obvious now that it had been a game all along. And when it was her turn, she made a stupid move, so he won. Why shouldn't he enjoy the thrill of victory and the excitement it had given him? Still gave him. Reviewing the murder was almost as exciting as the actual moment of her death. But maybe, as with Gretchen, the thrill would fade with time. Right now the newspaper article was brightening the focus on the picture, enhancing the color. Would there be follow-up stories? There would be at least one when they found out who she was. Then it would depend on whether or not the cops had any leads. Everyone knew that most crimes, especially murders, were solved because the police were tipped off by an informant, not because of brilliant detective work.

Well, there'd be no tips this time. The only one who saw him that night was the drunk he'd punched in the gut. Even if the dumb bastard remembered what had happened, he'd never come forward to admit he'd been with the whore that night.

CHAPTER 6

✝

UNTIL NOW JEANNE had been eager to face each day at her job. Harvest Films was a young company with young ideas. The producer, Brad Raven, was fast becoming Boy Wonder in a business where success was as sought and as elusive as the Holy Grail. He was an intense, difficult man who demanded perfection and antagonized people easily, but his genius had produced a box-office smash that reviewers likened to a collaboration between Hitchcock and DePalma. That Terry Faust got along with him was testimony to Terry's temperament and talent. He had managed to get Raven's approval to arrange the work schedule around Jeanne's need to visit Glenn every day. Jeanne was grateful, but she had the feeling that Raven was lying in wait to pounce on any mistake she made.

It was a miracle that everything had gone so smoothly until now, but today had been a series of disasters. First the continuity page for yesterday's shots had gone astray between the copying machine and the set. Callie Minette, who doubled as Harvest's receptionist as well as handling all the secretarial work, had endured the brunt of Raven's anger, but everyone on the set felt its sting. Then the first scene they shot needed seven retakes. Casting sent Anglo extras when the call had specifically been for Hispanics. A delivery kid ignored the lock-up light and barged in while they were rolling. One damned thing after another. Jeanne was exhausted and short-tempered and had all she could do not to take it out on a grip who had just run over a lighting cable, managing to disconnect it and plunge the set into darkness.

"Cut it," she called. The actor and actress on the set relaxed physically, but she could see the tension in their faces as the grip scrambled to reconnect the line. Jeanne took a deep breath, wishing that Brad Raven hadn't chosen today to stay on the set and watch every bit of action. His presence was as tangible as the Santa Ana outside, and crew and cast alike kept glancing over their shoulders. The rage in his face and stance was all too evident.

Terry stepped in front of the camera. "Let's take ten, gang. Everyone back on the set at twenty after." The talent and crew drifted away amid a murmur of voices. Terry came over to Jeanne. "Don't look so glum. Didn't your mother tell you there'd be days like this?"

"My mother was a schoolteacher. She wanted me to follow in her footsteps. I should have listened to her."

Terry grinned. "What, and give up show biz?"

Jeanne laughed, relieved to have the tension broken. She enjoyed working with Terry. He'd come a long way in the past few years since his teaching days in Minneapolis. His direction of *Dead Past*, the current production, was brilliant. He had an instinct for timing and setting up shots that brought out the best everyone had to offer. And he had a talent for restoring harmony amid the ranks at times like this.

Jeanne was impressed with the original screenplay by the author of *Death Pact*, who had once again created a masterpiece of obsession and the terrifying kind of madness that wore a veneer of respectability. The picture was going to be a smash, it couldn't miss. The casting was superb, especially Wray Jarvis, who played the lead. Jarvis was an unknown with an innocent, ordinary appearance that enhanced the menace of his role of a serial killer in the story. He had an uncanny talent for portraying schizophrenia and bringing out the fine differences between the intelligent, stable side of the character as convincingly as the irrational, inner fury that drove him to murder. The script's dialogue was crisp and believable, its action terse and dramatic.

Jeanne was impressed with Terry's directing ability, even though he was quick to give most of the credit to Brad Raven. Terry insisted that Raven's gut instincts about what made a good film were so on target that he brought in a winner every time.

Even if that was true, Jeanne wondered how Raven could be so completely lacking in sensitivity. Right now he was striding across the barnlike studio, his brows pulled in a tight scowl. His thin face, accented by high cheekbones and deep-set eyes, was Hollywood good-looking in the John Travolta mold. In appearance he was the perfect Hollywood image of a successful young studio executive.

"That was a stupid, costly mistake," he said.

Jeanne struggled with her reaction to the accusation. "It was an accident."

He stared at the dark set. "Terry recommended you very highly. I take it this isn't one of your better days."

Jeanne's spine stiffened. "*I* didn't yank the plug, Mr. Raven."

"It's your job to make sure no one else does," he said sharply, then strode off, yelling at one of the grips to coil a cable that snaked across the floor.

Jeanne clenched her teeth. What the hell was wrong with him? He'd do more harm than good if he started barking at people that way. Everyone was exhausted and tempers were short. He'd disrupt the whole picture if he kept it up.

She shivered, cold suddenly in the air-conditioning that was set to compensate for the heat of the lights that were now off.

Terry plucked a worn, gray cardigan from a chair and draped it across her shoulders. "You should keep a sweater on the set for times like this."

"I have one in my office." She watched Raven corner the soundman and take a stance with arms folded as he talked. She wondered if he was heaping undeserved blame on the technician too.

"Fat lot of good it does there. Keep one out here where you can grab it when you need it."

"Is he always like that?"

"Brad?" He followed her gaze. "No. Sometimes he's worse." When Jeanne turned to look at him, Terry grinned. "First you gotta get her attention."

She apologized. "Sorry. It's been a long day."

"You look pooped," Terry said, raising her chin with his finger as he peered at her. "Dark circles . . . pale. You need some sunshine. How about running down to the beach when we finish up?"

"Thanks, but I have to go to the hospital."

"You also have to take some time for *you*, sweetie. You're running yourself into the ground." When she didn't answer, he shook a cigarette from a pack and flared a Bic lighter to it. "How's the apartment?"

"Coming along. Thanks again for the advice. I'd still be wandering around those swinging-singles haciendas if you hadn't set me in the right direction. Los Feliz is charming."

"I've always liked it," he said.

"Do you know the neighborhood?"

He blew smoke. "I lived there when I was a kid. Of course, it was the edge of eternity then, way out in the sticks."

"It's hard to envision any part of L.A. 'out in the sticks.'"

"It was back in the old days."

She laughed. Terry Faust was only thirty-five. He was slender, with brown hair and a boyish face that crinkled when he smiled—which was often.

"Brad grew up in that part of town, too. We went to the same school. That's why we're using it for so many locations. The old neighborhood ain't what it used to be, but it's perfect for *Dead Past*."

She thought of the lovely tree-shaded houses up the hill as opposed to the seedy apartments south of Franklin, and she wondered on which side Terry and Raven had lived.

Glancing at his watch, Terry took a last drag on his cigarette and stubbed it out in a can of sand. Cameramen and technicians were filing back onto the set. Someone opened the door to the hall and yelled toward the dressing rooms. The set lights came up, and two electricians made quick rounds to inspect all the cables. When you worked for Brad Raven, Jeanne thought, it would be suicide to make the same mistake twice.

The late-afternoon sun was hot on her head and shoulders as she walked to the bus stop. The weather forecast was for more of the same, no relief in sight. Jeanne still found it hard to believe it was early October. In Minnesota it was a month of autumn leaves and approaching winter. Here it was temperatures close to a hundred and a hot, dry wind that made her edgy as it soughed in the palms like an animal crying in the night. Its heat was relentless and caustic with grit from the streets. A Santa Ana, they called it, and this one was setting a record. She wondered if she'd ever get used to it.

At the corner she muttered with disappointment when

she didn't see her bus looming in the traffic on Western Avenue. If it was late, she'd miss her connection on Beverly.

A white Thunderbird convertible, its top down, the tape deck pulsing strains of Mahler, pulled into the bus stop. Behind the wheel Brad Raven's expression was disguised by dark glasses. "Hop in, I'll give you a lift."

She hesitated, wondering if this was his way of apologizing for his earlier boorishness. "Are you sure it isn't out of your way?"

He made an impatient gesture and tapped the steering wheel. His mouth was a tight line the way it had been when he yelled at her on the set. Obviously Brad Raven was accustomed to getting his way.

"I know where the hospital is. Get in, I'm blocking traffic."

She was tempted to refuse but suppressed her resentment. She got in and barely had the door closed before the car shot away from the curb, swerving around people who were jockeying for position as the bus finally came into sight.

A faint taste of panic washed Jeanne's throat as she fastened her seat belt. She'd ridden with Caroline in the rental car without unreasonable terror, but Caroline was a conservative, midwestern driver. Brad Raven drove as if he had learned by watching chase scenes in cop movies. Ignoring the speed limit, he darted the car in and out of traffic with abandon. Jeanne clung to the seat nervously.

After a few blocks Raven glanced at her. "We're going on location next week. You're going to need a car. You do drive, don't you?"

"Yes."

"Then why the hell haven't you replaced the car that was totaled?" he demanded.

"I've had other things on my mind," she snapped in a tone to match his.

"We all do," he said coldly. "Starting next week, you'd

better find a way to give *Dead Past* number-one priority. Location work presents enough problems without trying to juggle schedules. Now that your husband's going home, your trips to the hospital will be over. You owe those extra hours to Harvest."

She struggled with roiling anger. "I'll have transportation. Please don't concern yourself."

"Anything connected with *Dead Past* concerns me," he said. "Beginning Tuesday, we're looking at the dailies after we wrap each day. I don't care what time it is. We've only got the street one day and Griffith Park two. We can't afford to waste any time. I want those scenes in the can, so everyone had better be on his toes every minute. Terry won't have time to taxi you back and forth, just remember that."

His tone infuriated Jeanne, but she bit back a sharp answer. Terry had done a lot to accommodate her, but whether she liked to admit it or not, nothing would have happened without Raven's consent. It was his responsibility to bring the picture in on schedule and budget, and now he was flaunting his authority.

"I understand."

"Good, then we'll get along fine." He glanced at her, and for a fleeting moment Jeanne thought he was going to smile, but he turned his attention back to his driving. After a few moments he said, "I want to swing around and catch the freeway. I'll drop you at the Emergency entrance."

Astonished, she realized they were already at the hospital. When the car squealed to a stop in front of the emergency doors, Jeanne thanked Raven for the ride and reached for the door handle. Raven leaned across and put his hand over hers before she could open the door. She felt the pressure of his arm across her body, intimate and insinuating. The unsettling intensity of his scrutiny as he looked at her, his face too close, was magnified by the dark glasses.

"I'm glad we had this little talk. I have the feeling we're going to get along just fine."

The wind made Jeanne's breath fiery in her lungs. She felt like an animal caught in a brushfire, aware of the need to flee but rooted momentarily by panic. His hand tightened on hers like pincers lifting molten iron from a furnace. Again she thought he was going to smile, but he let go of her hand abruptly and straightened behind the wheel. She opened the car door quickly and got out.

"Thank you," she said again, slamming the door.

Brad Raven glanced in the sideview mirror and pulled away without a backward glance.

Glenn's gaze was riveted on the doorway. His drawn, scowling expression didn't change when Jeanne came into view. When she bent to kiss him, he was almost indifferent as he stroked her hair with his unbandaged hand.

"It's getting late. I was worried."

She pulled a chair close, bending over to put down her purse and give herself a few seconds to adjust to his surliness. Actually she was early, but it wasn't worth arguing about.

"It's a jungle out there, sweetheart," she said in her best Bogart imitation. The traction pulley was twisted around one of the steel bars of the frame, out of the way until it would once more be attached to the cast on his leg and weighted. He was in traction only at night now, and his strained expression and deeply furrowed brow betrayed the pain he wouldn't admit.

His blue gaze softened and he touched the back of her hand. "It's a zoo in here, baby. Crowds of funny people in white keep staring at me. You don't know how happy I'll be to be sprung from this joint." He pouted suddenly, like a small child. "You still plan to bail me out, don't you?"

"As soon as I can. Oh, darling, it'll be so good to have

you home. I miss you." She ruffled his blond hair, then smoothed it with her palm.

He held her hand, still scowling. "I've got Dr. Ingerman pinned down to an indefinite maybe for Saturday. I'm doing great out of that damned contraption. Rehab came up to walk me and show me how to use the crutches. At this rate, I'll be able to dance out of here by Saturday."

She was elated by the news but worried that it was too soon for him to come home. His hospital excursions were brief and carefully monitored by nurses. Could he really manage by himself all day at home? Afraid of antagonizing him, she kept her doubts silent and forced herself to sound happy.

She lifted his hand and kissed his fingertips, one at a time, pressing them to her lips. "Wait until you see the apartment." She'd been giving him a humorous, day-by-day account of her progress. "The bedroom is getting absolutely respectable. Not the Ritz, but not bad, if I do say so myself. I hung some prints and the Guatemalan weaving Caroline gave us, and yesterday I saw an ad for some inexpensive drapes and a bedspread on sale at Bullock's. They're being delivered tomorrow. The building manager promised to cut a piece of plywood to put under the mattress so you'll have good support for your back. The mattress isn't all that bad, but I figured there was no harm in asking. And when I get——"

"It sounds like you're doing too much. We won't be there all that long."

She wanted to believe he meant in the apartment, not Los Angeles, but his tone held the familiar undercurrent of dissatisfaction she'd been detecting so frequently, as if he had already made up his mind the California experiment wasn't going to work and their return to Minneapolis was inevitable.

"You'll be spending a lot of time in the bedroom at first," she said. "I want it to be as cheerful as possible."

"Damned old coot in that pickup. I wish——"

"Please." She pressed her finger to his lips, not wanting to hear the refrain again. "First thing on our 'to do' list is get you home and well. Did Ingerman really say Saturday?"

"If I keep improving at this rate," he said. "And I will, don't worry."

In spite of her resolve she said, "Just don't push too fast. I know you're anxious to get out, but it's going to be a lot harder at home. I'll be gone all day and the therapist will only be there an hour."

Glenn's blue gaze challenged hers, but she couldn't read it. The open communication they used to have was cracked and faulted, and she didn't know how to repair the damage.

"How are you going to handle your job and take care of the apartment and an invalid?" he asked.

"One thing I won't put up with is that kind of talk, Glenn Donovan," she said with determined gaiety. "If you give me any trouble when you get home, you'll have more than a couple of broken bones to worry about." She leaned to kiss him. His response this time was eager, and his mouth opened to capture hers.

When she finally drew away, he grinned. "I've got plenty to worry about right now."

Relieved at his sudden shift in mood, she laughed softly, feeling an unexpected surge of desire and longing. "I'll have to ask Dr. Ingerman about that."

"The hell with Ingerman. Two clever people like us can work out our own solution." He took her hand, working her tanned fingers between his pale ones so they were clasped. "I promise no more grousing. And to behave myself. Now tell me what's been going on in the world."

She leaned comfortably on the edge of the bed and recounted her day, making a funny story of the minor and major crises that had filled it. Her description of Brad Raven's verbal attack about the cable made Glenn's face go moody, and when she told about his sudden appearance at the bus stop to give her a ride, Glenn's scowl returned full force.

"At least the stud's got an eye for beauty," he said.

"I think it was his way of apologizing," Jeanne said. "He's an odd man. Bright and successful and—"

"Good-looking?"

Remembering Raven's arm pinning her and the intensity of his gaze, she chose her words carefully. "Yes, I suppose, if you like the type." She wasn't sure if Raven had been making a pass or was just being his obnoxious self, but the last thing she needed right now was for Glenn to be jealous. "He's certainly temperamental. I find myself wondering if he treats everyone so brusquely or just the people who work for him."

"I thought Harvest Films was supposed to be one big happy family. Wasn't that the story Terry sold you?"

No matter what she said, Glenn was going to twist the meaning to suit himself. It was a mistake to even discuss Raven. "I've never worked for any other film company. Maybe one prima donna is *de rigueur*." She changed the subject. "I almost forgot. I met some of our neighbors yesterday." She told him briefly about Mrs. Saidlow and Mark Bonner, and of Mark Bonner's offer to find her a good used car.

Glenn's scowl returned. "I'm not trusting any joker to pick our car. I'll do it myself," he said.

"But Glenn—"

"Just forget it, Jeanne, I'm going to be out of here in a couple of days. I said I'll take care of it."

Her patience snapped. "Oh, sure, maybe on the way home from the hospital Saturday we can hit all the used car lots in Hollywood. You can spin a few out for test rides, then stand around and dicker price with—" She stopped, ashamed of herself.

Glenn was silent for a long time. Then he said sullenly,

"Okay. I guess you're right. Take the guy up on the offer, but make sure he lets you take the car to a mechanic to be checked before you commit yourself. Is his friend a dealer?"

Jeanne still felt guilty, but she was relieved. She tried to recall Mark's Bonner's exact words. "He didn't say. Is it important?"

"The seller has to guarantee the odometer shows the original mileage. Find out if there's any kind of warranty."

"I will, and I'll talk it over with you before I give him an answer, how's that?" His expression told her he expected that much. "Anyhow, it will take a few days to arrange, and you'll be home by then. We'll have lots of time to discuss it."

His fingers tightened on hers. "Jim Newell from the studio stopped by this afternoon. He says the job's waiting for me as soon as I'm ready."

She felt another surge of relief and wondered why Glenn hadn't mentioned it sooner. "Obviously he knows you're the best audio engineer in the business," she said.

Out in the hall a tray cart rattled. Glenn muttered savagely, "One thing I am not going to do when I get home is have dinner at six o'clock every night."

A young, chubby, blond-haired aide carried in a tray, set it down, and rolled the table where Glenn could reach it. "Can I get you some coffee or anything, Mrs. Donovan?" she asked.

Jeanne shook her head. "No thanks, I'll just watch."

"Lucky you," Glenn said, and the aide laughed as she went out.

Jeanne removed the cover from the soup bowl and unfolded the napkin while Glenn adjusted the head of the bed. When Jeanne handed him a spoon, he ate dutifully.

"You don't have to hang around, honey," he said. "I know you're beat." His voice lacked conviction.

"I'm too tired to hassle those buses right away. Besides, maybe it will cool off a little."

"As long as you get home before dark, okay? This town's full of creeps. Tell you what, as soon as—what's his name?—Bonner lines up a car, call me. Maybe we can save some time that way."

"If he's home tonight, I'll ask him to see what his pal can do." She thought about the luxury of driving. Los Angeles traffic would take some getting used to, but her confidence would grow. She realized she was actually looking forward to driving again.

CHAPTER 7
✝

TOO TIRED TO shop, Jeanne began the long ride back to the apartment. The apartment was on a convenient and direct busline to the studio, but it meant backtracking to and from the hospital. In a few days she was already sick of the tiring commute.

Well, she wouldn't have to make it much longer. She was excited at the prospect of having a car. And she was delighted with the news that Glenn was coming home soon. She was, she told herself, she really was, but nagging worry picked at her conscience. Glenn looked so tired today she couldn't help wondering if he was pushing himself too hard. She made up her mind to telephone Dr. Ingerman and put the question to him bluntly.

Alighting from the bus, she stood back from the wave of hot exhaust that spewed over the sidewalk when the vehicle lumbered across the intersection. Her throat stung with the sharp tang of it. The evening was still cruelly hot, and although the temperature had dropped a few degrees, heat clung to the sidewalks and radiated from the buildings. The tree-shaded streets of Los Feliz were cooler than the concrete canyons of the commercial areas of the city, but with the relentless Santa Ana blowing, it would be another uncomfortable night.

Entering the apartment building, she glanced at the mailbox, not expecting anything and only slightly disappointed when nothing was visible behind the slots. She crossed the hall to knock on Mark Bonner's door. Behind her the door of 101 opened a crack and an old woman peered out.

"Mr. Bonner isn't at home," she said in a voice that carried clearly, though it was soft and well-modulated. The bit of face visible in the narrow opening was lined like wrinkled silk and topped by a smooth puff of white hair.

Jeanne smiled. "Oh."

The door opened farther. The woman was small and erect, with a regal bearing that commanded attention. "It is none of my business, Mrs. Donovan, and I do not wish to interfere, but I feel it my duty to say that Mr. Bonner is hardly suitable company for a young lady whose husband is recovering from serious injuries."

Annoyance and amusement vied for Jeanne's tongue. "Thank you, but—"

The old woman shut the door. Jeanne shrugged and walked down the hall, sighing at the idea of having a busybody to contend with in addition to all her other problems. As she unlocked her door, the telephone began to ring. Inside she dropped her briefcase and purse and ran to grab it.

"Hello—"

"Jeanne? How are you? You sound breathless. If I caught you at a bad time, I can call back."

"No, it's wonderful to hear your voice, Caroline." Jeanne sank onto the sofa and kicked off her sandals. "I stopped at the hospital after work. I just walked in."

"How's Glenn?"

"Coming right along." She told her sister the news that he was going to be released in a matter of days.

"That's marvelous. Are you sure you'll be able to handle it when he comes home?"

"I'll be so happy to have him out, I'll be able to handle anything. The hospital is arranging for a therapist to come every day."

"But with your job——" Caroline fretted.

Jeanne smiled. Caroline always fussed over her. Their mother had died when they were young, Caroline ten and Jeanne seven, and Caroline had stepped into the role of little mother willingly and expertly. The domestic one, Jeanne thought, loving her sister more for it.

"I promise to let you know if I need help. Glenn's the one who'll have the rough time. He's going to be alone all day except for an hour with the therapist."

"Maybe he should stay in the hospital until he can manage better on his own. A change of scene isn't going to work magic to improve his disposition, no matter what he says. You don't know what you're letting yourself in for, hon. When I took care of Dad those last months, it wasn't easy."

As an invalid, their father had been crochety and impatient with the fast-moving world he could no longer share actively. Glenn *was* impatient, but Jeanne was sorry she had confided his frequent irritability to her sister, yet it had been natural at the time because she needed to unburden herself.

"But you did it and you did it very well," Jeanne reminded her, "so I'm sure I can handle this. Glenn will be able to get around on crutches. This apartment is about one-tenth the size of the nursing station he's on. It's only a few steps to the bathroom, and there's a phone right by the bed. Besides, they've been getting him up for a couple of days now. By the weekend he'll have plenty of practice."

"Promise you'll call me if it gets to be too much. I can take some time off——"

"I promise, now stop worrying." She wouldn't, Jeanne knew. Worrying and caring came naturally to Caroline. Having her baby sister move two thousand miles away had been a traumatic experience, and Caroline would worry even if Jeanne and Glenn were comfortably settled in Beverly Hills with servants catering to their every whim.

Caroline asked about the apartment, and they slipped into relaxed conversation about ordinary things. They talked for twenty minutes, and when Jeanne hung up, she sat savoring the pleasure her sister's calls always brought. The room was remarkably insulated from the street noises outside. Gazing at the armchair covered by the bright multicolored Guatemalan throw that was another souvenir of Caroline and Peter's trip to Central America three years ago, Jeanne realized the room had taken on a comfortable hominess. Despite the lack of bright natural lighting, it looked pleasant and inviting. All the packages she'd carried home had been worth the effort.

Suddenly the peculiar feeling of being watched riffled along the back of her neck, and she turned. A shadow flitted past the door she'd failed to close in her haste to reach the phone. Jumping up, she glanced both ways along the hall, but it was empty. Her hands trembled as she snapped the lock and the dead bolt. It was probably another tenant headed for his apartment or the laundry room in the basement. She was jumping at shadows again. She had never lived in an apartment and wasn't used to a building where she shared space. The condo in Minneapolis had been a complete unit, with private access from the garage or the small garden court in front. As kids, she and Caroline had grown up in the big, old house near Lake Harriet where Caroline and Peter still lived.

Resolutely she walked through the rooms unlocking windows and fastening the safety chains so each opening was limited to a scant two inches. In the bedroom she clicked the lock on the patio screen door several times but couldn't convince herself it would hold against any kind of force. Was it possible to install a chain similar to the ones on the windows? Or block the track in some way? Suddenly she remembered seeing two lengths of wood in the back of the closet. She pulled on the light and rummaged behind Glenn's things, which she'd hung in a neat row. When she found the dowels, she carried them back and tried them in the bottom track of the sliding glass door. They wedged tightly, apparently designed for that purpose. If one were a few inches shorter, she could set the door so the opening was too narrow for anyone to get through, yet wide enough to allow a decent flow of air.

Carrying the pieces of wood, she returned to the living room and picked up her keys before she crossed the hall to knock on the manager's door. After several moments the door opened. A gray-haired, pale-faced, scowling woman stared at her.

"Mrs. Crenshaw?" She hadn't met the caretaker's wife. "I'm Jeanne Donovan in 104. Can Mr. Crenshaw cut a couple of inches off one of these dowels for me?"

The woman's drawn face twitched. She looked older than Crenshaw. She was thin and stooped, and her hands darted restlessly. "He's not here." There was no friendly overture in her tone.

Jeanne refused to be dismissed so easily. "Will you ask him to see me when he comes in?"

The woman seemed to ponder the request. Behind her someone appeared at the end of the hall from the rear of the apartment. Jeanne had only a glimpse of a rangy figure with a shock of unruly hair. Alerted by some instinct or sound, Mrs. Crenshaw swiveled her head, then quickly said, "I'll have him call you." The door was shut before the words finished.

Jeanne stood for a moment, the two dowels in her hand. That was the second time one of the other tenants in the building had shut a door in her face. For a moment she was tempted to bang on the Crenshaws' door, but instead she turned and walked down the hall and knocked at Mark Bonner's again. She glanced over her shoulder at the apartment behind her where the woman had eavesdropped earlier, but the door stayed closed. Listening to the faint sound of music from one of the upstairs apartments, Jeanne waited several minutes then knocked again, but there was still no answer. Sighing, she returned to her apartment and tossed the dowels on the sofa. Could she rely on Mrs. Crenshaw to relay her request? If the caretaker didn't call by nine, she'd call him. It wasn't as if she was asking something outrageous.

She changed into jeans and a T-shirt and slipped on a pair of neon-yellow thongs. In the kitchen she grabbed the top frozen dinner from the stack in the freezer. Veal parmigiana. She lit the oven and leaned against the sink while she read the cooking directions, then tore open the carton. Putting the tray in to heat, she poured a glass of chardonnay from the chilled bottle in the refrigerator. No work tonight, she told herself. Glenn was right, she was wearing herself to a frazzle. She'd soak in a warm tub and go to bed early. She still had a couple of days to finish what had to be done before Glenn came home.

She poured a second glass of wine and sipped it while she ate the uninspired meal directly from the container. Sitting at the small round table in the kitchen, she vowed that when Glenn came home, she'd go back to cooking decent meals. She enjoyed fussing in the kitchen when there was someone to share the food, but it seemed too much effort for only herself. Lazy. Caroline would scold and nag if she knew. Loneliness overwhelmed Jeanne momentarily, and she had to stop herself from running to the phone to call her sister and admitting how much easier it would be to have her there.

She dropped the empty tray into the plastic-lined garbage can under the sink, then washed the wineglass and her coffee cup and egg dish from breakfast. As she dried her hands, there was a knock on the door. She went to it and paused with her hand on the dead bolt.

"Who is it?"

"Mark Bonner."

She snapped the lock and opened the door. Dressed in jeans and blue T-shirt with the sleeves cut off, he glanced past her.

"Am I interrupting anything?"

Jeanne said with a smile, "No, I just finished eating. I knocked on your door earlier." She wondered if she should invite him in.

"I just got back. Got something to show you. C'mon." He motioned down the hall.

Jeanne hesitated.

"I brought home the car for you to look at," he said. "I hope you don't mind. I know I'm being pushy, but there's no obligation, as they say. Come on, take it for a spin so you can see how it handles," he coaxed.

Jeanne laughed nervously, suddenly wary of such overt friendliness. He'd taken it for granted she wanted to look at the car he mentioned. It was presumptuous, to say the least. She tried to formulate a refusal, but the lure of ending the abominable daily bus jaunts was too tempting.

"Okay," she said, "let me get my keys." She grabbed them from the bookcase and shoved them into her pocket as she pulled the door shut. Mark Bonner walked ahead, then waited for her in the foyer, shifting his weight from heels to toes as if accustomed to utilizing every spare moment with exercise. He pulled open the outer door and stepped aside, holding it for her.

"It's that one across the street," he told her. "Parking's a bitch around here."

They walked twenty yards up the block and crossed to a maroon Toyota Tercel parked at a small stretch of curb between two driveways. "This is it," Mark said. He opened the door and handed her the keys. "It's got standard transmission. I should have asked if you can handle that."

"No problem." She was still ecstatic at the possibility she might not have to ride the buses much longer.

"It's an '80. Seventy-two thousand miles, but it's in good shape." He motioned for her to get behind the wheel, then leaned through the open doorway, pointing to levers and buttons. "Headlights, wipers, radio, blower. This little baby even has factory air." His arm brushed hers as he showed her how to regulate the air-conditioning, and he stepped back, embarrassed. "Go do your shopping or whatever."

Jeanne tried to remember all the questions Glenn had told her to ask, but Bonner slammed the door and was walking away before she could frame them. Shaking with nervous excitement, she inserted the key in the ignition, disengaged the clutch, and started the engine. It sprang to life and she sat listening to the smooth cadence. Test-drive . . . ask the questions later. Taking a deep breath, she released the hand brake, put the car in gear, and pulled away from the curb smoothly, and without butterflies or jitters.

She and Glenn had sold her Honda before they left Minneapolis. This car handled with the same ease. She felt completely at home behind the wheel. She drove up the steep hill, turned at the corner, and came down the next block. Without her purse shopping was out of the question, but Mark's offer was generous. She liked the feel of the car and considered going for a longer ride, but she decided not to risk losing the parking place, which was miraculously still vacant when she came around the block. She parked and locked the car, then walked back to the apartment building with a spring in her step. The last daylight was fading rapidly, and the hall lights had been turned on. Mark Bonner answered her knock as if he'd been waiting for it.

"Well?" He tilted his head, watching her with a smile.

"It seems fine," she said, holding out the keys.

He jammed his hands in his pockets. "Keep 'em. Drive the car to work tomorrow. Have a mechanic check it out and talk it over with your husband before you decide. My friend's asking two thousand dollars, but he'll take a couple of hundred less if you offer him cash." He rocked on his heels slowly.

"Oh, I can't do that," she protested.

"Why not? I trust you. You're not going to skip town, are you? Besides, my friend really wants to sell the car. If you buy it, he doesn't have to run an ad and go through all that hassle."

"You're sure?" When he nodded, she said, "Well, all right, but I don't know how to thank you." He had answered all the questions Glenn had raised. Maybe the same details were important to all men when a car was at stake. She smiled apologetically. "I would like to have a mechanic check it, just to be sure."

"Hey, that's only being smart. There's an honest station over on Western and Franklin."

Jeanne clamped her hand around the keys. "Well, if you're sure—"

"Positive. No sweat."

"Thanks again, really. I'll let you know tomorrow night, okay?"

"No hurry. I'm going down to San Diego for the weekend." He cocked his head and grinned. "A buddy of mine set up an interview with an agent who likes my composite. I'm an actor. I haven't done much yet, just a couple of bit parts and a few commercials, but I'm taking classes. This agent in San Diego has a great reputation. I'm not crazy about the idea of driving back and forth, but if he can line up jobs for me, it's worth it. I need the exposure, you know? Any credits I can get will look good on my resume."

"That's wonderful! Good luck."

He grinned. "Thanks. I probably won't drive back until late Sunday. I know a girl down there, and we're going to hit the beaches."

Jeanne thanked him again and waved as she went down the hall. When she entered her apartment, a chill wrapped around her like swirling fog. The two wooden dowels she'd left on the sofa were laid across each other in the middle of the floor to form a cross. In its center a crushed rose lay in a pool of red petals.

CHAPTER 8
†

AIR ESCAPED HER lungs in painful little gasps. Unreasonable fear like that created by the shadows in the patio swamped her, and she shivered as if the temperature had suddenly dropped. Her mind searched for a logical explanation as she fought the urge to run. When she realized she was cowering against the door, she bit her lip.

She'd locked the door before she followed Mark Bonner down the hall. She distinctly remembered twisting the knob, a ritual she'd established right after moving in. Had someone left the entry door open and a sneak thief broken in opportunely? There really hadn't been time. She was only gone a few minutes, and part of that time Mark Bonner was in the hall.

Not Mark surely. Someone else in the building then? Another tenant? The building manager had keys to all the apartments. Had Crenshaw come about the dowels? If he knocked and got no answer, would he use his key?

A sound disturbed the silence pressing around her. Her fear returned in a wash as she realized the intruder might still be in the apartment. Wiping her sweaty palm on her jeans, she felt for the doorknob. Trembling, she yanked open the door and ran out into the hall. She started for the Crenshaw apartment, then thought better of it and raced to Mark Bonner's instead. She pounded on the door, glancing nervously back along the dim corridor until he answered.

"Oh, hi— Hey, what's the matter?"

She tried to keep the hysteria from her voice. "Someone was in my apartment while I was out driving."

"What?" He looked as incredulous as when she told him she didn't have a car.

Panic was brassy on her tongue, and she tried to slow the bursts of breath escaping from her lungs. "I know it sounds silly—"

"Hey, no, I didn't mean that. C'mon, I'll have a look." He pulled his door shut and led the way down the hall. At her apartment he glanced at the door she'd left ajar, then poked it with a fingertip so it swung open. He went in and looked around the living room. Motioning her to stay where she was, he walked toward the kitchen, pausing in the hall to examine the small panel through which, long ago, some dairy had delivered milk. It was securely nailed, and the layers of paint over it were unbroken. He opened the closet at the end of the hall and pushed aside the few jackets and coats hanging in a space too cramped to hide anyone. With a glance at Jeanne, still standing in the doorway, he disappeared into the kitchen. She held her breath while she listened to his steps on the linoleum. Finally he came through the dinette back into the living room.

Motioning her again to stay put, he completed his circuit of the apartment. Jeanne heard him pull aside the shower curtain in the bathroom, open the linen cupboards, and go through the closets of the den and the bedroom. She caught a glimpse of him kneeling to look under the bed.

When he came back to the living room, he said, "No one here. What gave you the idea someone was?"

Feeling more foolish by the moment, Jeanne pointed to the dowels on the floor. "I wanted Mr. Crenshaw to cut one of those so I can keep the patio door open for air, but he wasn't home. When I came back, I dropped both sticks on the sofa, I know I did. They were there when I went out with you."

Bonner studied the cross formation with a puzzled frown. "I never heard of a thief leaving crushed flowers. Maybe you better check and see if anything's missing."

Jeanne walked through the rooms nervously, taking mental inventory of the few possessions she had so recently arranged. Everything seemed to be in place. There was so little of value, a thief would be wasting his time, she thought. Belatedly she thought to check her purse. Her wallet was intact. When she told Mark, he looked relieved.

"That's something," he said, giving her an encouraging smile. He bent to pick up the dowels. "They couldn't possibly have rolled from the sofa clear over here."

She was grateful he wasn't laughing at her fears.

"Did you lock the door when we went out?"

She nodded. "Yes."

"Did you set the dead bolt?"

She thought a moment. "No." She was eager see the car, and she hadn't stopped to use the key.

Mark went to the door, opened it, pushed the snap lock several times, then bent to examine the keyplate. "According to police and security outfits, locks like this are pretty easy to get past. You'd better make a habit of the dead bolt."

Her earlier thought about the building manager resurfaced. "Suppose someone has keys?"

Bonner's brows lifted. "You mean Crenshaw?"

"The outside door is supposed to be locked, but he has keys to all the apartments, doesn't he? Does he do things like that, just walk in when people aren't home?" Maybe she was right to dislike the stocky building manager.

"Not that I know of, unless it's to repair something. Besides, you said he wasn't home."

"What about his wife or the other man?"

Bonner frowned. "What other man?"

Jeanne hugged her arms. "I only caught a glimpse of him. He was tall and thin, with bushy hair." She waggled her hands around her own smooth hairdo to indicate fullness.

"Young? Maybe twenty-four or five?"

"He could have been. I didn't get a good look at him. Mrs. Crenshaw practically slammed the door in my face."

Bonner pursed his lips in a silent whistle. "I didn't know he was home."

"Who?" Jeanne's anxiety took shape again.

"Sonny. The Crenshaw kid. His real name's Norman, I think. They don't talk about him much." He gave Jeanne a serious look. "He's in and out of hospitals all the time. The guy's not playing his tape deck at full speed." He tapped his temple suggestively. "According to them, he's not dangerous, but he sure as hell is strange. He spends a lot of time watching movies and TV. He got in trouble picking flowers over in the park, and he's always talking about evil spirits and crap like that. This is the kind of dumb stunt he'd dream up."

"You mean——" Her mouth was dry.

"Hey, I didn't mean to scare you. Just a warning. If Sonny's around, well—— Lucille and Harry are usually pretty careful about making sure he doesn't roam the building. They've had complaints from tenants before and they're sort of on probation with the owner. I'll see what I can find out. In the meantime, be sure you use the dead bolt, okay?"

"Yes, but if he can get the keys——"

Mark's gnawed his lip. "You should have a chain so you'll feel safe."

"What about the other tenants?" she asked. "I haven't met any of them except Mrs. Saidlow. Would any of them do this?"

Mark knuckled the side of his chin. "There's never been any trouble as long as I've lived here. A guy named Russ Talbot lives over me. He's an accountant or something. A real milk-toast type. Hardly ever see him, and he's not very friendly. Likes his privacy." There was no condemnation in the comment. "The Saidlows are across the hall from him. In 204 over you is a guy named William Zimmerman. I don't know anything about him except he'll bang on the floor if you play your TV or stereo after ten o'clock. He used to bug the hell out of the guy who lived here before you. Above the Crenshaws are the Vernons. They're middle-aged and both work. They're gone most weekends." He calculated silently. "And last not but not least, across the hall from me is Pearl Gannon. She's pushing eighty from the other side and has been here since the building went up. She was an actress back in the heyday of Hollywood. If you fall for an invitation to tea, you're in for a couple of hours of old pictures and stories about how she once worked with Barrymore." Mark smiled to show his gossip wasn't malicious. He gave Jeanne a searching look. "That's the roster. Not exactly a den of iniquity, wouldn't you say?"

"I guess you're right. Still, I would feel better with a chain on the door." She hesitated, then summoned the courage to say, "I know I'm imposing, but could you put one on for me? You said you were handy with tools. I really hate to ask, but if Mr. Crenshaw doesn't come home soon, I'll be a nervous wreck."

A frown banded Mark's face but was erased quickly. "Sure, I'd be glad to. There's a hardware store over on Vermont. I can pick one up and be back in twenty minutes."

Pointing at the dowels, Jeanne said, "Could you get them to cut one of those?"

He tossed one dowel to the sofa. "Sure, but what you really need is a bolt that locks down into the metal frame. One should have been put in, but I guess nobody ever bugged Harry about it. He has to account to the owner for every cent he spends, and the old geezer who owns the building never volunteers anything. He doesn't want to admit this neighborhood isn't what it used to be. I wouldn't send the A-Team out after dark on the other side of Franklin."

He grinned as he spun the dowel like a baton. "This will do the trick tonight, and I'll ask Harry about a bolt in the morning." As he opened the door, he cupped his hand to his mouth and whispered melodramatically, "Two shorts, three longs. Don't open for anyone else, and whatever happens—don't let them get to the radio, as they say in the movies." He winked with exaggeration and sidled into the hall, pulling the door shut behind him.

Jeanne snapped the dead bolt. Even though Mark was trying to allay her fears, she was still nervous. His descriptions made the other tenants sound harmless, but to her they were unknown quantities. When the phone shrilled suddenly, she jumped. Her knees were weak when she lifted the receiver.

"Yes?" It came out a frightened whisper.

"Jeanne? Is something wrong?"

"Oh, Glenn—" Her relief was so immense, she slumped into the chair.

"What's the matter? Are you all right?" He sounded worried.

Jeanne pulled herself together quickly. "Of course I am," she fibbed. "I was pondering the difficult decision of where to hang a picture. It took me a second to get my head together."

"Are you sure?" He sounded dubious.

Jeanne leaned back. "Absolutely. You know how I am when I'm lost in thought."

"You said you were going to call." His tone verged on petulance. "Did you talk to that guy about the car?"

Guilt swamped Jeanne. She should have called Glenn—

and Dr. Ingerman too. She forced a chipper tone. "Matter of fact, that's one of the things that got me distracted. Mark Bonner wasn't home when I knocked, then I had a lovely phone call from Caroline. She sends her love."

"What about the car?" Glenn persisted.

"Well, a little while ago Mark knocked on the door. Would you believe he had the car keys in his hand? He actually brought the car home for me to look at."

"You're kidding."

"Nope. It was parked across the street, and he insisted I take it for a test drive. I'm not an expert, but it seems to handle fine. It's an '80 Toyota Tercel with standard transmission—"

"How many miles on it?"

She told him, and the asking price as well as Bonner's comment they could probably get it for less. "He wants me to drive it to work tomorrow. He even told me a good place to have it checked by a mechanic."

Glenn was silent a moment, then said, "This guy sounds too good to be true. Maybe the mechanic is a buddy of his."

"Oh, Glenn—" She stopped herself from accusing him of paranoia. "I'll take it anywhere you say."

Glenn said, "I'll call Jim Newell. He'll know someone."

"Fine. I have to admit, now that I've actually driven the car, I like the idea of having one again. The first thing I'm going to shop for is a fan. When this place is shut up all day, it gets stuffy."

"Jeanne?"

"Yes?"

"I miss you, baby."

He sounded so wistful, she forgot all the unloving thoughts she'd been harboring. "Oh, darling, I know. I'll be so glad to have you home. Promise me you won't overdo now and have any setbacks."

"I'll be a model patient."

"The days will go fast."

"Not fast enough for me."

Jeanne heard a voice in the background of the hospital noise. A moment later Glenn said, "My remark about being a model patient was overheard by the enemy. They're ready to put me back in my slingshot. I have to go. I'll phone Jim in the morning. Call me about eleven and I'll let you know about the mechanic."

"Okay. Good night, darling." Jeanne hung up the phone and with her head still resting on the back of the chair, glanced around the room. The red flower petals on the floor were the only reminder of her fear. Even the dowel on the sofa was only a piece of wood. Her panic had been totally irrational. She would talk to Crenshaw herself, without accusing, of course, and make it understood that she didn't want anyone coming into the apartment without her permission.

The new chain would calm her nervousness tonight, and when there was a sturdy lock on the patio door, the apartment would lose the forbidding atmosphere she had allowed her loneliness to create.

It was after ten when Mark finished installing the chain, but he assured her he had plenty of time to get to his job as a night security guard. Jeanne felt a little sorry for him, knowing he was a struggling actor, but right now she was grateful for him as a friendly neighbor. When he left, she went through the apartment and locked every window despite the lingering heat.

CHAPTER 9
✝

HE KNEW IT was late, but time was no long measurable in the soft, hot embrace of the night. It had no meaning when he was walking. It passed and changed nothing. He wasn't tired. Just the opposite. Walking helped dissipate the restless energy that festered inside him like an infected wound when he was cooped up too long. Even though he made no attempt to keep track of his random choice of dark streets, he knew his car was at the end of the block. He walked one direction until some inexplicable urge, as if he were receiving silent orders, made him turn a corner. Sometimes it was the shape of a hedge surrounding a yard. Sometimes it was shadows cast by the streetlights. But no matter how many unknowns coaxed him to alter his route, instinct kept him within range of the car.

In the middle of the block he stopped to stare at a long-haired gray cat crouched on a wall. The streetwise animal regarded him with eyes like polished steel, its taut body ready to spring at the first sign of danger. When he tired of the silent, staring battle of wills, he leaped at the animal with a hissing noise and a swinging hand. Soundlessly the cat vanished among the overgrown shrubs.

He laughed silently. Power. It surged through him, filling his mind and banishing the tormenting discontent. He felt exhilarated. He could walk all night without getting tired. He was safe in the night. Safe and strong. He owned the city. He could go anywhere, do anything. On the dark streets no one paid attention to him. He was invisible and invincible.

Even in his random pattern he avoided going down the same streets too often. On hot nights like this people sat by windows to catch the air. He didn't want anyone getting curious about him. There wasn't much chance of anyone calling the cops for something less than murder or mayhem in this neighborhood, but it was smart to be careful. The fancy area a few blocks away was a different story. People in big houses got nervous easily. He found that out one night when he came around a corner and bumped into a Chicano maid putting out the trash. She screamed a torrent of terrified Spanish and dropped the garbage can lid as she ran inside. A second later lights flooded the yard and the driveway. He barely had time to duck out of sight as a burly man in a tuxedo with the tie undone emerged from the house.

Since then, he stayed clear of the hillside blocks and stuck to the area farther south and east. Besides, he was more comfortable here. He'd grown up in this area, only then it was a decent, middle-class neighborhood. It went to seed so gradually he never noticed until it had happened. It was like seeing a picture on the wall for years and taking it for granted, then one day stopping to examine it closely only to find that the sun had faded the colors and a gradual buildup of dust had obscured the details.

It wouldn't be long until these blocks would be as tacky and run-down as the stretch between Hollywood and Sunset. The telltale signs of decay were already showing through the veneer of respectability. Once the erosion began, deterioration would be swift, as it had been elsewhere. It wouldn't be safe to walk the streets at night or even to park your car.

The restless energy he thought gone began to gather again like a rolling cloud. Gray spikes of depression penetrated his thoughts. He shoved his hands into his pockets and hunched his shoulders. He'd go back to the car. Drive somewhere. Maybe up to the reservoir where he used to play as a kid. Maybe up in the mountains, where only the silky sky and stars blanketed the landscape.

A few houses down the street, a woman wearing shorts and a peasant blouse emerged from a lighted house. He stopped and watched her move down the walk, peering under the bushes bordering the yard. She was whispering and spreading branches as she searched. Curious, he moved closer, his hands still in his pockets.

"Suki—here kitty, kitty—" Her whisper floated softly in the night. She must have heard him because she turned suddenly, then darted up the path to the house.

She was scared. He smiled. "You looking for your cat?" he asked in a friendly tone.

She waited until she reached the safety of the door before she looked back. "Yes. A Siamese. Have you seen her?"

"Kinda small?" He took his hands from his pockets and held them apart a cat's length.

"Yes. My boyfriend left the screen open and she got out. She's been declawed. She's not supposed to be outside." She sounded close to tears. Her hand was still on the door, but she didn't open it.

If she worried so damned much about her cat, why hadn't she made sure the screen was latched? She was probably too busy screwing her boyfriend. In that outfit, it was obvious she was a slut. Heat pressed behind his eyes. "I saw a cat just a minute ago," he said, pointing toward the corner. "It ran that way."

"Oh—" The woman glanced over her shoulder at the closed door, then down the dark street.

"I'll see if I can find her for you." As if he had nothing better in the world to do, he continued down the block, darting a gaze sidelong in time to see the woman start down the porch steps. He stopped to check a row of rose bushes along a rail fence around the corner yard and peeked again to see if she was following him. She didn't have on any shoes, and her bare feet made tiny slapping sounds on the pavement. Her thighs and shoulders were tawny against the tight white shorts and low-cut blouse. He stopped when he reached the corner.

"There she is," he said with just enough excitement to make her quicken her steps. "Damn!"

She was right behind him now. "Where? I don't see her. Where is she? Suki—?"

"She ran under that car. I guess I scared her. She doesn't know me." Crouching to look under the car, he closed his hand around the incredible equalizer in his pocket, his fingertip on the magic button that would shoot out the powerful blade. "There she is. *Sssssst*, here kitty, kitty . . ."

The woman knelt, unmindful of the rough, dirty pavement. The neckline of the white blouse sagged under the weight of her breasts. He could smell flowery perfume mingled with her sweat and the musky odor of sex. Her voice was little-girl plaintive. "Suki, here Suki—"

Panting softly through his mouth, he took the knife from his pocket and slipped off the fitted cap with a flick of his thumb. Moving as swiftly and silently as a cat, he grabbed her before she realized what was happening, forcing her head back so her throat was stretched tight and she couldn't yell. He got up, dragging her to her feet. When she began to claw and kick, he raised the knife where she could see it and snapped the release button. Click. The beautiful tapered blade shot out. Her eyes opened so wide he could see white all the way around the dark centers. He brought the blade close and let the finely honed tip nick her cheek. Meaningless whimpers came from her gaping mouth. He shifted the knife to his other hand so the point pressed under her chin would puncture her if she moved. With his free hand he got out his keys and unlocked the car. He opened the door and slid across the seat, dragging her with him, yanking her legs up so he could reach back to slam the door. When his hand touched her warm, bare flesh, he began to tremble.

He was out of breath. He didn't dare let go of her or she'd scream. How was he going to drive? His gaze studied the dark, quiet street as he tried to think. A scene from a movie script he'd read a long time ago flashed in his memory. Smiling, he jammed his feet against the floorboard to raise his hips. Gripping her by the throat, he shoved her head under his thigh. Her hair came loose from its pins and spread across his jeans like moonlight. He grabbed a handful and twisted hard to force her face against the upholstery. She gagged as he let his weight down to hold her. Then using both hands, he wedged the knife handle in his crotch so the point of the blade touched one of her nostrils. In the faint reflection of the distant streetlight, he saw the stark terror in the single eye staring at him. Still smiling, he started the car and turned on the radio before he pulled away from the curb.

CHAPTER 10
✝

IN THE MORNING Jeanne made sure she keyed the dead bolt in place before she went down the hall even though common sense told her that if someone had used a key to enter the apartment last night, he more than likely had a key for the dead bolt as well. The thought wasn't comforting. In the foyer she glanced around nervously as a slightly balding, bespectacled man came down the stairs. He nodded politely. He was younger than she thought at first, no more than thirty, with a thin face under rounded cheekbones, and pale eyes behind the wire-rimmed glasses. Hardly anyone's image of a sneak thief, Jeanne told herself. He crossed the foyer and held the door for her.

"Thanks," she said.

He offered a smile as if it was not something he had a great deal of practice doing. "You must be the new tenant."

"Yes, Jeanne Donovan."

"I'm Russ Talbot. I saw you move in. I heard about the accident. Is your husband getting better?"

"Yes, thank you. He's coming home this weekend."

"I'll bet you're happy. I think you'll like it here. It's a

nice quiet building and a good neighborhood." He stepped out into the morning sunshine behind her, nodding politely again as he walked to a white Ford Escort parked in front of the building.

Jeanne crossed to the Toyota. Tossing her purse and briefcase across the seat, she got behind the wheel and studied the dashboard to refamiliarize herself with the controls. When she checked the gas gauge, the tank was full. Once again she had the uncomfortable feeling that she was taking advantage of Mark Bonner's easygoing nature.

She'd forgotten to reset the alarm last night. She'd be early, but she needed time to get used to the traffic. She had to find out about parking too. The studio had its own lot, but she'd never asked about a card or permit to use it. She'd park on the street while she went up to the office to talk to Callie, then move the car before they viewed yesterday's dailies.

Major studios were extravagant places with huge back lots, private dressing rooms, and plush offices. Harvest Films was housed on the third floor of a converted warehouse that took up an entire city block, except for two fenced areas designated for parking. It had four direct entrances from the street, each leading to a security desk where everyone had to sign in before they could pass through to the inner environs. The main entrance opened to a tiled reception area with the head security desk. A uniformed guard was on duty at all times, and he scrupulously checked identification badges. Anyone without one had to wait while he phoned to make sure the visitor was expected. Two hallways branched at right angles behind the guard's desk, and across from it was the elevator that serviced the upper floors.

The caged elevator was a relic of bygone years. Warehouse-sized, the original grillwork had been covered with reflective metal panels that distorted multiple images of the interior. It reminded Jeanne of the old fun house at Lake

Minnetonka when she was a kid, where angled and curved mirrors cast back dozens of misshapen images.

On the third floor the elevator doors opened directly to the reception room of Harvest Films. Callie Minette, the attractive, young, black receptionist-secretary sat behind a chrome and glass desk that held a modern phone-intercom system in black plastic, stacked, alternating black and white plastic trays for correspondence and memos, a pristine black pen in a chrome holder, and a single white rose in a slender black ceramic bud vase. The effect was early Hollywood, pre-Technicolor, and it never failed to impress visitors. Terry claimed Brad Raven designed it with the cinematic effect in mind.

As if she were part of the decor, Callie dressed in black and white. Today she was elegant in draped, white gauzy cotton with a wide, black patent leather belt and chunky black beads that looked like polished coal. She smiled when she saw Jeanne.

In the few weeks Jeanne had been at Harvest, she and Callie had become friends. From the first day when Callie had given her the grand tour of the studio and introduced her to people, they had gotten along well. Callie had been with Harvest since the company formed, and she knew not only the business side of the company, she knew the business. Without a doubt she kept the wheels oiled and rolling. Several times Callie had given Jeanne a ride to the hospital when they were leaving at the same time.

"How's it going, hon?"

Jeanne jangled the car keys, grinning. "I've got wheels!"

"Hey, all right!" Callie returned the grin.

"It's on trial," Jeanne said.

"What car isn't? Mine's facing the death sentence."

Jeanne laughed. "I hope this one lives up to its advance billing. One of my neighbors lined it up for me. Glenn didn't like the idea of letting someone else pick a car for us, but I pushed him a little."

"Good for you," Callie said. "You've been letting him get away with murder. It's time you stood up for your rights."

"Oh, Callie—"

"Sweetie, don't 'Oh, Callie' me. You know I'm right. Giving in to bad temper doesn't solve problems, it just shoves them under the rug temporarily. You and Glenn are going to have to talk and work this thing out pretty soon."

Jeanne sighed. "I know, but—"

Callie waved a hand. "You'll do it when the time is right. Just don't put it off too long, sweetie. Is the doc still talking about letting him out this weekend?"

Jeanne nodded. "I hope he's not pushing too hard." Guilt sobered her as she realized she hadn't called Dr. Ingerman.

"Stop worrying," Callie said. "Pain is a great teacher. If he overdoes, he'll learn fast enough."

"I know, but—" Seeing Callie's expression, she abandoned her argument. "You're right. Besides I haven't got time to worry about it now. Where do I park my wheels?"

Callie opened a drawer, pulled a parking permit from a file, and signed it. Handing it to Jeanne, she told her how to get into the lot, then said, "Brad cut a scene from today's shooting." At Jeanne's look of dismay, Callie raised a hand. "Not to worry. It's one of those last-second things he does. He told Terry but you were already gone. It doesn't change any of talent calls. He's expanding the murder scene. I put all the information on your desk."

Brad Raven had never said a word about the change during the ride to the hospital! Not one word! She wondered if it gave him some kind of perverse pleasure to make everything as difficult as he could for others.

"I tried calling you last night, but you weren't home,"

Callie said, seeing her expression. "Listen, don't worry about it." She glanced at the black-and-white art-deco clock behind the desk. "Terry won't be ready in the viewing room for fifteen minutes. You'll have time to go over it."

"Raven picked me up at the bus stop and gave me a ride to the hospital last night," Jeanne said angrily. "Why the hell didn't he mention it?"

"He's an odd duck. You just have to accept that. Maybe it's the price of genius."

"I feel sorry for his wife."

Callie laughed. "Wife? No woman would stay married to that one. Brad's a loner, sweetie. I don't think he's ever been married."

"That doesn't surprise me," Jeanne said.

"We don't even have an address on him—can you believe that? Only a phone number, and it's an answering service. He comes and goes without accounting to anyone, but by God, he's one hell of a producer. He's turned down offers from Paramount and Warner. He likes being independent."

And mean, Jeanne thought. The phone buzzed, and Callie tapped a lighted button as she picked it up. "Good morning, Harvest Studios."

Jeanne pushed the call button for the elevator, and the mechanism clanked like rattling sabers. The elevator door opened, and Jeanne had to step back as Brad Raven strode out. Seeing her, he stopped with his back against the door so it didn't close.

"So you got a car," he said.

Jeanne found the fragmented multiple images of his face in the metal panels disconcerting. Surprised, she asked, "How did you know that?" When he pointed to the gate pass and keys in her hand, heat crept along her neck as she struggled to control her embarrassment and the remnants of irritation. "Yes, I did. I always do what I'm *ordered* to do."

The sarcasm was lost on him. "Get it parked so we can

start the dailies on time." He moved away, and the door gave a noisy clatter as it started to close. Jeanne darted inside. When she turned, Callie gave her a thumbs-up sign and a wink before the doors closed.

Brad Raven got to her without half trying, Jeanne thought, and she let him. Calling him difficult was an understatement if she'd ever heard one. He was impossible. Well, from now on, she wouldn't give him the satisfaction of seeing her sweat. Damned if she would! The elevator jerked to a stop on the ground floor and she walked across the lobby, aware of her sandals clacking on the tiles and the security guard's gaze. She pushed open the heavy glass door and stepped out into the rising heat of the Santa Ana.

CHAPTER
11
✝

"WHAT THE HELL have the weirdos got against us?" Parch grimaced as he turned away from the mutilated corpse sprawled on the broken plasterboard, concrete, and wood. He'd left his jacket in the car. His short-sleeved blue shirt was damp and wrinkled, and a faint sheen of perspiration glossed his face. The sun was climbing above the palms east of the vacant lot, and the few degrees of coolness that had come with night were already vanishing as the wind picked up. Flies droning around the blood-encrusted body in the dumpster sounded like heavy equipment warming up for the day.

Remembering the bloated corpse in the closed apartment, Nasty said, "At least we're out in the fresh air." Despite the weather forecast that offered no relief from the Santa Ana, he was dressed more like a bank executive working in an air-conditioned office than a homicide detective. His pale-gray suit was tailored to fit his slender frame, and a knit tie was precisely knotted under the collar of his white shirt.

It was the second time in a week they'd been called out on a murder. Blame it on the Santa Ana. During any hot spell, murders came in batches. Usually they were crimes of passion committed as tempers rose with the thermometer. And usually they were violent. This one was par for the course.

Nasty glanced at the two workmen leaning against a backhoe smoking nervously. "Let's take their statements."

"Shit, let's take 'em in. It's cooler at the office."

Complaining was as natural to Parch as Nasty's unruffled disposition was to him. Nasty learned to ignore it long ago. "Let's finish up before their foreman gets here. He's not going to be happy about the job being held up."

Parch followed Nasty across the uneven ground where a row of small bungalows built in the 1930s had been leveled. The last of the debris had been loaded into dumpsters, ready for hauling. Lines staked out the measurements of the new building, a twenty-four-unit condominium with underground parking. The bright-yellow backhoe with CLARK CONSTRUCTION stenciled on the side was ready to continue excavating as soon as the uninvited corpse and the police left the premises.

When they first teamed up as partners, Parch urged Nasty to handle the note-taking. "Good penmanship is like surgery," he argued. "You gotta have the hands for it. Mine are like baseball mitts compared to yours. Hell, Nasty, my writing's so bad even I can't read it."

Actually, Nasty didn't mind. He was justifiably proud of his neat, small handwriting. Each letter was clearly formed and precisely executed if he could count on the pen not to skip. He hated retractable ballpoints because they made marks like chicken tracks across a dusty yard, so he always used an accountant's black, fine-point pen, and he always carried two backups in his shirt pocket.

Lopez uncapped the pen and opened the report book to a page he'd already headed with the date and the time the call was received. He wrote rapidly as they questioned the two men. It didn't take long, and they didn't have any information that was helpful. They were two innocent schmucks who turned up for work on time and had the bad luck to discover a murder victim. The little guy, Ulster, spotted the body in the dumpster when he climbed up onto the seat of the backhoe. His face was still pale as he told the story, and he chain-lit another cigarette with shaking hands.

Harmanski had even less to offer. He'd taken one look at the corpse when his partner yelled, then used the company truck's radio phone to call the dispatcher, who, in turn, called the job foreman and the police. Harmanski hadn't studied the corpse's face, didn't want to, thank you, but he was positive he didn't know her. Ulster nodded emphatic agreement.

The coroner's wagon and a blue and white van with the Clark Construction Company name and logo on the door pulled up at the same time. The foreman jumped out and hurried toward the men standing near the backhoe, as if it were imperative for him to reach them before the coroner did.

"What the hell's going on?" he demanded. "I'm Clyde Jeppson. I'm in charge of this job. Christ, we're losing money by the goddamn minute. We're already an hour behind schedule." He glanced around as the coroner's assistant moved toward the dumpster. "This business has nothing to do with us. Anybody could have been here during the night, fer crissake."

Lopez returned to the dumpster, leaving Parch to handle the irate foreman. The tall, thin coroner's assistant greeted him.

"This makes twice this week, Nasty. What are you guys doing, going for a new city record? Don't you ever find bodies at a decent hour of the day? I had only four hours' sleep last night."

"She's already attracting flies. In another hour or two, she'll be really ripe," Nasty said.

"Well, let's get it over with. I'll need something to stand on. Damned if I'm going to climb in there with her." Kroeger glanced around, saw a metal milk carrier, retrieved it, and braced it firmly against the side of the dumpster. Lopez stepped back to let him do his work. Kroeger balanced his black bag on a corner of the dumpster and opened it. Pulling on rubber gloves, he selected instruments with the intensity of a surgeon, then leaned over the body.

Lopez was glad he couldn't see what Kroeger was doing. Despite his outward calmness, he wouldn't have Kroeger's job on a bet. He'd seen a lot of dead bodies in five years in homicide, and he'd almost gotten used to it. Almost, but not quite. But he didn't want to touch them. He wouldn't admit it, but it made his insides churn to think about it. He glanced at Ken and saw he'd calmed down the foreman, who now was in earnest conversation with the two workmen near the truck.

Parch came over to the dumpster. "I convinced him it would be awhile. He's trying to con them into taking the morning off, but they're not falling for it. Now that they're over the shock of seeing Miss Pretty, they're ready for a l-o-n-g coffee break." Another van pulled up behind the parked vehicles. "Here's the crime unit."

Parch and Lopez walked to the van, and after acknowledging the greetings of the other men, gave them what little information they had. One man began tying yellow plastic ribbons to rope off the area. Jeppson was apoplectic when it included the backhoe and the excavation site.

"Jesus Christ, how long you guys gonna tie me up like this?"

No one answered.

Ten minutes later Kroeger dropped his instruments into

a plastic bag and put it in his case. He climbed down, holding his hands out like a scrubbed surgeon.

"From the liver temperature, I put the time of death around midnight. Don't quote me until we get her on the table, but cause of death is probably stabbing. She's got two heart wounds, either of which could have been fatal. From the semen in her pubic hair, I'd say she was raped. The way her clothes are slashed fit the picture. If you want an off-the-record guess, it might be the same weapon that killed that hooker a few days ago. The size of the slits and pattern, if you can call it that, are the same, and she's got bruises on her neck. The killer probably held her down while he had his fun, just like the hooker."

Lopez capped his pen slowly. Parch shook his head like a enraged bull eyeing a red cape. "Aw, c'mon, Kroeger," he pleaded, "say it isn't so."

Kroeger shrugged. "Forget I said it. I'll let the coroner take the rap when he releases the report."

"One killer, two bodies?" Lopez asked of no one in particular. Parch began to whistle "In the Good Old Summertime" off-key.

"Thanks, Kroeger," Lopez said. "I hope you're wrong this time, but you've got me worried. I can't remember the last time you made a mistake, even guessing."

Kroeger nodded and walked back to the dumpster, where he spread a black body bag on the ground and motioned to a uniformed cop to help him lift out the corpse. The officer glanced at Nasty, who nodded, then pulled on the gloves Kroeger held out to him.

"A weirdo baying at the moon two nights in one week?" Parch asked with a pained expression.

Lopez said, "If he's right, we'll be able to work on both cases at the same time."

"Yeah, sure. Let's hope to hell that's all it is. The last fucking thing we need in this heat is Son of Jack the Ripper."

CHAPTER 12
†

THE HUNCHED FIGURE staggered to his feet and stared down at the sprawled woman. Her legs were a pale blur against the blanket spread on the floor of the empty room. The yellow skirt pulled up around her hips was soaked with blood. She lay motionless as the camera panned slowly across the torn blouse and exposed breasts before closing in on her face, which was marked with oozing cuts. Her mouth was pulled back in a rictus of terror, and her eyes stared blankly. The camera dollied back to a long shot framed by the knife in the man's hand.

"Cut it."

"We're cut."

The lockup buzzer blared twice to open the set. Jeanne took a deep breath. The actors had held her spellbound, and her heart was racing as though she'd witnessed a real murder. Wray Jarvis was terrific. The changes Brad Raven had made in the scene were nothing short of genius. He had honed the emotional impact of the murder scene to stunning perfection. The actors felt it. Everyone on the set did. The shot went without a hitch, and they had a perfect take on the first try.

"Good work, team. You did a hell of a job," Faust said, moving toward Jeanne as the cameramen pulled back. The actress playing the victim scrambled to her feet and joined Jarvis as he walked off the set.

Jeanne raised her voice. "Your call is at three Monday." Jarvis smiled and waved acknowledgment.

Terry grinned at Jeanne as he lit a cigarette. "Good day," he said.

"Good? It was fantastic. Working with you is better than going for a Ph.D. And mad as I was about Brad's last-minute changes, I have to admit they made the killer so believable I was shivering. The scene is one of the best I've ever seen."

Terry grinned. "I told you he was tops."

"That you did. You also told me he was 'difficult,' and I won't argue with that either."

"Maybe we're all hard to get along with at times. Brad's got to answer to the money men. He's under a lot of pressure."

"I suppose," she said grudgingly. It was hard to forgive Raven's rudeness.

Terry changed the subject. "What's the status of talent for Monday?"

Jeanne said, "Velasquez, Dryden, Stave, and Decker are on call for eight-thirty, Jarvis and Bart for three. We've got five atmospheres for the apartment scene at ten-thirty. We should finish up with Velasquez and Dryden by then. If not, we can shoot out of sequence."

"You make my job easy, Jeanne. It's great working with you." Faust blew a set of lazy smoke rings onto the darkened set as electricians began to coil cables and push light standards against the wall.

"That's actually the other way around, but you always were modest."

Faust considered the ash on his cigarette before he flicked it on the floor. "How's Glenn doing?"

Jeanne's voice lost some of its bantering tone. "Fine. He's coming home tomorrow."

"That's great." He looked at her candidly. "Going on location next week means rotten hours, Jeanne, no way around it. Are you going to be able to handle everything?"

Terry had gone out of his way for her and she appreciated it, but Brad Raven had already made it clear she'd get no more special treatment. "I'll work it out, I promise," she said. "Thanks for worrying."

"Hey, you and I go back a long way, kid." Terry squeezed her shoulder and winked before he walked off.

Jeanne slid from the high, canvas chair that bore not her name but the inscription #1 AD, as if to humble her by hinting a replacement could easily be accommodated. When she turned, she was startled to find Brad Raven standing at the rear of the studio watching her. His bright-yellow shirt stood out against the shadows. She wondered if he'd been listening.

She walked over to him. "I haven't had a lot of experience with features, Brad, but that had to be one of the most powerful scenes ever put on film. I'm proud to be part of Harvest. I mean that sincerely."

"It was good," Raven said. "Jarvis has talent. He may go places if he doesn't let success rush to his head." He paused, as if he realized he'd been chatting amiably. He started to walk away, then looked back. "Make sure someone double-checks the caterers for locations next week."

Someone like me, Jeanne thought. But it was her responsibility, and at least Raven was being civil.

Around the set, lights went off. Shadows lengthened in the big room. Raven was silhouetted momentarily against the brightness of the hall as someone pushed open the door.

As the door swung shut, Raven became a shadowy figure again.

"On Monday I want Terry to take you out to see the locations we'll be using next week so you can do all the setups ahead of time. We can't afford to waste any good light. And get the schedule blocked out over the weekend." He hesitated, then said, "Unless you have something more important to do?" His voice was heavy with sarcasm.

Jeanne nodded, not trusting her tongue. So much for being civil, she thought.

"Good." With that, he walked away. His footsteps echoed in the cavernous room as he headed not for the hall leading to the offices but for the door beside the storage room. Jeanne didn't know where it led, but right now she hoped it was to a sheer drop of three stories.

Brad Raven was a pompous ass, but angry as he made her, she had to admit that he still had a team that was willing to do its damnedest for the picture. In spite of his high irritability quotient, Raven had mastered the winning combination of artistic and practical talents. His suggestions gave that last scene an aura of terror she wouldn't have thought possible. There was no doubt about it, this picture would keep audiences on an emotional brink. She had the feeling it was going to make the success of *Death Pact* pale by comparison.

She watched the grips store the last of the equipment. When they finished, the number one grip glanced around. Seeing Jeanne, he raised his hand in salute.

"Want me to leave the lights on, Mrs. Donovan?"

"No, it's okay, Bill. I'm on my way."

"It was a good day," he said, grinning.

Jeanne smiled. "You have a great crew."

Bill left, snapping off all but one panel of ceiling lights near the door. Jeanne glanced around the empty studio. Shadows lurked along the walls and in corners. The booms were dark outlines like hovering aliens. The studio had been constructed on the upper floor of the building where there was no ceiling other than the rafters and roof. Overhead, exposed wiring and ductwork crisscrossed like webbing spun by a gargantuan spider. On poles hanging down fifteen feet, black curtains slid along tracks that roughly outlined divisions of small sets that could be sectioned off. Behind the folds of drapery, movable sets were lined up like wooden soldiers.

Few changes had been made in the original layout of the warehouse when it was converted to a studio. One end of the room was walled off for storage space. In the center of one of the long walls, a utility room housed circuit breakers, power controls, and the air-conditioning unit. Opposite it was the main entrance from the dressing rooms and the lounge, which was no more than a wide area of the hall with several chairs and couches. Except for the equipment pushed against them and a dimly lit door marked FIRE EXIT, the other two walls of the big room were bare.

This was reality, Jeanne thought. Here in Hollywood and across the country there were hundreds of studios like this. Empty space, lights, camera and sound equipment. The heyday of sprawling megastudios was over. Home video, network TV, and pay cable had supplanted superstars and studio moguls. A picture that wasn't a smash at the box office could make it through other outlets. Harvest had proven its ability to win audiences with *Death Pact*. It was going to do the same with *Dead Past*. And she was part of it.

Picking up her clipboard, she opened the door to the lounge and snapped the light switch as she went out. Then she turned as she heard something at the far end of the studio. She snapped the lights back on.

"Anyone here?" Her voice echoed in the dim cave of shadows. Faintly but unmistakably, one of the black curtains suspended from ceiling tracks swayed. Jeanne had only a glimpse of the figure that moved behind it, but she couldn't mistake Brad Raven's yellow shirt.

The garage Jim Newell recommended to Glenn was only a few blocks from the hospital. The mechanic hooked up the Toyota to a diagnostic machine and put it through its paces while Jeanne watched from the waiting room. When he finally detached the last cable, he spread a length of white paper across the driver's seat before he got behind the wheel, backed the car out of the garage, and turned onto the street. Ten minutes later he was back.

"It's a good buy at two grand," he told Jeanne. "It uses a little oil and may need a valve job down the road six or eight months, but if you change the oil regularly, it shouldn't give you trouble. With the kind of mileage it's got, it's probably been used mostly for city driving, but someone's taken damned good care of it." The mechanic, whose coveralls had the name "Tony" embroidered over the pocket, grinned. "As is, I could sell it tomorrow for twenty-two five. If you decide not to take it, ask your friend to give me next crack at it."

Relieved, Jeanne thanked him and paid the bill. She was pleased, and she hoped the report would put Glenn's mind at ease about the car. It certainly made her grateful she had met Mark Bonner. She still couldn't believe her luck.

At the hospital Glenn's supper tray had come and he was eating without enthusiasm. She told him the news in a burst of excitement. Pushing aside his tray, he began to talk about practical things, such as the pink slip and getting the registration signed over.

Jeanne moved the tray back in front of him. "You can talk and eat at the same time."

He tried to slide it away again, but Jeanne wedged it firmly in place. "You've barely touched it. Come on, I know it isn't gourmet, but it's got all the calories and good stuff you need to get well." In her excitement she hadn't noticed how pale he was. Worried, she leaned closer and touched his cheek. "Are you all right? Nothing's happened, has it? Guiltily she recalled her failure to call Dr. Ingerman. *As soon as I get home tonight,* she promised herself.

"I'm bored with this damned place. You're working and having cars checked and doing everything while I lie here like a lump of sod. I feel stupid and helpless. I need to get out and back to work."

"Then eat your dinner." At his quick scowl she sighed. "Please don't be difficult, Glenn. You know you have to keep up your strength. I want you home well and strong."

He picked up his fork and poked at a slice of overdone beef smothered in gravy. "I'm sorry we ever left Minneapolis. I hate L.A."

Jeanne's hands clenched in her lap. "All you've seen is a crowded freeway and the less-than-spectacular view from this window. I don't blame you a bit." She was determined to stay cheerful. "Too bad you don't have a roommate. That bed's been empty the whole time. I thought hospitals were supposed to be overcrowded."

"People are dying to get out of this one."

She grimaced at his horrible joke, and he gave her a weak smile.

"Sorry, I'm grumbling again, and I promised not to. It's just that I really am sick of this place, and I worry about you being alone. The newspaper is full of stories of robberies, rape, and murder. It worries me. Just a couple of days ago they found a woman murdered in Los Feliz. Isn't that where the apartment is?"

She studied him with suspicion, hoping he wasn't going to give her a hard time now about the apartment. He was searching for things to worry about. Or was he actually upset about something he wasn't telling her? Surely Dr. Ingerman would have let her know if anything serious had come up. She renewed her vow to check with him tonight to be sure.

"And you worry me," she told Glenn in a firm tone. She had been too busy to read a newspaper since she moved into the apartment, but murder was hardly big news in L.A. "Gory stories sell newspapers. Don't read them if they upset you. You are fine, I am finer, and when you come home tomorrow, we will be the finest! Now stop worrying. That's an order!" She held out the fork he'd put down. "Now eat. That's an order, too!"

He sighed heavily. "Okay, okay. I'll eat, you talk."

Hopeful that his black mood might be lifting, she decided not to tell him about the strange incident in the apartment last night or the new chain Mark Bonner had installed for her safety. Instead, she gave an amusing account of her day's work, elaborating here and there as she would its telling a bedtime story to a child. She was careful not to be overly enthusiastic about how well the film was shaping up for fear of renewing his irritability about his own inactivity. She didn't mention Raven by name, but Glenn interrupted to ask if the producer had made any more passes at her. Jeanne treated it as a joke by saying Raven had been too busy being Wonder Boy to do more than growl.

While Glenn ate peach cobbler, Jeanne asked, "What about your day? How did it go? Did you walk?"

He made a face.

"What happened?" she asked quickly.

"They say I'm doing fine, but my feet still feel like they're on fire. I was only up twenty minutes and I *asked* to go back."

"Twenty minutes is wonderful!" She coaxed him to talk about it. Who had helped him? How far had he gone? She drew words from him as she would a sulky child. Her praise finally had him smiling, but she knew his progress had not met his expectations. She was careful to hide her disappointment.

"Ingerman wants to send me home in an ambulance," Glenn said, scowling again. "But as long as you've got a car, you can take me."

"Oh, Glenn, I don't know. It'll be hard for you to get in and out."

An angry tic jerked the corner of his mouth. "I'm not a helpless cripple. I'll manage."

His tone was knife-edged, and Jeanne withdrew in hurt silence. After a moment Glenn went on as if nothing was wrong.

"That way I'll be able to have a look at the car, too. If its really a good deal, you can tell Bonner we'll take it. If it's the bargain everyone says it is, we better grab it before the guy changes his mind. We'll offer him eighteen hundred. No sense going any higher unless we have to. You'll have to get a cashier's check, but don't hand it over until he signs the registration, you hear?"

She couldn't believe this was her husband she was listening to. Did he hear himself? She didn't trust herself to say anything, and when he finally wound down, she picked up her purse and rose to go.

"Hey, you're not leaving already?" He reached out a hand as if to stop her.

"I have to, hon." The endearment came out of habit, not her emotions of the moment. "I have a million things to do before you get home." She bent to kiss him, and he turned his cheek and closed his eyes.

In the car she sat trying to stem her resentment. Damn it, she was tired too. Glenn rattled off orders like a drill sergeant one minute, then pouted like a two-year-old the next. She didn't care if he was in pain, he was being impossible. When she called Dr. Ingerman she was going to ask him point-blank if Glenn was really ready to be released. If Ingerman had so much as a single qualm, she'd ask him to keep Glenn in the hospital awhile longer——for her sake as well as his.

On Hollywood Boulevard, Jeanne knew she should stop and do the grocery shopping, but the supermarket parking lot was packed and she didn't have the energy to fight the crowds. She'd do it in the morning. With the car it wouldn't take long. Behind her a horn honked impatiently and she realized the light had changed. *Pay attention, kiddo,* she warned herself, *or you'll be trampled in the rush.*

Cars lined both side of the street bumper to bumper. Jeanne realized it didn't pay to be the last one home if you wanted a parking place in this neighborhood. She drove up the hill without finding a spot, then went around the block and down the route she'd taken the night before. The two streets came together at a Y just below a Victorian-looking apartment building with high, old-fashioned mullioned windows. She found a spot not far from the corner and eased the car in on the first try, despite the hill. Remembering to angle the wheels, something that was rarely necessary in Minneapolis, she locked the car and walked around the corner. The sun had set and the pink-blue twilight was deepening rapidly. Pale splashes of streetlights magnified shadows of leaves whipping in the overheated wind. The temperature still hovered in the nineties even though the stinging glare of the sun had yielded to twilight. Maybe she should have gone shopping. With another stifling night in the offering, a fan would be a godsend.

As she crossed the street, lights of a car coming down the hill splashed over her. She hurried to the curb, but the car stopped fifty yards up the street in front of a driveway. The headlights went out and the purr of the engine hovered in the quiet gloom, but no one got out. Jeanne crossed the sidewalk and unlocked the door, anxious to be inside.

The mailbox yielded a letter from Caroline and an advertising circular. Inside the apartment she set the dead bolt and the chain, then dropped onto the sofa. Caroline's letter was full of chatter and interesting tidbits about people they both knew. Jeanne's new address and phone number had been given to one and all, as well as changed on the mailing lists of the Guthrie Theater and Orchestra Hall so the transplants would stay informed on what was happening back home. Caroline had visited Glenn's father in the nursing home, and he was doing fine even though he didn't want to admit how much he missed his son and daughter-in-law. Knowing it was difficult for the old man to write at any length, Caroline had left a stack of stamped, addressed postcards so he could send one off every few days to California.

When she finished reading, Jeanne felt better. Caroline's letters had that effect, even though they left Jeanne with a faint touch of homesickness. Determined to banish it, she told herself they could—*would*—have a good life here just as they had had in Minneapolis. And there'd be no more snow to shovel or cars to jump-start at thirty below zero. No more windchill factor, no more hot, muggy summers and hungry mosquitoes.

She got up and went through the apartment opening windows. In the bedroom she saw that Mark Bonner had kept his word about having Crenshaw install a bolt on the sliding glass door. She knelt to examine the shiny steel contrivance. A bolt slipped into holes drilled through the metal track. There were two, one that would fasten the door open two inches, a second two inches farther back. She experimented with the door at each position and decided she was more comfortable with the narrower opening when she was alone in the apartment.

While her dinner was heating, she forced herself to phone Glenn to tell him she was home safely and to say good night. At his lack of enthusiasm she was sorry she had bothered. She placed a call to Dr. Ingerman's exchange and asked that he return her call at his earliest convenience. The oven timer buzzed, and she took out the linguini with clam sauce that was her blindman's-bluff choice of freezer food tonight. Sitting at the table, she found a pad and pencil and began to make a list while she ate.

Grocery shopping. Buy a fan. Check the Thomas Brothers map book for an alternate route to the studio and the hospital. Today she had gone along the bus route and had run into several pockets of heavy morning traffic. She was sure she could find side streets just as direct and a lot faster. Do laundry. Crenshaw had told her there were coin machines in the basement, but so far she had not used them. Things would be hectic next week with Glenn home. She considered doing the laundry tonight, but the thought of venturing into the as-yet-unexplored basement wasn't appealing, so she earmarked yet another chore for morning.

The shrill of the phone in the quiet apartment made her jump. It was Dr. Ingerman. Glenn was making excellent progress, he assured her, though it would be some time before his bones were completely healed. It would be a week or two before he should be out of bed for very long at a time, and an additional two weeks until he attempted to resume activity on any normal scale. However, the doctor was convinced that going home would bolster Glenn's spirits and constitute a form of therapy as valuable as any the hospital could offer. Arrangements had been made for a physical therapist to begin working with him on Monday at home. All Jeanne had to do was stop at the rehabilitation department tomorrow and complete the necessary forms.

Jeanne hung up with a sense of relief and vague disappointment. It was disloyal to wish Ingerman had suggested keeping Glenn longer, but she realized she had been hoping just that. In light of his positive outlook, she could hardly suggest it. She prowled the apartment restlessly. It would take most of Saturday to get Glenn home and settled. He'd be exhausted, she knew. And Brad Raven wanted the schedule ready by Monday. Doing it would take a good chunk out of Sunday, and she'd have to leave Glenn to his own devices. She glanced around, wondering nervously if he'd like the apartment. She wished there were some way she could stay home until the therapist came Monday just to make sure Glenn could manage.

Stop worrying, she told herself. Glenn would be fine. Maybe it would do him good to be alone awhile. Right now she'd better not waste time. She set about cleaning the kitchen, then went through the apartment like a whirlwind, dusting and vacuuming until it was spotless. Promptly at ten o'clock her upstairs neighbor banged on the floor, and Jeanne remembered Mark Bonner's admonition about the curfew. She stuck out her tongue at the ceiling and put away the vacuum.

A relaxing soak in the tub and the luxury of reading in bed for a while before she went to sleep were in order. She started the water and propped open the bathroom window with a small block of wood. She discovered after moving in that the cord of the double-hung window was broken. The top portion was sealed shut by layers of paint, so the only way to get air was to prop open the bottom. The block of wood obviously had been left for that purpose. Despite the fact that the window was seven feet above the walkway, Jeanne pulled the worn, cracked shade down as far as it would go, which was almost to the sill. While it was fresh in her mind, she found a tape measure in the den and measured the shade so she could put a new one on her shopping list.

In the morning she'd do the laundry, shop for a fan, the shade, and a few other household items, and go to the market. She'd stock the cupboards. No more quickie frozen meals. Saturday night would be candlelight and champagne. Cornish game hens stuffed with wild rice and mushrooms?

No, something that required less cooking so the apartment wouldn't overheat. Lobster salad and fresh artichokes. She could prepare everything ahead and buy some of those chocolate-covered wafers Glenn liked for dessert. A light, nourishing dinner would be perfect.

Pulling a towel from the rack, she patted drops of moisture from her skin, then let her body air-dry. Despite the open window and door, the bathroom was steamy, and she had to rub the mirror with a corner of the towel so she could see to apply moisturizer to her face. Pulling off the terry band holding up her hair, she brushed it until it curled damply. As she reached for the batiste nightgown she'd hung on the hook behind the door, a sound made her whirl. Outside, the scraping noise was followed by a soft thud and a muttered curse. Heart racing, Jeanne snapped off the light as she heard the sound of someone running along the walkway between the buildings.

BODY OF WOMAN FOUND IN DUMPSTER

The mutilated body of a woman was discovered in a dumpster at a construction site in Los Feliz by workers early yesterday morning. The woman suffered multiple stab wounds, according to the coroner, who estimated the time of death between 12 and 2 A.M. The body has been identified as that of Vicki Ewing, of 400 Talmadge Street, who was last seen about midnight. Police refuse to comment on similarities between Ewing's murder and that of a woman whose body was found two days ago in an apartment in Los Feliz, not far from the site of yesterday's discovery. The earlier murder victim has now been identified as Lily White, a known prostitute. So far police have not uncovered any connection between the two women.

CHAPTER 13
✝

HE READ THE story a third time. Lily White. Now he remembered her saying her name was Lily, but she never told him about the "White." He would have laughed right in her face. Wouldn't you know she'd pick a name like that. Her johns probably got a good laugh whenever she pulled it on them.

And the other one, Vicki Ewing. That was almost as phony. The newspaper didn't say she was a prostitute, but it should have. Even if she didn't pick guys up on the street it amounted to the same thing. He knew as soon as he saw her in that skimpy outfit, with her hair all tousled because she had just climbed out of bed. They didn't fool him, not since Gretchen. There weren't any nice girls in this town. There were plenty who looked okay, but when you got to know them, the masks fell away and you saw the bitches for what they really were. He'd seen plenty. Sometimes he made a game of watching women when they didn't know it. It was the best way to learn what they were really like. Catch them when the thoughts running through their minds were exposed on their faces. When they thought they didn't have to play a part.

Not that there was anything wrong playing a role. He did it like everyone else. It was part of the game. Like the other night when he pretended to—what the hell was her name? . . . he glanced at the newspaper—Vicki Ewing that he'd seen her cat. He knew the gray cat he chased wasn't her Siamese, but for a minute it made her happy to think it was. And it made her follow him.

He scrubbed the ridge of his jawbone with a knuckle. Had he wanted her to follow him? Certainly he hadn't planned it, no more than he'd planned to kill Lily. He didn't know Vicki Ewing would be on that street right then. But she was. That was the invitation to start the game. What would he have done if she had run back into the house when she saw him? Nothing. Not a damn thing. Hell, if she didn't want to play, he'd have walked on. But she did want to play, and she made her move. She believed him about the cat and followed him to the corner. Then he got her into the car. His move.

He had considered taking her up to the reservoir or some other isolated place, but that wasn't much of a challenge. So he decided he'd find a place within ten blocks. Ten blocks from where he found her would be the board for the game. All games had limits and rules. The more he thought about it, the more excited he got. And when he spotted the construction shack, he knew he'd found exactly what he wanted.

The girl was too scared to do anything with the point of the blade touching her nose that way. One little move and *zap*—just like Jack Nicholson in *Chinatown*. When he parked on the dark street near the construction site, she didn't even try to make a break for it or yell. It was her choice, and *that* was a stupid move. He knew then that he was going to win.

The tears running down her cheeks like dirty water left

smudged tracks of mascara on her skin. Her eyes were so puffy he could hardly see the pupils. When he dragged her out of the car, she was almost choking on sobs, but she kept nodding and moving her lips, trying to tell him she'd do whatever he wanted. He made her carry the blanket while he kept the knife against her neck. When he asked her something, she was shaking too hard to answer. He remembered laughing and asking her if it was hot enough for her, and she even pretended to laugh at the stupid joke. It was astonishing what people did when they were scared. He practically had to hold her up as they scrambled across the lot. She was crying so hard she kept stumbling and sliding.

The little fool cowered like a kicked puppy while he forced the padlock on the shed door, then stepped right inside when he told her to, like an actress taking directions from off camera. For kicks, he made *her* spread the blanket. She had to know what was coming, but still she didn't scream. What a stupid broad. The game moved very fast after that. His memory was out of focus, but the feel of his hand on her throat was vivid, and the look of terror on her face. He fueled his excitement by telling her over and over how the blade would zap out when he pressed the release. Christ, she almost wet her pants. Chicken-shit whore. Her flesh was pale and flabby when he cut away the tight shorts and panties and the low-cut blouse, using only the tip of the blade, but pretending he was going to push the button. When she wouldn't stop whimpering, he pricked her a couple of times until finally she lay still, completely subjugated, waiting. Damn, he'd been excited. He was excited now thinking about it. He closed his eyes and breathed through his mouth until the exquisite pain passed.

He picked up the *Times* and read the story again. "Police refuse to comment on similarities between . . ." What similarities? Two completely different girls in two separate places. Those freaky cop doctors probably could measure wounds and tell what made them, but could they tell for sure it was the same weapon? For a moment his elation drained. He jumped up and went to the closet, shoving aside things on the shelf so he could reach the cloth-wrapped bundle. He carried it back to the light and unwrapped the silky white cloth and took out the beautiful weapon he'd cleaned and polished so carefully. He ran his hand along the handle, flicked off the plastic cap, then caressed the release button with a feathery touch before he pressed it. The click was loud in the quiet room, and even though he was watching for it, the blade shot out faster than his eye could track it. One second there was only an inch of slender, tapered steel. A hundredth of a second later, the six-inch shaft glistened in the light. He was hypnotized by the beauty of the slim rod.

His fears vanished as if a surgeon's blade had exorcised a malignant growth. Elation returned in a heady rush. Let the cops run their tests. Let them find their damned similarities. He wanted them to know it was the same weapon. Even if they knew what it looked like, it wouldn't do them a fucking bit of good. The stupid cops hadn't even caught on to the name of the game. They didn't have the slightest idea what he'd do next.

Savoring his triumph, he ran his fingertip down the length of the triangular shaft. The warm steel was as provocative as a woman's silken breast. He stroked it lovingly before he reset the plastic tip guard and exerted the force of his other palm to shove the blade into the hilt so the lock caught. Rewrapping it in the silky material, he returned it to its hiding place, then turned off the light and sat in the dark room, remembering . . . remembering how he felt at the instant Vicki Ewing died.

CHAPTER 14

JEANNE WOKE AT five-thirty. She was sweating and headachy from uneven sleep filled with dreams of shadowy figures stalking her. Too much imagination born of working on a film about a serial killer, she told herself. She got up and dressed in shorts and a tank top. It was time to reestablish some semblance of her normal habits. A brisk jog would stretch her muscles and clear her head.

Heat lay in pools along the street, which was stagnant in the calm early hour before the city stirred and the Santa Ana gathered force to sweep down with the ferocity of a brush fire. The sun that had not yet scaled the San Bernardino Mountains cast a flat, molten glow across the sky.

She walked up the hill, increasing her speed gradually until at the top she found an easy jogging pace. She chose streets at random until she reached Los Feliz Boulevard, then circled east until she reached Vermont. It felt good to be out, but she had too much to do to explore the neighborhood fully, though she was impressed by the size and grandeur of some of the homes she passed. All in all, the area was a pleasant mixture of upper and very upper middle class.

She cut back across Franklin to the apartment. If she didn't get busy, the morning would be gone and she wouldn't have everything done before she had to pick up Glenn. She realized she was nervous about his coming home. She wanted him to be in a good mood. She wanted him to like the apartment. She wanted everything to be perfect, and she wanted everything to go smoothly next week when her long days on location began.

At the front door, curiosity got the better of her and she crossed to the walkway that ran along the side of the building. Last night when the first paralyzing wave of panic had subsided and she'd shut and locked the bathroom window, she tried to convince herself the sounds she'd heard were something quite innocent. Judging by her restless sleep, she hadn't succeeded.

So take a look, she told herself.

The walkway angled from the wide frontage on the street to the narrower rear of the lot. Standard rectangular lots took up the base of the Y to the corner of Franklin. Uphill, the remaining lots were also rectangular, leaving this oddly shaped piece of property that called for architectural ingenuity. The building had been designed in the shape of a triangle, with one straight wall from the right angle, the other a slanted hypotenuse.

Glad that Mark was out of town so he wouldn't see her skulking past his windows, she saw that his apartment varied only a couple of feet in width from front to back. The difference was more pronounced in her apartment. The walk and the building's outer wall slanted at nearly a forty-five-degree angle. The concrete path sloped downward with the natural terrace of the lot, and it was bordered on both sides by narrow plant beds that looked remarkably healthy even though they got so little direct sun.

She had left her kitchen and living room windows open on the chains, and she was relieved to discover it was impossible to see inside the apartment. Straining on tiptoes she could glimpse only narrow slivers of wall and ceiling through the openings. The kitchen window was as high as her head, the others even higher. Across from her living room there was a door in the building on the opposite side of the walkway. It was two steps below the level of the path, and the metal was filmed with dirt and fingerprints. A fire exit or the door used to carry out the trash. Hardly sinister.

She stopped under the bathroom window. When she stretched her arm, her fingertips barely brushed the sill. A basketball player or circus freak might be tall enough to raise himself to it, but anyone else would have to stand on something or be a human fly. She glanced around, but there wasn't anything to stand on. *All right, scaredy cat,* she told herself, *you let your imagination run away with you. You're too immersed in the script of* Dead Past, *admit it.* The noise had come from somewhere else. The tunnel formed by the buildings bounced sounds. They could have come from anywhere. The most logical spot was the basement door of the other building. Someone came out, stumbled, and then reacted in a perfectly normal way by muttering as he hurried off. She was going to have to get used to strange noises, that was all there was to it.

The space between the buildings widened near the back of the lot, and the builder had taken advantage of it by putting in the small patio deck off the bedroom. From the walkway there were three steps up to the gate. There was no latch on the outside, but a cord was strung through a hole. The latch clicked when she pulled it, but to her relief the gate didn't open. She reminded herself to check the slide bolt every day.

Beyond the patio, the rest of the building was blank except for a small dusty window. Judging by the distance from the bedroom, it had to be in the hall behind the apartment. Probably a storage room of some sort. At the back of the lot the adjoining property facing the next street dropped off several feet. It was surrounded by a fence overgrown with bougainvillea and oleander. All she could make out beyond it was the roof of a garage.

The walkway went around the rear of the building where a flight of steps led to the door with the fanlight. It was locked, but her building key opened it. In the back hall the basement door under the stairs was ajar. Opposite it was another door. She had assumed there was nothing beyond the wedged closet in the bedroom, but it made sense that what would otherwise be dead space had been utilizied. Not sure why, she tried the knob, but it didn't turn. She went back to the basement door and snapped on the light. Taped directly above the switch was a hand-lettered sign: SHUT ALL LIGHTS OFF WHEN YOU LEAVE THE BASEMENT!!

Jeanne held the wooden rail as she made her way down the dimly lit steps. At the bottom it was as dark as a cave. Two small windows were so covered with grime and dust she could barely make them out. She felt for another light switch before she dared move. This time several lights came on. The one directly overhead showed the wire-grill-enclosed storage spaces Mr. Crenshaw had told her about. Toward the front of the building, a brighter fluorescent light illuminated the laundry room. She headed for it. One washing machine and one dryer. There'd probably be a traffic jam on weekends when tenants were off work. She read the instructions on the machines to see how many quarters she needed, then glanced around for rules about hours the machines could be used. There were none.

No time like the present, she decided. She could run two loads and be finished in an hour and a half. Remembering to snap off the lights as she reached the top of the stairs, she went back to the apartment to collect the laundry basket and detergent. Ten minutes later she was back in the basement sorting clothes and feeding soap and quarters into the washing machine.

Jeanne showered before she ran downstairs to put the clothes in the dryer and throw the second load in the washer. Standing at the stove, she eyed the clock as she drank a glass of orange juice while her egg fried. Twenty-five minutes for the washing machine . . . the delicates would be dry by then. Say a half hour to dry the heavier things. She could be at the supermarket before nine, back by ten.

The charge nurse on Glenn's station said he couldn't be released until after the doctor made rounds. On Saturday that usually was about noon. Jeanne knew how irritable Glenn would be if she wasn't there even if they had to wait. Well, she didn't have time to waste sitting around. She'd get there at eleven-thirty. That would be plenty of time, and it would give her a chance to get everything done here first. In the Minneapolis condo she would have gone shopping while the laundry was churning, but she didn't want to tie up the machines if someone else needed them. The last thing she wanted was trouble with their neighbors.

She slid the egg from the pan to a plate. What she really was hoping for were friendly neighbors who would look in on Glenn from time to time. She was sure Mark Bonner would if she asked him, but given Glenn's attitude, it might cause more trouble than it was worth. The Crenshaws? She doubted that Glenn would want them popping in. Harry Crenshaw wasn't a brilliant conversationalist by any stretch of the imagination, and his wife could double for the Wicked Witch of the South. And from what she knew about Sonny, she didn't want to know him better or have him hanging around. And that was it. She'd barely said hello to Mrs. Saidlow and Russ Talbot. They seemed friendly enough, but she really didn't know them. The tenants of the other upstairs apartments were complete strangers, and there wasn't much chance that the old woman who had opened the door of 101 to chastise her would be any help.

She carried the plate to the table and opened the window wide before she sat. The sun, bright at the mouth of the walkway, was only a slash high on the building next door. Her windows were in cool shade. That's what kept the apartment from getting unbearably hot, she thought. Those sunny, boxlike places she'd passed up in her apartment searching would need air-conditioning all day. Another plus for this place. She smiled sheepishly as she realized she was gathering ammunition to ward off any faults Glenn might find. She ate, then carried her plate to the sink and rinsed off the egg yolk before it set. She filled a bright blue mug with coffee and checking the clock again, sat to drink it.

The past few weeks had been a strain. She knew she was being defensive in anticipating problems that might never occur. It wasn't like her. Problems had always been something to be handled if they came up, not sought out beforehand. Had she fallen into the habit because of the terrible disruption of their lives caused by the accident, or was it more? Glenn was so different, he forced her to be defensive. If things didn't change, how would she be able to juggle her career and a faltering marriage?

Stop it! she ordered herself. She was getting worse than Glenn looking for things to worry about. The best cure was to stay busy. She carried her coffee into the bedroom and set it on the dresser while she made the bed with clean sheets from the linen closet. Done, she saw it was time to check the laundry.

Both the washer and the dryer had stopped. She transferred the second load to the dryer and reset the timer. Carrying the basket of dry clothes, she crossed the basement. When she snapped off the switch and started up the steps, a sound under the stairwell drew her attention. In the murky light from the landing, his face bisected by one of the steps, Sonny Crenshaw was watching her.

CHAPTER 15
✝

VICKI EWING WAS killed in the small construction shack at the corner of an excavated lot. The padlock on the door had been forced and loosely reset afterward. The single room was empty except for two folding chairs and a table covered with blueprints and specifications. Four cheap metal ashtrays overflowed with cigarette butts. Forensic found small amounts of blood that matched Vicki Ewing's and semen on the rough wood floor, and two microscopic khaki fibers that came from an army blanket of World War II vintage, the type that could be purchased in any Army & Navy store or found in Salvation Army thrift shops. Scuff marks indicated the body was dragged outside on the blanket and thrown like a sack of garbage into the dumpster. The mobile crime unit found another fiber from the blanket caught in a bit of sharp metal at the corner of the dumpster. The blanket itself was not found.

The autopsy report confirmed Kroeger's "guess" that the stab wounds that had tortured and killed Vicki Ewing were made by the same instrument used on Lily White. The fatal heart wounds were distinctive: triangular in shape and a hundred and fifty-three millimeters deep. In both cases the point of penetration of the heart had a smaller circumference than the entry wound, which indicated the blade had a tapered tip approximately twenty-eight millimeters at its widest where it met the three-sided shaft. The thirty-eight punctures, forty-two in Lily White's case, varied from pinpricks to a depth of twenty-eight millimeters, the same length as the tip of the blade. Most were perpendicular to the point of entry, indicating a stabbing motion. They were in a random pattern across the victims' faces, arms, and torsos. Some of them were surrounded by impact bruises, also indicative of stabbing. The deep wounds had punctured Vicki Ewing's heart in the right ventricle, severing the semilunar valve, and in the left atrium. Either one could have caused death, and they had been inflicted within a very short time of each other. The bruises on her throat occurred before death and were incidental to it, not a contributing factor.

Detective Lopez glanced at the coroner's signature and the notation that Dr. Sherman Kroeger had assisted. Kroeger must have gotten a kick out of the whole procedure. He didn't miss much. Hell, the department could skip the damned autopsies and just let him just write the reports based on his "guesses." A good man, Kroeger.

Nasty reached for the can of Tab on his desk. The rotten coffee that stagnated in the office pot soured his stomach, but he needed caffeine to survive the long days in Homicide, which seemed longer than usual right now.

Sipping from the can, he reread the report, turning his brain power on analytical as he tried to think like Kroeger. It was a game Nasty played. He admired Kroeger all to hell for his sharpness of mind and ability to go directly to the heart of a problem. His brain was a computer that stored information and was able to sort it on demand. While Nasty and Parch were still trying to keep down their breakfast, Kroeger had spotted the pattern of the stab wounds and realized they meant something. If Kroeger had written the autopsy report, he probably would have drawn a picture of the damned weapon, because sure as hell he knew what it looked like. He'd call it a guess, but he'd be right. Again. The coroner didn't have the luxury of including guesses or personal opinion in his report; he had to stick to bare facts. "Triangular-shaped weapon eight millimeters in diameter, six inches in length, with sharp, tapered point measuring twenty-eight millimeters."

Nasty leaned back, letting his chair tip like a recliner. His small frame was too light to keep the heavy spring stretched that far, so he braced his feet against an open desk drawer. No knife or switchblade fit the description. An ice pick? Screwdriver? Nasty wasn't a handyman, and his knowledge of tools was limited to what he'd seen in the academy or police property room. He was sure he'd never come across anything like the one in the report.

He caught his negative feedback. That was the wrong approach. He had to work with the positives and view the problem from all angles. Okay, pattern. A few nicks, but the significant wounds were the same depth. Even if the victim was being held by the throat, the killer couldn't be that precise. Not even the luckiest bastard in the world could plunge a weapon to the same depth every time by chance. Yet the same blade apparently had made the much deeper hits to the heart.

Nasty swung his feet off the drawer and the chair came forward like a rocket. Damn! The weapon was used to puncture the victims until the killer tired of the game, then ZAP! A clean thrust six inches deep instead of one. The superficial pricks were teasers to frighten the woman into submission, or maybe just for the pleasure they gave the attacker. Maybe both. Then as the action got more frenzied, the killer plunged the sharp tip in as far as it would go. When he was finally ready, he struck two full thrusts right into the heart. Six inches deep. Same blade that left a triangular wound.

It had to snap out! And with enough force to sink through flesh and muscle. A spring mechanism was the only possibility. Nasty grimaced as he imagined the woman's terror as she heard the click. He hoped to hell she didn't know what it was or that she was lucky enough to have passed out.

Okay, he had the weapon. What about the killer himself? Why two hits to the heart? Insurance? Loss of control? Dead is dead. Why the overkill? What kind of thrill did the bastard get from it? Nasty couldn't come up with an answer to that one, so he went back to the weapon.

His conclusions fit the autopsy picture, but a plunger with the strength to penetrate flesh and muscle six inches had to have one hell of a heavy spring behind it. Nasty had never seen anything like it, he was sure. Granted that didn't rule out the possibility, but it also probably meant they were dealing with a very clever murderer, not some garden-variety psycho with a sudden urge to kill.

Reaching for the phone, he dialed the coroner's office. He hit it lucky; Kroeger was in. While he waited for the assistant coroner to come on the line, Nasty polished off the rest of his soft drink and lobbed the can into the wastebasket.

"Kroeger."

"Lopez. Glad I caught you in on a Saturday."

"What can I do for you, Nasty? I have a dead wino waiting for me down in Echo Park."

"The White and Ewing cases. Could the weapon be spring-loaded?"

There was a pause before Kroeger said, "It could be. It would account for the deep, clean wounds if he held it up against her flesh and snapped the blade out. Both hits were as straight as plumb lines."

Nasty felt as if he'd just gotten a gold star in arithmetic. "Ever seen anything like it?"

"It's a new one on me. I don't think you'll come up

with a similar MO when you run it through, at least not in L.A."

Nasty took Kroeger's words as gospel. Kroeger had been with the coroner's office eighteen years, and he'd seen just about every kind of violent death on the books. And what he hadn't seen personally he'd either heard in office shop talk or read in reports. And the information was in his mental computer.

"You got any ideas?" he asked hopefully.

"It sounds like a precision job to me. Try machine shops or tool and die makers."

Nasty had already thought of that. It was a long shot, and there were enough shops in the city to keep them busy for months.

"One other thing, Lopez. You remember one of the White woman's shoes were missing? Vicki Ewing didn't have any underpants."

Nasty ran his glance down the page. "Maybe she didn't wear them," he said hopefully.

"There were faint red marks across her abdomen and hips that are consistent with the kind elastic makes. It's in the report."

It had to be important or Kroeger wouldn't mention it. "Could she have taken them off when she got home from work?"

"Under normal circumstances, the line would be gone in thirty minutes."

So the killer had taken them. Nasty sighed. "Thanks, Kroeger."

Nasty dropped the phone to the cradle and stared at it balefully. Same weapon. Souvenirs. The trademark of a serial killer. If that's what they had, this snap-happy slasher was a walking time bomb who'd probably kill again.

It was going to be a long, lousy hot summer.

CHAPTER
16
✝

JEANNE CONCENTRATED ON maneuvering the Toyota through the Saturday-afternoon traffic. In the backseat Glenn was silent, his face strained despite the pain pills he'd been given before they left the hospital. It was his own fault, she thought angrily. If he wasn't so stubborn, he could have made the trip by ambulance. He never considered how hard this was on her.

She sighed and tried to erase the gloomy, self-pitying thoughts. She'd been on edge since the incident in the laundry room. Catching Sonny Crenshaw watching her that way had frightened her, and she raced upstairs as if he'd chased her. She felt foolish about it now. The boy had every right to be down there. If she hadn't been so preoccupied, she probably would have heard him come down. Still, she wondered why he'd been hiding, and she couldn't help wondering, too, if it had been Sonny outside the bathroom window last night.

Even though she had arrived at the hospital ahead of schedule, Glenn was irritable and petulant. He barely picked at his lunch. Dr. Ingerman was late, and it was after two by the time the discharge papers were signed and Glenn was transported by wheelchair to the ambulance entrance where Jeanne brought the car. After the struggle of getting him into the backseat, he was too exhausted to do more than grunt at her attempts to keep his spirits up. Irritated, Jeanne let the tense silence fill the car. Her stomach was rumbling with hunger, and the air-conditioning was blowing against her shoulder. She could feel her muscles stiffening, but she knew Glenn would complain if she turned off the air-conditioning and opened a window. She'd be glad to get home.

"How much farther is it?" Glenn asked.

She glanced at his reflection in the rearview mirror, wondering if he was criticizing again. His face was so drawn, she felt remorse.

"Not much," she said. "Are you okay?"

"I'm fine."

It was a lie, but a brave one. Dr. Ingerman warned them Glenn's pain would be aggravated temporarily by movement and by the exercise he needed to get his muscles strong again.

Jeanne turned a block before the apartment so she could come down the hill and let Glenn out at the front door. She glanced at the mirror again and saw his surprised interest as they went up the steep street with its attractive, comfortable houses, neat yards, and huge old trees that spread dappled shade. *He didn't think it was going to be so nice,* she thought, gloating.

There were a few parking spots on the hill but none close to the building, so Jeanne double-parked. "This is it," she said, turning off the ignition and opening her door. "I'll help you inside then come back and park."

"I can manage alone."

Jeanne got out. "No arguments. I'm taking you in first." Coming around the car, she opened the back door and watched nervously as he shifted the awkward cast and swung his legs through the doorway. She handed him the crutches.

He slid to the edge of the seat, braced himself, and struggled up. He had trouble because of the low head clearance, but when Jeanne tried to help, he waved her off impatiently. When he finally managed to get to his feet, he leaned against the car to catch his breath.

"Take your time," Jeanne said.

"I'm okay," he snapped.

Jeanne gritted her teeth and watched him push himself upright again. Then she led the way between a green Chevrolet and a blue Buick parked several feet ahead of it. At the curb she watched apprehensively as Glenn positioned the crutches carefully and got his balance before he lifted his weight. He grimaced in pain. Jeanne turned away, pretending not to notice. By the time they reached the front door, Glenn's face was filmed with sweat. The door swung open before Jeanne could use her key. Mark Bonner was holding it.

"I saw you drive up," he said, glancing first at her then at Glenn.

Surprised, Jeanne said, "I thought you were in San Diego."

"I was. I just got back a few minutes ago." He grinned. "My girlfriend had other plans. I should have called first, I guess."

Glenn paused at the step. Mark looked from Jeanne to him and back at Jeanne again.

"This is Mark Bonner, Glenn," Jeanne said.

"Hi," Mark said eagerly.

Glenn didn't look up. "Hi. Sorry I can't shake hands."

"Hey, no sweat. Need any help?" Mark offered.

"No. Jeanne, do you mind if we get inside?" Glenn began to maneuver himself up the step.

Jeanne was embarrassed, but Mark's smile didn't fade. He held out his hand. "Give me the keys and I'll get your door open for you."

With a glance at Glenn, who was trembling with exhaustion, Jeanne dropped the keys in Mark's hand. He sprinted down the hall while she trailed behind Glenn, praying he wouldn't fall. His progress was slow, but he made it to the open door of the apartment.

Standing aside, Mark bounced the keys on his palm. "I'll park the car for you. Anything you want brought in?"

"Some stuff in the backseat," Jeanne said gratefully. Bonner bounded down the hall. The outer door banged shut as Glenn leaned against the living room wall and looked around.

"Well, what do you think?" Jeanne asked.

"He's a little too friendly, if you ask me."

"Oh, Glenn, don't be absurd," she said. "He's just being nice. Besides, I meant about the apartment." She was close to tears.

Glenn glanced around. "Not bad, but do you mind if I skip the grand tour? I'm beat."

"Sure," she said, struggling not to be hurt. "The bedroom's this way." She walked ahead of him, looking back to make sure he was okay. He barely glanced at the den or the bath as he passed. She pulled back the covers on the bed, and he sank onto it with an explosion of breath. She knelt to take off his shoe and help him lift the heavy cast.

He closed his eyes as he lay back. "Thanks."

She put a pillow under his leg to help support the weight. She'd bought him a pair of summer pants with a drawstring waist and wide legs that would slip over the cast easily. When she started to undo them, he pushed her hands away. Jeanne went around the bed to open the sliding door, set the new bolt to the wider position, then adjusted the blinds and turned on the fan she'd bought that morning at a drugstore. Glenn's eyes stayed shut. She unplugged the phone and closed the door as she went out.

Mark Bonner was standing by the front door.

"Is he okay?"

She nodded without meeting his gaze. "Mark, I'm sorry about the way—"

"Hey, it's okay. I understand."

She gave him an apologetic smile. "He's exhausted. The ride really did him in, but he absolutely refused to come home in an ambulance."

Mark pursed his lips. "Sure, I can understand that. It would make a guy feel pretty helpless. I wouldn't like it either."

Jeanne had never thought of it that way, but she was still upset. "It would have been a lot easier," she said.

Bonner cocked his head in the boyish way he had. "Yeah, but sometimes what's going on in your head is more important than what's happening to your body, you know?"

She wasn't sure she understood, but he was being so nice, she was willing to concede the point. She smiled. "Well, thanks again for your help. I really appreciate it."

"No sweat." He held out the plastic personal-property bag from the hospital and Jeanne's keys. "Anything else I can do for you?"

"No. You've been great." Guiltily she recalled the purpose of his trip to San Diego and asked him about it.

Mark grinned. "The agent thinks he can get me some industrial shoots. He handles a lot of in-house sales demo tapes and stuff like that. It's not exactly what I've been hoping for, but it's a start."

"I'm sure it will lead to something better," Jeanne said.

"I sure hope so. Look, I don't want to hold you up. You sure there's nothing else I can do for you—need anything from the store?"

She shook her head. "I shopped this morning, thanks to your friend's car. Incidentally, we're going to take it. Will Monday be all right to handle the details? You said—"

"Sure, that's fine. I'll tell him."

As he turned to go, Jeanne thought of something.

"Mark?" He looked around. Hesitantly she asked if he had spoken to the Crenshaws about Sonny.

"I mentioned it to Harry. Why?"

"Oh, nothing, really, I guess. I saw Sonny in the basement this morning. He scared the life out of me."

Bonner's face clouded. "Where was he? What did he say? Did he do anything?"

She felt foolish. "He was standing under the stairs, and I didn't see him until I started up. I didn't hear him come down. It scared me seeing him unexpectedly like that. He never said a word. If I hadn't noticed him, I would have gone up and turned off the light and left him there in the dark."

"That wouldn't bother Sonny," Mark said. "He's always prowling around in the dark. I'll talk to Lucille. If she can't keep an eye on him, I'll tell the landlord."

"Please don't," she said quickly. "I don't want to get him in trouble." It was true, but at the same time she realized she was afraid it might have been Sonny she heard outside the bathroom window last night. She decided not to mention that. Mark frowned. "The thing is, he'll be in plenty of trouble if other tenants start complaining. I'll actually be doing him a favor. Don't worry, I'll handle it carefully."

Jeanne was sorry she'd brought it up. It was nonsense to blame Sonny Crenshaw for everything that made her nervous. "Please, I'd rather you didn't."

"Well, okay, if that's the way you want it. But listen, if he scares you again, you tell me, okay? I'll talk to him."

"All right. And thanks again for your help. I really appreciate it."

"Jeanne!" Glenn called querulously from the bedroom.

Jeanne's smile vanished.

"I gotta go," Mark said quickly. "See you." He hurried down the hall.

Jeanne went into the bedroom. The sheets were already

twisted under Glenn, and he was propped on one elbow trying to work his way out of bed.

"I need another one of those pain pills."

"Are you sure? It's only been two hours—"

"Yes, damn it, I'm sure!" He fell back, grimacing.

Jeanne went back to the living room and retrieved the prescription bottle from her purse, then went to the kitchen for a glass of ice water. Bringing them back to the bedroom, she gave them to Glenn without a word. He tossed back a pill, drank, then held out the glass to her. When she took it, he fell back against the pillows, his eyes closed once more. Jeanne stood looking down at him, close to tears, wondering how this could be the same wonderful man she had married.

CHAPTER 17
✝

HEAT HUNG IN the room like fog. He was sweating, but he didn't turn on the fan or open a window. He sat in the corner, his back against the wall, his arms wrapped around his knees, his eyes staring across the dim room at the closet door. The quiet was chipped by small sounds that irritated him like pinpricks. A surge of canned laughter from a TV show . . . strains of stereo music . . . a dog's sharp yip . . . voices at a distance that blended them to a murmur of secret words. Although he hadn't moved for what seemed like hours, he hadn't been able to dispel the restlessness mushrooming inside him.

Discipline. He had to stay in control. He wouldn't move until he was sure he could handle the power that was gathering force like the Santa Ana breathing across the city. He had to discipline himself. Concentrate.

Sweat trickled down his jaw and dripped onto his bare chest. The hot, stale darkness squeezed him like a fist and forced air from his lungs in small explosions. His eyes burned as if he'd been staring into a roaring bonfire. Cocking his head, he listened again to the night sounds. Voices had been added. Faint. Distant. Arguing. He couldn't make out the words, but the cadence had a pattern of anger. He got to his feet and began pacing. When he realized he was rubbing his hands together, he jammed them in his pockets. Control. It had grown dark, but he didn't turn on a lamp. He knew the room well enough to make his way around blindfolded. Four paces to the closet. Opening the door, he reached to the shelf and picked up the package, then held it against his chest until his breathing slowed. He went to the pale rectangle of window illuminated by the streetlight. Slowly he unwrapped the bundle.

Lifting out the knife, he put the wrappings on the windowsill while he balanced the weapon on his palm. It was warm and felt alive when his hand closed around it lovingly. His thumb settled as lightly as a dust mote on the release button. The inferno inside his chest flared.

Was it really too soon if he planned carefully? The police would be out in force. Doubling the number of men on the streets was the way they conned the public into thinking they were doing something. Manhunt. Killer watch. He snorted. They didn't know what to look for . . . or where. If they put fifty men in the neighborhood, they still couldn't cover every street and alley. It was an interesting idea, though . . . a challenge. It would make the game more interesting. Of course, the cops weren't hard to outsmart. They were pretty stupid when it came right down to it. The added risk would make the game more exciting. All he had to do was plan carefully and move cautiously. He'd stay ahead of them every step of the way.

Hadn't he figured out what the similarities they'd found were? The shape of the blade left distinctive marks on the two bodies. Two. Not Gretchen. They didn't even know about Gretchen, who had started it all. They didn't connect the deaths of the whores to Gretchen because they didn't have their stupid little clue. What a bunch of assholes. Christ, he could stay ahead of them without even trying. He was calling the plays. He was in control. And now he had a master game plan. A script to follow. The idea began to form when he saw the dumpster outside that construction shack. He picked the shack by chance, because it was within the arbitrary boundaries he'd set as his game board. The inside of the shack reminded him of the empty room in the script of *Dead Past,* but it wasn't any more than a passing thought until he spotted the dumpster outside. He'd been laughing the whole time he hauled Vicki Ewing's body out to it.

It was his game, he thought, smiling. He was timekeeper and scorekeeper and everything else. Why shouldn't he go out tonight? *They'd* think it was too soon. *They'd* figure that because he had waited five days last time, he had a pattern. That was the kind of dumb thinking they did. Losers. All of them.

He raised the knife and flicked off the cap. Then, holding his breath, he pressed the release button. In silhouette the triangular sides didn't show, but he could see them as clearly as he had the day he shaped it. He'd started with a screwdriver but nicked the shank while he was grinding it. The flaw had marred its perfection, and in his determination to smooth it, he saw the possibility of creating the unique triangular blade. He'd done it for the hell of it. Now the shape was the only clue the police had. He laughed quietly. Let them try to figure it out. They never would, not in a million years.

In those confusing days after Gretchen, he wasn't even sure why he was making the blade. Maybe it had been something to calm his nerves. Or maybe he'd been trying to clean the shaft of the dark stains left by her blood. It didn't really matter. He made it. And he knew how to use it.

He reset the cap over the needle-sharp point. He designed the cap so he'd have a way to reset the blade without dulling the tip or breaking it off. None of those exotic Oriental blades had that. He pressed the smooth rounded plastic against his palm and exerted the pressure of his hand. The shaft forced back the heavy spring and clicked the lock. He picked up the pieces of cloth from the windowsill and put them back on the closet shelf. He slipped the knife into his pocket.

He picked a spot only two blocks from where he'd found Vicki Ewing, right in the center of the gameboard, and parked the car under a drooping bottlebrush tree. When he turned off the engine, he put the keys in the back pocket of his jeans and zipped it closed. Most houses on the street were already dark, and the steady hum of air conditioners blended into the stillness. He had driven around the area for twenty minutes to see if there was any unusual police activity. More patrol cars than usual were cruising Vermont Avenue, but not as many as he expected. The cops didn't have it all together yet. Stupid asses.

He chose that street to park because he knew mostly middle-aged people lived there. That lessened the risk of any swinging young singles coming home at this hour, or some stupid senior citizen who had trouble sleeping deciding to sit by a window. He got out and shut the door softly so the noise wouldn't attract attention.

He headed for the six-way intersection a few blocks away. It would be easy to find a woman there. He could have his pick of the hookers who stood around in hot pants and tight, low-cut shirts or strolled past the porno movie house offering men the real thing instead of a film. It was a well-patrolled area because of the cluster of medical complexes on Sunset, but the emphasis was on protecting hospital employees and visitors, not hassling the handful of hookers who had begun to filter across from the more competitive Hollywood turf farther west.

At the corner he slowed to a saunter and shoved his

hands in his pockets. Sure enough, there were three whores within a hundred feet of each other near the cheap adult bookstore and theater. They kept moving, pretending they were walking past or waiting at the bus stop, but their darting glances and slow smiles at every male within range gave them away. Without turning his head, he looked both ways along the street for cops. No uniforms in sight, but he spotted a vice cop making his way toward a car that had slowed so the driver could proposition a black whore. She saw him too. The car took off with a squeal of rubber, and the stupid vice cop was left with the hooker, who started an argument that made the other two whores split in different directions. One came right around the corner where he was standing.

It was almost too easy.

CHAPTER 18

✝

GLENN SPENT A restless night. Jeanne moved to the lumpy daybed in the den about midnight. For a long time she heard him tossing and turning in search of a comfortable position, and when at last she fell asleep, the pillow under her cheek was damp with tears.

She woke stiff and out of sorts, wondering if their lives would ever be the same. She put on her running shorts and rummaged in the small dresser for the tank top she'd washed yesterday. Annoyed when she couldn't find it, she decided she must have left it in the bedroom. She put on a white T-shirt and carried her shoes to the living room. When she looked in on Glenn before she left, he was sleeping on his side, his face pressed into the pillow, his body curled awkwardly as though he'd tried to roll onto his stomach. The cumbersome leg cast was tangled in the sheet, and even in sleep his forehead was marked by deep furrows that made her heart wrench.

She let herself out and locked the dead bolt before she slipped the keys onto the Velcro fastener at her waist. Concentrating on the mundane task, she didn't see Sonny

Crenshaw holding the handlebars of a ten-speed bicycle that he'd been walking down the hall.

"Oh!"

His face molded itself into a frightened expression. "I'm sorry, Mrs. Donovan," he whispered. "I didn't mean to scare you."

She was annoyed to find her hands shaking. She tried to smile, but her face was stiff and unresponsive. All she could think of was that he was taller than she remembered. Tall enough to pull himself up to the high bathroom window?

She forced words out. "Hello, Sonny."

When she started down the hall, he wheeled the bike after her. There was only the faint whir of the bike wheels turning, but she felt Sonny's presence like a sudden shift of barometric pressure before a storm. *He's harmless*, she told herself. Mark Bonner said he was harmless. At the front door he hung back like a whipped puppy, and Jeanne felt as if she'd kicked him. Chagrined, she held the door open and motioned for him to go ahead. He picked up the bike and hurried out.

"Thank you, Mrs. Donovan," he said as precisely and politely as a child reciting a lesson. His hair was a tangled mop of dark curls around his thin face, and he seemed to be all bones and joints poking awkwardly from a tattered T-shirt and faded blue shorts with a dark patch where an emblem had been torn off. His running shoes were scuffed and the laces had been knotted so many times they went only halfway up.

"You're welcome," Jeanne answered. Poor thing. He was so pathetic, how could she have been frightened of him? He was an adult whose mind had not grown with his years. She turned up the hill and began to walk at a brisk pace. Sonny ran to catch up with her, the bike pedals spinning as he steered the bike beside him.

"I'm sorry about yesterday," he said. "I didn't know it

was you in the basement. Then I was afraid to say anything. I didn't want to scare you, but I did, didn't I. I'm sorry, honest."

His hair had red highlights in the morning sun, and his face was tortured by a tight puzzled look that centered in his deep-set eyes that tunneled to some empty place.

"It's all right, Sonny," she said gently. "It was my fault. I wasn't paying attention."

For an instant a faint spark glimmered in the void of his expression. His mouth twitched in an unpracticed smile, and his face flushed. Abruptly he turned and stared straight ahead. Jeanne felt sorry for him again. She couldn't ignore him, but she wondered if she should encourage him. *Don't be silly,* she scolded herself. There was no harm in being nice. From what Mark said, she suspected most of the tenants in the building gave the mentally slow youth a hard time. But when she thought about the dowels and the crushed flower, she was nervous again. She glanced sidelong at Sonny and wondered if she should confront him about it. Before she could make up her mind, they reached the top of the hill, and Sonny waved as he veered off, swinging his leg over the bicycle seat and catching the pedals as they spun around. A moment later he was halfway down the quiet block. Jeanne turned the other way on the curving, tree-shaded street and broke into an easy jog.

She ran for a half hour, exploring curving, hilly streets while she expelled the cobwebs from her mind and sweated out the remnants of her bad night. The peaceful morning was hers to enjoy despite the heat that quickly had her perspiring. The streets were quiet, with only an occasional sign of a household stirring. Los Angeles was not a Sunday-morning city. When she began to tire, she slowed her pace to cool down on the last few blocks.

Dripping with sweat and still breathing hard, she unlocked the front entrance. As she came into the foyer, the door of 101 opened, and Pearl Gannon beckoned to her from the doorway. Jeanne glanced down the hall, knowing she should get back to Glenn, and not wanting to let herself in for busybody gossip. The old woman gestured again with an imperious command meant to be obeyed without question. Jeanne crossed the hall. Pearl Gannon flipped her wrist as if pulling a cord to yank Jeanne through the doorway. Pearl shut the door behind her.

Jeanne looked at the room in amazement. It could have been a set out of a Woody Allen movie portraying middle-class Hollywood of the 1930s. A front apartment, it had windows on two sides of the square living room. Facing the street, a set of French windows opened to a small balcony covered with a variety of plants of every imaginable size and shape. A philodendron in a pot on the floor snaked vines up the wall and across the window frame. A hanging spider plant trailed a profusion of wiry stems that ended in bursts of new growth. The windowsill held a colorful assortment of crotons, dracaena, geraniums, and wandering Jew. In a corner a four-foot Norfolk pine looked like a green crown rising from an elaborately decorated Chinese pot.

The other windows had old-fashioned window shades, complete with fringed edges and ornate tasseled pulls. They were raised, but hanging plants filtered the light so the room resembled a shadowed jungle. A dark Oriental rug covered the floor, and the furniture was an eclectic collection of antiques and junk. An overstuffed chair, a lovely Queen Anne sofa with faded rose tapestry upholstery, a bronze *torchère* with an alabaster reflector, a piecrust table holding a genuine—Jeanne was sure—Tiffany lamp, and an ugly coffee table in dark veneer with rounded edges and corners of the once briefly popular waterfall design. Magazines racks—one, Early American wood spindles; another, cheap brass with ugly patches of marred finish—overflowed with magazines, *Daily Variety* and the *Hollywood Reporter*.

Jeanne remembered Mark's warning about the woman's ability to chatter. "I can't stay. My husband—"

Pearl glanced at the closed door. "How is the poor dear? I won't keep you, but I wouldn't have a minute's peace if I didn't warn you," she said in a quiet voice that had an iron spine. Not waiting for an answer, she went on, "You must be careful, my dear. I'm sure things are different in the Midwest. Heaven knows they were here in California when I was young, but times have changed. It isn't wise to be too trusting. This used to be a lovely building, but now you can't be too careful." She glanced out the window with an expression of incredible wistfulness.

Considering Pearl's earlier criticism of her friendship with Mark, Jeanne wondered if this was a generalization or if the old woman had something specific in mind. Obviously she watched the comings and goings of her neighbors through the screen of greenery that faced the street. How else could she know Jeanne was back from her jog and have opened the door with such perfect timing? Had she seen Sonny Crenshaw go out with her earlier?

Jeanne smiled politely. "Thank you, Mrs. Gannon. I'll be careful, I promise. Now I really must—"

Pearl raised her hand like a school teacher demanding silence from second graders. "Another murdered woman was found this morning. I heard it on the news. Not ten blocks from here. That's the third in a week."

Jeanne looked at her in astonishment. She was expecting vague insinuations about Sonny Crenshaw, but Pearl's mind had skipped to murder.

Pearl shook her finger. "You haven't taken time to listen to the news or read the papers, have you? No, you young people are always in a rush. Oh, I realize you've been busy with your husband in the hospital and all, but you *must* think of these things. Now that he's home, I hope you won't be coming in alone at all hours. And you must be careful. Be sure to keep your door locked. And don't invite that boy in. You never know." She touched Jeanne's arm and her blue-veined hand was cool on Jeanne's sweaty skin. Pearl's wrinkled face looked like a museum masterpiece due for restoration.

"There's evil in this city," she said. "Hollywood has become something sordid and cheap. Not at all like the old days. Not at all. Such a shame. In my day, there was a clear-cut line between good and bad. Now one can no longer depend on the old standards."

Jeanne was too confused to reply. She wondered if Pearl Gannon was out of touch with reality, and this was the babbling of a senile, old woman.

"Thank you for the advice," Jeanne said with careful politeness. "Please don't worry, I'll be careful. Now I have to go. My husband needs me. He isn't very strong yet."

"Poor dear. Of course. I do wish you could stay for tea. You must come back another time. Now don't rush off—wait a minute." She walked stiff-spined to the kitchen and returned with a foil-wrapped package that she thrust upon Jeanne. It was warm. "Fresh-baked coffee cake."

"Why, thank you, Mrs. Gannon. That's very sweet of you."

The old woman's tapered hand brushed away the compliment. "I'm always up early. At my age, one doesn't waste a lot of time sleeping." She reached for the doorknob and smiled. "It's *Miss* Gannon, or *Ms.* today, I suppose, though I really am uncomfortable with such a modern appellation. One gets accustomed to old habits, you know. Please, call me Pearl. Everyone does. Darryl Zanuck chose the name for me. He said I was a jewel. I have always loved the name." Her smile grew from some long-ago memory. She opened the door, still smiling. Jeanne heard the chain slide into place as soon as the door closed.

She went down the hall shaking her head. As she

reached her own door, Mark emerged from the basement carrying a box of detergent. He grinned and hurried to her.

"How's it going? I saw Pearl nab you. I warned you about her." Like Pearl and Sonny, he kept his voice low, as if an unwritten law of the building decreed that no one disturbed late sleepers on a Sunday morning.

"I think she was lying in wait for me," Jeanne whispered, laughing.

"She's always snooping on people. What'd she want?"

Jeanne held up the foil package. "Coffee cake for Glenn's breakfast."

"Good old Pearl," he said, shaking his head. "How's your husband? I was going to call last night to see if there was anything I could do, but I figured I'd better not disturb you."

"He had a rough night. I hope he feels better today."

"Well, holler if you need any help. I'm just bumming around today." He indicated the box in his hand. "Laundry and that kind of stuff."

"Thanks. I guess I'd better see if Glenn's ready for breakfast. Might as well have Pearl's coffee cake while it's warm. Did Darryl Zanuck really pick her name?"

Bonner shrugged. "Could be. She was one of his starlets, and in those days the studio renamed just about everyone."

"I wonder what her original name was?" Jeanne mused.

"She's never said. It must have been a dilly."

Jeanne unlocked the door as Mark continued down the hall. The bedroom door was open, and the sound of the shower running in the bathroom surprised Jeanne. Glenn up and showering without help? He was the only one who could judge his strength, but she prayed that he wouldn't overdo again. She went to the kitchen to start the coffee. Despite his restless night, Glenn seemed to be in a good mood, judging from the song bellowing above the sound of the shower.

Maybe Dr. Ingerman was right about the therapeutic value of his coming home. She hoped so. To celebrate she set up two lawn chairs and a small folding table she'd bought at a discount store on the patio and carried dishes out on a tray. When Glenn emerged from the bathroom with a towel wrapped around his middle, he looked fresh and handsome. He caught Jeanne and pulled her into his arms.

"You have a miserable bastard for a husband. I don't know why you put up with me. I'm sorry as hell about the way I acted yesterday. Forgive me?" He gazed at her with an intensity that surpassed longing.

"Oh, Glenn, of course. There's nothing to forgive. You were exhausted—"

"I had no right taking it out on you." His blue gaze held hers, pleading.

She put her arms around him gently and pressed her face against his cool, damp skin. How desperately she wanted everything to be all right. "I forgive you. And I love you." She raised her face and her lips parted as he kissed her long and satisfyingly, a renewal of promise. She snuggled against him, careful not to throw him off balance. "How did you manage to shower?"

"Wrapped a garbage bag around the cast. A trick the therapist showed me, garbage bags compliments of a friendly nurse."

"Not too friendly, I hope," she murmured. In answer he lifted her face, and he kissed her again. Sighing, she said, "Go put on a robe so you don't shock the neighbors. We're having breakfast on the patio. It will be ready in a minute. I hope you're hungry. I'm making your favorite omelet, and we have homemade coffee cake, a gift from our neighbor, Pearl Gannon."

"The old-time-movie Pearl Gannon?"

"So I hear. Do you know her?" She searched her own memory for a clue. Glenn was more of an old-movie buff than she was and had a collection of videos from the late show, fortunately safely stored at Caroline's in Minneapolis.

"She was a starlet back in the thirties. Her career was pretty short, but she played in *Starstruck, The Way Back, Sam's Girl*—a dozen others. I've got 'em all on tape."

As he named the pictures, vague memories came into focus for Jeanne. "The tiny blond with the big, dark eyes in *Starstruck* who played the roommate of the understudy who got her big chance?" When Glenn nodded, she said, "Of course. I'm surprised I didn't recognize her. She's still got those eyes, believe it or not. I guess I didn't expect her to be living here. Beverly Hills maybe, or at least the Motion Picture Retirement Home."

Glenn eased away and Jeanne realized how long he'd been on his feet. She helped him put on a striped cotton robe and hobble out to the patio where she settled him in a chair with his cast close to the fence, out of the way as she went back and forth.

Glenn was still thinking about Pearl Gannon. "I read somewhere she had a crooked manager. There was a lot of that in those days. A lot of those early stars didn't know how much they were making or what their expenses ran. Pearl's career didn't last long enough for the actors' pension fund to take care of her, but her last husband was a businessman, if I remember right. He must have left her some kind of little nest egg. Tell me all about her," Glenn said eagerly. "She must be quite a gal."

"Let me start the omelet first. I'll be right back." She ran to the kitchen, lit the burner under the omelet pan, and gave the egg mixture a few whips before she poured it into the melted butter. Opening the refrigerator, she took out the bottle of champagne she had chilled for last night's celebration, which Glenn's mood had canceled before she suggested it, then removed two chilled glasses from the freezer. Checking the omelet, which had begun to bubble, she went back to the patio and handed Glenn the bottle.

"Orange juice for mimosas on the way." She darted back inside and returned with a tray laden with a pitcher of orange juice, the omelet, and Pearl Gannon's coffee cake under a warming cover. The champagne cork popped and hit the fence before it fell into a dusty-leafed jade plant.

They toasted Glenn's homecoming. Over breakfast Jeanne described her encounter with Pearl. Glenn laughed until Jeanne mentioned Pearl's strange admonition about evil.

"Is that true about three murdered women in the neighborhood?" he asked with a worried look.

"I don't know. She's right about my not reading the paper. I haven't had time."

Glenn frowned. "I read about one murder victim they found in Los Feliz. Maybe this area is a dangerous part of L.A."

"Oh, Glenn, don't get paranoid. Remember that university coed in Minneapolis? They found her body on Thirty-sixth Street."

"That was different—"

"Less than ten blocks from our place," Jeanne insisted. "Los Angeles is bigger so it has more murders, that's all. Besides, Pearl is probably exaggerating. She's a typical lonely, gossipy woman. Any excitement is grist for the mill."

He didn't look convinced, but he let the subject drop. Jeanne supposed it was natural for him to worry about her when he was helpless and tied to the apartment. She bit off a piece of coffee cake and almost choked on the crumbly, dry concoction. She sipped some mimosa quickly to wash it down.

Making a face, she said, "If Pearl's knowledge of the news is as bad as her baking, we have nothing to worry about."

Glenn laughed, but his worried expression didn't disappear. "Did you buy a morning paper while you were out?"

"I never thought of it, but I'll tell you what. If you behave yourself and rest after breakfast, I'll run over to the 7-Eleven and get one."

"It's a deal, as long as I don't have to eat my coffee cake." Grinning, he reached across the table to take her hand and kiss the palm. "Maybe I'll be so rested we can think of something else to do when you get back."

Jeanne lay semistuporous, staring at the ceiling, totally relaxed. Beside her, Glenn was breathing heavily from the exertion of their lovemaking. They had both been so engulfed by need and desire they forgot about the heavy cast and their awkwardness. They came together eagerly, passionately, desperately, and satisfyingly.

"I'm going to have to shower again," she said lazily.

Glenn drew his hand across her naked belly. "I like you sweaty."

She turned and rolled into his arms, burying her face against his chest. Passion had erased her fears and hurt briefly, but now they wanted to creep back. She tried to fight them off. "It's good to have you home. I missed you." The words were muffled against his flesh.

He lifted her chin and kissed her with tender hunger. "Only half as much as I missed you. The worst part was knowing you had to hold everything together and I couldn't lift a finger to help. I've never been helpless before. I don't like it."

Still searching for assurance, she traced a finger along his jaw. "You're not helpless anymore. As a matter of fact, I'd say you've been throwing your weight around very effectively. Look at the tangled mess this bed is."

He kissed her again, then slapped her bare buttocks

playfully. "In that case, I'll let you shower first and you can remake it while I hobble into my garbage bag."

As Jeanne rolled from bed, Glenn watched her with a stir of renewing desire. When he heard the shower, he reached for the Sunday paper she'd gone out for but which they'd tossed aside as her innocent move of lying beside him turned into an opening for passion. He peeled off the front section and punched the pillows under his head until he was comfortable. Scanning the headlines, he paused to read a brief, boxed story that had made the late edition, headlined: "Third Victim Found in Los Feliz."

When he finished, the room, which had seemed too warm minutes ago, was suddenly cool. Pearl Gannon's warning to Jeanne had been about these murders. According to her, this was the third one in a week. Glenn felt a chill even though he was sweating.

THIRD VICTIM FOUND IN LOS FELIZ

A woman was found stabbed and strangled in an alley behind a row of commercial buildings on Virgil Avenue in Los Feliz last night, another apparent victim of a killer stalking the streets of Los Angeles.

The partly clad body of Suzette Amy Miller, 27, was discovered shortly after midnight by police, who were called by the manager of a cocktail lounge who reported a woman screaming in the alley. Police officers who responded to the call found the dead woman a few yards from the rear door of the lounge.

Similarities to the murders of Lily White and Vicki Ewing, who lived within a one-mile radius of the latest murder site, indicate the same person may be responsible for all three deaths. Like the stabber's earlier victims, Miller had been sexually assaulted and bore signs of attempted manual strangulation as well as repeated stab wounds.

Police cordoned off the area and conducted a house-to-house search, but no sign of the killer was found. Police are continuing the investigation in the hope that someone in the vicinity may have seen the killer make his escape after he was frightened off by Miller's screams.

Police refuse to comment on the possibility of the murders' being the work of a serial killer.

CHAPTER 19
†

HE DIDN'T EXPECT the story to make the news so soon, but then he hadn't expected that damned whore to scream and fight the way she did. At first she'd been terrified just like the others, but somewhere along the line she must have decided she had nothing to lose. Or maybe he had relaxed his hold on her throat without realizing it. He already had her skirt and blouse cut away, and he was engrossed in telling her the wonderful things he was going to do, getting himself excited to fever pitch. Did he forget to watch her closely? Or was it a mistake in his game plan to make such a bold move? Sweat trickled down his temples when he realized how close Suzette Amy Miller had come to ruining everything. Stupid whore. He should have taken her to some isolated spot like the last one. He would have enjoyed her agony and given her something to yell about. Instead he had to finish the job quickly.

Christ, he'd been excited. Adrenaline pumped through him in such a rush he could hardly breathe in those final moments. He plunged himself and the blade into her at exactly the same instant, but there wasn't time to reset the blade and put a second hole in her heart. With all the racket she made, he had to get out of that alley fast. He'd run like hell, zipping his pants as he went, leaping over a fence behind the restaurant, then scrambling through a block of backyards to the street where the car was parked. He didn't even notice the blood on his shirt until he ran under a streetlight. Damned bitch. She'd robbed him of a clean kill.

He was proud that he hadn't panicked. He had the sense to think out his moves carefully. When the cops hit the scene, he knew they'd comb the neighborhood and start checking cars. Get out of the area fast.

Hunched over the wheel to hide the bloodstains, he had headed for Vermont Avenue and took it down to Hollywood Boulevard. They wouldn't expect him out in the open that way. When he heard sirens after a few blocks, he pulled over like a good citizen. The police car raced by in the other direction.

He got home without incident and stripped off the bloody shirt before he got out of the car. He wrapped it around the knife and carried the bundle under his arm. Inside, he cleaned the weapon carefully and put it back on the shelf in the closet. Then he fell across the bed and passed out as though he were drugged.

When he woke in the morning, he heard the story on the radio. He considered going out to get a paper so he could savor the story in detail, but the early edition would have gone to press before midnight. The story might make the late edition. He'd wait.

His wait paid off. The story was boxed on the front page. Grinning, he wondered what they had pulled to make room for it. "Killer stalking the streets . . ." They hadn't dubbed him with a nickname yet, but they would. As soon as the reporters got wind that the same weapon had been used, they'd come up with a tag for the killer. They always did. It sold newspapers.

Maybe he should think up one himself. Write one of those indignant letters to the editor about the killings people were always sending. Unsigned, of course. Make sure it couldn't be traced to him. Mail it from some other part of town. Beverly Hills would be a nice touch.

He leaned back and laced his fingers behind his head. The Avenger? Too much like a sleazy, low-budget film title. The Slut Sticker? He liked that one, but it was too gutsy for the media. The Civil Liberties Union would jump on them like starlets on a producer. The Sidewalk Stalker? That wasn't too bad.

He explored the letter idea from different angles and reluctantly had to admit it was too risky. Even if they couldn't trace it to him, the police might find a way to use a letter. Analyze the handwriting, or trace the paper or envelope. They were always coming up with shit like that. So no letter to the editor, at least not yet. Not when he was enjoying the game so much. The kill was the important thing, and the thrill of getting away with it. He could play the game as long as he wanted and change the rules whenever he felt like it. At the same time, he was cleaning up the neighborhood. He was doing the city a favor, when it came right down to it. He was making the streets safe for decent people.

Tomorrow he would pick up the *Herald*. It used more lurid headlines. Maybe some reporter there had nicknamed him.

CHAPTER 20

✝

THE CALL WOKE Nasty shortly after midnight. He grabbed it on the first ring, hoping it wouldn't disturb Estrella, but by the time he came out of the bathroom, a mug of steaming coffee was waiting for him.

"You shouldn't be up," he whispered. He hated night calls that made her lose sleep. She had her hands full with the baby's teething.

She smiled serenely to say she was where she wanted to be.

He sipped the coffee. It made going out after only two hours sleep a little easier. Estrella's coffee was fantastic because she ground dark, Mexican beans fresh for each pot. It was one of the reasons Nasty couldn't stomach the swill in the homicide office. From the day they were married, Estrella had gotten up and had coffee ready before Nasty was ready to leave, day or night.

"Go back to bed, *querida*," he whispered, slipping his arm around her and kissing her cheek.

They had been married eight years, and if anyone had asked Nasty, he would describe her as the best thing that had ever happened to him. If anyone had asked Estrella, she would have described herself as a good wife. Petite and pretty, she was often mistaken for a teenager when she was with their three children, ages seven, five, and nine months. She looked more like their sister than their mother. Her skin was honey colored, her hair glossy black with soft waves that lay across her shoulders like draped silk. Her obsidian eyes glittered like Fourth of July sparklers.

If it upset her to have her husband called out in the middle of the night when he had had only two hours sleep, she never said it aloud. Estrella was determined never to become a nagging policewife. She had seen too many marriages fall apart under that kind of pressure. She wouldn't let it happen to hers and Ignacio's. Never. But still she worried about him . . . and she did what she could to make his job easier.

Nasty swallowed some more coffee and took Estrella in his arms. "Go back to bed, *querida*. I'll call you when I can."

She kissed him and accepted the promise lightly. He always made the promise. He kept it when he could, and when he didn't, she accepted that too. She didn't like his erratic hours any more than he did, and she worried when he was exhausted.

"I will take the children to my mother's after mass," she told him as they walked to the front door.

He nodded. It wouldn't do any good to argue. She always kept the house quiet if there was a chance he might find time to come home and sleep. He gulped the rest of the coffee and she took the mug, then stood with it between her hands as if to capture the warmth his fingers had left as she watched him sprint across the yard to the car in the driveway. He drove off without looking back, his mind already on the crime to which he'd been called. When the car disappeared around the corner, Estrella closed the door and went back to bed.

*   *   *

Nasty and Parch spent two hours in the alley. The dead woman's name was Suzie Miller, occupation: prostitute. A Vice detective who heard the call confirmed the identification. Suzette Amy Miller's rap sheet covered three years. Each time she was picked up, one of the bailsmen known to work for a small-time pimp named Charlie O posted her bail. Just being on the corner near Le Sexe Shoppe was enough to mark her as one of Charlie's girls. Nasty had Vice round up every known prostitute in the area for questioning. Although a few admitted they had seen Miller, no one had noticed her with anyone in particular. Two of Charlie's women had been killed in less than a week. The rest were nervous, but not nervous enough to admit to anything that might get them in trouble with Vice or Charlie O. One thing they were sure of: Suzette had been wearing two gold-hoop earrings that night. Only one was on the body when it was found. The mate had been ripped off, tearing the lower portion of the earlobe with it.

It took a few hours to run down Charlie O. Nasty's eyes burned and there was a dull ache across the back of his head. At nine in the morning he felt as if he'd been up twenty-four hours. Charlie O's sharkskin sportscoat took on a silky glow under the harsh fluorescent lights of the homicide room, making him look like a beached shark dying in the sun.

"I told you, man, I don't know nuthin'. Sure, I seen Suzie around, but that don't mean I know nuthin' about her getting killed."

Charlie O was a little man with big ambitions. He hadn't been able to worm his way onto the more lucrative ends of Hollywood Boulevard or the Sunset Strip. Small in stature, his fish-belly-white, pockmarked face was dominated by a bulbous nose and ferret eyes that were almost hidden by shaggy black brows. He compensated for his physical ugliness by wearing flashy, expensive clothing and an onyx and diamond ring on his little finger.

"Just like you didn't know anything about Lily White?" Nasty said. Charlie had been brought in for questioning after White's murder, and he'd claimed complete ignorance. Now he retreated behind a blank stare. Nasty wagged his head and sighed. "What would you say if I told you we made your prints in Lily White's apartment?"

"I'd say your fingerprint boys made a mistake. I ain't never been in that apartment," Charlie said flatly.

"We have a positive ID on you in that building." Parch linked his hands and stretched his arms until his knuckles cracked.

Charlie's shaggy brows pulled together. "What was that address again?"

"You know where she lived."

"You brung me in last week to talk about Lily White," Charlie said. "I didn't know nuthin' then, and I don't know nuthin' now. I'm real sorry, Mr. Detectives, I'd like to help you, but . . ." He shrugged and smiled a fleeting, thin-lipped grimace.

"You went to Lily's apartment last Tuesday."

"No, sir. Maybe I was in the building, like you say. This guy—he's lookin' for an apartment, ya know? I'm helpin' him out, checkin' a couple of places, just sort of friendly like."

The building manager's statement about a neighbor complaining about the smell hadn't washed. When Nasty and Parch had questioned the tenant who allegedly reported the smell, they knew Harris was lying. He had pulled her name out of a hat in the mistaken belief that she would back his story. The girl, Sheri Walker, was another of Charlie's girls, but what Harris didn't know was that Walker had been booked for soliciting and spent the night in the tank awaiting arraignment. Questioned again, Harris said he *thought* it was

Walker on the phone, but he must have made a mistake. The caller hadn't given a name. Thinking it over, Harris decided he couldn't even swear it had been a woman.

The booking sheet showed Walker was picked up less than two blocks from where Miller's body was found. In that area, it was a foregone conclusion she was one of Charlie's women. And she lived in the same building as White. Nasty didn't believe in coincidence, at least not until he ruled out every other possibility. When latent prints came up with a partial that was a possible match with Charlie's but didn't have enough points to stand up in court, Nasty was using it as a bluff. He was willing to bet Charlie had gone to Lily's apartment to find out why she wasn't working. He used his key, found the body, then told the manager to call the police.

"What's your friend's name?" Nasty asked.

Charlie squeezed his eyes shut, and his face became all nose and brows. "Can't rightly recollect. Just some dude I see around."

"How do you explain your fingerprints on White's doorknob?"

"It must have been outside. I maybe touched it walkin' down the hall. You know how you do sometimes."

He was too sure of himself. The partial had come from the outside knob. The inside one and the doorframe had been wiped clean. There were enough prints inside the apartment to paper a wall. They were being run through, but Charlie knew his weren't among them.

Nasty turned away. "Okay, Charlie, you can go. Stay in town in case we feel like talking again."

As Charlie got to his feet, Parch slid from his chair and stood behind him, dwarfing the little man, who, after a quick glance over his shoulder, kept his gaze on Nasty.

"Just put out the word, man. I'll be here."

"We'll really appreciate that, Charlie," Nasty said, ending the interview.

Charlie had to sidle around Parch to get out. Parch watched him strut down the corridor. "The little shit. What do you think, Nasty?"

"Even if he was in the apartment, we don't have anything to hold him on. Let him worry awhile. We gave him plenty to think about. If a killer is working his turf, Charlie's got a problem."

"You think this kook has a thing about whores?"

Nasty shrugged. "It gives us a place to start." He found the small notebook in his desk and flipped through the pages. It was his private file of snitches. Every cop had one, and Nasty's had been compiled over his five years as a detective. The names were abbreviated so no one else could make sense of them, but Nasty read them as easily as a primer. If a detective wanted to keep his sources, he protected them.

He found what he was looking for and glanced at the clock. It would have to wait. The Saturday-night girls were off the street by now, either in gainful, all-night employment or crashed after a long night. He dropped the notebook back into the drawer as the phone rang.

Parch lifted it, listened, then said, "There's a guy named Haslett from Weapons out front looking for you."

"Send him in."

Parch spoke into the phone, then wheeled his chair to the doorway so he could wave. "Down here, Haslett."

Jack Haslett was a small, slight man with dark hair and a thin mustache. He shook hands with both detectives and accepted the cup of coffee Parch offered him.

"Sorry to get you out on a Sunday," Nasty apologized.

"No problem. I'm on my way up to Ojai. They're trying to link a couple of guns they found in a car trunk to a slaying last month. The guy has an arsenal of exotic weapons."

Nasty laid a copy of the flyer being circulated to machine shops in front of Haslett.

"This what your man is using?" Haslett asked.

"It's an educated guess based on the autopsy reports. Ever seen anything like it?"

Haslett studied the specifications and the sketch. "Not the way it's drawn here, but there are a couple of possibilities. What makes you think it's spring thrust?"

Nasty told him about the autopsy findings.

"I guess it could be," Haslett said, "but it's new if it is. On the other hand, I came across something a couple of weeks ago that could give you the same effect."

Parch hitched his chair. Nasty turned a hand for Haslett to go on.

"A new wrinkle in ninja weapons. First time I've seen it, but if there's one, you can bet there are others. Ninja is the latest fad in martial arts. Schools are opening all over the place, and most karate joints have added it to the classes. You can't pick up a martial arts magazine without seeing an article on it. Ninja weapons are a hot market. These days, kids are spending their allowances on swords, chains, butterfly knives, blowguns, *sheung dao, ashiko, shuko*—"

"You're losing me," Nasty said.

Haslett put aside the coffee cup and settled back. "Ancient Oriental weapons, all potentially deadly. There's a lot of crap floating around about mental and spiritual aspects of ninja, but the ninja were really cowboys. They were mercenaries. Cold-blooded assassins who took jobs no one else wanted. Killers for hire. Put them up against today's mafia or soldiers of fortune and the ninja would wind up showing them a few tricks. These damn kids who are into it today don't care about mental and spiritual discipline. Come downtown and see the heavy equipment we take away from street gangs. You'll feel naked with only a thirty-eight."

"What are those ninja weapons you mentioned?"

"*Sheung dao* is a light steel blade, slightly curved and sharp pointed. You've probably seen pictures of them in fancy ceremonial cases. *Ashiko* are foot spikes, meant for use in climbing. A couple of well-placed kicks and they can tear up a man as effectively as grenade fragments. And *shuko* are technically climbing claws for the hand, but they can dig into flesh just as easily as they can a cliff."

"Jesus . . ." Parch let his breath out noisily.

"Which one fits our murder-weapon pattern?"

"A variation of the *shuko*. Did you guys hear about that rumble down in Lincoln Heights a few weeks ago? Two of the kids were wearing modified *shuko* that had only one spike on the palm side. They were a little thicker than your tip here, but they made the same kind of wound." He slapped his palm against the desk. "Then when you want to get down to business, you close the fist and it lifts a longer spike on the knuckles, heavy-duty, sharp, and with the same needlelike tip. What you have is brass knuckles with a built-in six-inch stiletto. One kid was hospitalized with a puncture wound that nicked his aorta."

"Were these things homemade?" Nasty asked.

Haslett shook his head. "That's the real scary part. Both the ones confiscated were exactly alike, ordered by mail from an outfit in San Francisco. Maybe that particular model doesn't match your picture, but if there's one variation out there, you can bet there are others. You could be looking for a modified *shuko* any kid with ten or fifteen bucks and a postage stamp can send for."

Nasty shook his head. "It's possible, but I don't think our guy could get those clean punctures that way. He has to punch straight down, pull the blade, and hit again with the same precision? I don't think it can be done, but it's a direction. We'll check out subscriptions to those magazines. Can you give me a list?"

Haslett nodded. "I can't come up with anything else, Sergeant. It's very possible you're right about the spring thrust. I haven't seen anything like it, but the guy could have made it himself." Haslett started to pick up the coffee mug, then changed his mind.

"How? Where?" Nasty wanted to know. The flyer had been sent out to every tool and die maker and machine shop in the city without results so far.

"He could do it in a home workshop," Haslett said. "It's sophisticated but not all that difficult once he's got the idea. He'd have to know his way around metalworking tools, but any hardware store in the city carries them."

"What kind of tools?"

"Grinder, vise, drills, saws. If he started with a round shaft, it would be a simple grinding job."

"Why'd he make it triangular?" Parch asked. "Wouldn't anything with a point work?"

"You say your first two victims had two heart wounds incurred within seconds of each other. If the blade is spring-thrust, it has to be retractable so he can use it the second time, otherwise the wounds aren't going to be the same, right?" When Parch nodded, Haslett went on. "A triangular shape will give him extra strength to take the pressure when the blade is pushed back into the hilt. We're talking about a hell of a thrust, which means an equivalent amount of pressure to reset it."

"He made it tough for himself, if you ask me," Parch said.

"I don't know what makes the guy tick," Haslett said. "Maybe he just likes fooling around with tools."

Parch moved his chair into the direct flow of cold air from the vent near his desk. "We don't have a chance in hell of finding a home workshop."

"Your flyer may still produce results," Haslett said.

"How so?" Nasty queried.

"He may have decided to have the blade case-hardened."

Lopez gave him a quizzical look.

Haslett traced the sketch on the paper. "He's got a sharp instrument with enough spring-power behind it to drive six inches through flesh and muscle, not to mention the risk of hitting bone. He needs a heavy-duty spring to guarantee that kind of thrust. But he's got to reset the thing for his second strike, and that means pushing it back with an equal amount of force."

Nasty was following the weapons expert's logic. "Yet he does it easily in a few seconds. How about some kind of ratchet?"

"Any kind of gear mechanism would make the thing cumbersome to carry and handle. If the wounds are made less than a minute apart, the method of retraction has to be fast and easy. The simplest answer is retraction by pressure. He holds the blade against something and pushes. It may have a locking gear or rachet to grab it at intervals, but no matter how it works, the guy wants to be damned sure the blade doesn't break while he's resetting it. His best bet is heat-treated and case-hardened steel. It gives him a little more insurance it won't snap."

"So he case-hardens or whatever," Parch said.

Haslett nodded. "Right, but even if he made it himself, it's a pretty sure bet he had to send it out somewhere for hardening. He's not apt to have a cyanide bath sitting around."

"Machine or tool and die outfits do that?" Nasty asked. When Haslett nodded, Nasty considered the whole picture again. "Okay, he's got the weapon and the woman. What does he push it against to reset it?" He was having trouble envisioning the killer in the act of rape and murder pausing to reset the weapon. It was crazy. The damned thing wasn't an automatic with a loaded clip.

Haslett scratched his ear. "The ground would be too soft, so would wood. Some kind of plastic or metal maybe."

"How about concrete?"

Haslett looked doubtful. "It would have the strength, but it would dull the tip. That wouldn't diminish the killing potential, but there'd probably be particles of concrete in the second wound."

Suzette Amy Miller was the only one killed in an alley where there was plenty of concrete, and the killer had been scared off before he could put a second wound in her heart.

"Rule out concrete. I don't buy this guy leaving it to chance," Nasty said. "Whatever it is, he carries with him."

"That makes sense," Parch agreed.

"One other thing," Haslett offered. "He's got to protect the sharp tip. If he presses it against something, it's going to dull and he runs the risk of it snapping off. My guess is he's got a fitting of some kind that goes over the point and spreads the pressure back on the shaft while he's resetting the spring. If that's the case, the tip can't retract completely, but it's protected inside the cap so the guy can carry the thing in his pocket."

"Jesus, this guy's gone to a hell of a lot of work!" Parch rolled his eyes.

Nasty grunted. "Anything else you can give us, Haslett?"

"That's about it." He got to his feet. "If I come up with any more ideas, I'll call you."

When he left, Parch rubbed his eyes. "You think this nut plans to keep on killing?"

"Three in a week? What do you think?"

"I think we have ourselves a serial killer. I'll give you three to one the lieutenant appoints a special unit."

Nasty picked up the flyer and tapped his fingertip on the sketch of the weapon. "This intrigues me. I have the feeling this guy's not a nut in the usual sense of the word. He's crazy okay, but he's sane and clever at the same time. He picks victims at random, but he takes them all from a very small area. Almost like he's cleaning up the neighborhood." He glanced at Parch.

"His last job left a bloody mess."

"Maybe he didn't intend to kill her there. Maybe they were on their way to her room and something tipped her off that she'd picked up a weirdo, so she starts screaming."

"If he's smart, he's not going to take time to screw her. He's going to kill and take off fast as possible."

Nasty tossed the flyer back to the desk. "So he planned all along to do it in the alley? Why? White was killed in her apartment. Ewing was killed on the floor of the construction shack then tossed in the dumpster. Now suddenly the killer comes out into the open and makes what looks like a stupid move? It's like a chess player deliberately putting his queen in jeopardy."

"He's getting careless?"

"Or bold?"

"He wants to keep us off balance?"

"Change strategy . . . unexpected moves . . . He's playing a damned game," Nasty said.

Parch closed his eyes, then opened them wearily. "Just what we need, summer games."

CHAPTER
21
✝

AS JEANNE GOT off the elevator, Callie gave her a cheerful grin. "Hi, sweetie. How was the weekend? Did Glenn get home?"

Jeanne nodded. "It was hectic, but we made it."

"How's he doing?"

"Good news and bad news," Jeanne said, sinking into the chair beside Callie's desk and setting her briefcase on the floor. "Saturday was a nightmare. He was exhausted by the time we got home, and it didn't do much for his disposition."

Callie looked sympathetic. She was wearing a pencil-slim white dress with wide shoulders and black piping at the neckline and waist. She'd done her thick, glistening hair in a smooth upsweep topped by curls that completed a Joan Crawford silhouette.

"He was feeling better Sunday morning, but he got pretty tired before the day was over and was bristling again. He's got me walking on eggshells." She felt guilty complaining, but the pleasant euphoria she'd enjoyed Sunday morning had eroded as the day wore on. Glenn's irritability focused on petty complaints about everything from the heat to his nervousness about the murder story he read in the newspaper.

"Hey, sweetie, it's better for him to keep trying than to lie around babying himself."

Jeanne sighed. "You're right. At least it gave me time to get my homework done." She reached into her briefcase and took out the schedules and call sheets.

Callie glanced through them, turning pages quickly. She would have them typed and copied by the time the production staff finished in the viewing room. Jeanne glanced at the clock and picked up her briefcase. "Brad and Terry in yet?"

"I haven't seen Brad, but Terry's in the editing room."

Jeanne walked to her office and leafed through the few papers in the basket on her desk. A pink memo slip read, "Review scene 37." There was no signature. Frowning, she found the notes she'd used to make up the schedule for the week. Scene 37 was set for Tuesday. She rifled through her working copy of the script.

Scene 37 was a location shot in an alley, a dramatic murder scene that bridged the action to the picture's climax. She hoped Terry wasn't going to make drastic changes. She thought the scene read well and accomplished what it was intended to do. As if she had conjured Terry by her thoughts, he leaned in the doorway.

"Hey, you survived the weekend. How's Glenn?"

"Good, thanks."

"You look tired."

"I am a little." She held up the message slip. "What's this about?"

He plucked the slip from her hand to read it. "You've got me. That's our location shoot tomorrow. What gives?"

"Didn't you write it?"

"Nope."

She frowned. "Brad?" She wondered if he'd had another flash of artistic brilliance at the eleventh hour.

Terry ticked the paper with his fingernail. "This doesn't look like his writing."

Surprised, Jeanne said, "Who then?"

Terry shrugged and dropped the slip onto her desk. "If it's important, you'll find out sooner or later." He perched on the edge of her desk. "Brad wants me to give you the grand tour of the outdoor locations today. It's a fantastic excuse for us to do lunch. How about it?"

Jeanne nodded. It sounded great if they could fit it in the day's tight schedule.

"Wait until you see the alley we've got for that scene." He pointed at the memo. "It's got everything—grime, filth, cracked pavement, and overflowing garbage cans."

Jeanne laughed. "Sounds terrific. It should go well with lunch."

"I know a great restaurant only a few blocks from there. You like Thai food?"

"I've never tried it."

"You'll love it. The restaurant's on Hillhurst, not far from your apartment as a matter of fact."

Jeanne made a face. "Which means that your quaint little garbage-filled alley is also not far from my place."

He grinned. "Ah, but consider the bonus of easy access. Five minutes driving time, no hassle with traffic. Tell you what, after we see the quaint little garbage-filled alley, we'll run by your place to say hi to Glenn if we can squeeze it in before the three-o'clock call. It'll give him a nice break, and at the same time reassure you he's surviving without you. Maybe it will erase some of those worry lines from your pretty little face." He patted her hand.

"Sounds wonderful."

Terry glanced at his watch and got to his feet. "Time to look at Friday's footage. Brad wants a quick production meeting after we finish the morning's shooting, then we can take off. C'mon. Let's not keep the mighty guru waiting."

Jeanne crumpled the message slip and tossed it into the wastebasket as she got up.

The Thai restaurant was small and unpretentiously decorated in delicate pastels with an Oriental flavor. Crisp white tablecloths and slim vases with tiny pink- and salmon-colored lilies enhanced the Eastern atmosphere, and the proprietors had the good sense to leave the decor at that. There were two rooms; the smaller one, a step up and facing the street, had obviously been an expansion to the adjoining building as business increased.

Alerted by Terry to the spicy selections on the menu, Jeanne chose a mild chicken salad, which she found delicious. She preferred not eating a big meal at midday, and the Thai food was filling but not heavy. She also skipped the glass of wine Terry suggested for fear that, combined with the searing heat of the unrelenting Santa Ana now in its eighth day, it would make her sleepy. She and Terry had spent a half hour in Griffith Park looking at the location they'd be using. On the hillside where the final night scenes would be shot, the wind had been so hot the air was painful to breathe. She didn't envy the crew of the motion picture company filming that day.

As Terry promised, the restaurant was not far from the apartment. She had taken the Vermont Avenue bus when she apartment hunting, and Hillhurst was only two blocks beyond that. After lunch Terry drove south toward Sunset and parked on a side street. "We can walk to the alley from here."

Hot air engulfed them. The sun-baked sidewalks reflected the heat so even the shade of an occasional tree offered little relief. Jeanne's eyes burned behind her sunglasses, and the skin of her bare arms seemed to be shrinking under the sun's glare. She'd have to cover up on location so she wouldn't burn.

As they neared a six-way intersection, pockets of sleaze encroached on the aging neighborhood. The blight was reminiscent of what Terry had helped her avoid when she was apartment hunting: once-pleasant residential streets, gritty with blowing dust, bordering on major avenues that had fallen from grace and were now sprinkled with automobile body shops, strip shopping centers, and cocktail lounges. On one corner a windowless building had ADULT THEATER printed above the corner entrance and LE SEXE SHOPPE and ADULT BOOKSTORE on a long expanse of brick wall that had been painted garish pink.

The alley was half a block from the intersection. It hunkered in heat-permeated shade between a row of commercial buildings and a sagging wall of grape-stake fencing screening off the bungalows that occupied the rest of the block. The alley was littered with paper and debris skittering restlessly in a draft created by the rattling exhaust fan of a Chinese restaurant. The air was thick with the odor of hot grease and an unpleasant underlying stench of garbage.

"Well, what do you think?" Terry held out his hands as if framing the alley for a long shot.

"Yuk. It's perfect."

He laughed. "What did I tell you? Can I pick 'em? Come on, I'll show you our spot." He propelled Jeanne down the alley as she grimaced in the gusting breeze. "The place is perfect for the cameras. We couldn't do better if we had it made to order." Beyond an open door marked THEATER FIRE EXIT ONLY, where dark velvet drapes billowed in a crosscurrent of air, Terry pointed like an explorer claiming new land for the crown.

A building squeezed between the theater and a cocktail lounge was ten feet shallower and formed a small cul-de-sac. A door with two steps leading to it and a small, high window covered with heavy wire mesh were the only breaks in the dirty stucco wall. A green dumpster beside the door overflowed with cartons and packing materials. Near the alley, bits of yellow plastic were caught on the wall of the theater.

"What do you think?" Terry asked.

Jeanne studied some faint white marks on the pavement. "Aren't you going a bit overboard?"

"What do you mean? It's perfect. This is exactly the atmosphere the scene demands. We'll set up the number one camera there, and the dollie can go—"

"Of course it's perfect, Terry. Absolutely. I meant the chalk marks are a bit premature."

"What?"

She pointed to the smudged white line on the concrete. "The body outline doesn't come until the police scene."

Terry moved closer to the chalk marks and knelt to run his finger across them, then studied it as if it had been dipped in blood. He stood up.

Jeanne laughed at his comical expression. "Don't worry, the prop men can erase them."

Terry frowned at the smudge on his fingertip. "It wasn't here Friday." He made a fist and struck his forehead. "Jesus—" He blew out a breath. "Of all the eff-ing places in the whole damned city!"

"What are you talking about?" Jeanne asked.

He pointed to the chalk outline. "Realism, baby. I have picked the perfect spot for murder, only someone beat me to it. This is where that prostitute was killed Saturday night."

Jeanne stared at him, openmouthed. Yesterday Pearl Gannon had told her, *Third murder in a week. Less than ten blocks from here.* And Glenn had confronted her with the newspaper story when she emerged from the shower. Jeanne had laughed it off then, but now the reality was too sharp to ignore.

She heard herself whisper, "My God."

Terry took her arm. "Let's get out of here."

Jeanne let him propel her back to the street. He slowed

his long stride when she tugged at his arm because she was running to keep up with him.

"Sorry," he mumbled absently. "Damn, I hope this doesn't louse up the permit. The police must be finished with the crime scene or there'd be someone here, but we'd better check it out so Brad doesn't blow his cork."

Distracted, Jeanne barely heard him. Something else was swirling in the murky depths of her thoughts. The memo this morning had called her attention to the murder scene that would be shot in this alley. Coincidence? Terry had scouted locations in this neighborhood because he'd grown up here and knew it. Brad Raven, too. . . . And a murderer had chosen the same spot. Coincidence . . . or connection?

She was silent during the ride back to the studio, all thoughts of stopping to see Glenn forgotten. Terry headed directly for Raven's office. There was a message on Jeanne's desk that Glenn had called, but she set it aside and picked up the script that was open to scene thirty-seven. She read the scene through, then retrieved the crumpled memo from the wastebasket and went to the reception area.

"Callie, this was in my basket this morning. Did you put it there?"

Callie glanced at the pink slip. "Nope. I don't recognize the writing. Is it important?"

"I don't know. Do you still have the morning paper?"

"Sure." Callie reached to a shelf behind her desk and held out the *Times*. "I'm finished with it. Just toss it when you're done."

The story was on the front page.

CHAPTER 22
✝

SUDDENLY COLD IN the air-conditioning, Jeanne hugged her arms. The lightheartedness with which she had dismissed Glenn's fears yesterday was replaced by chilling apprehension. She opened the script of *Dead Past* and put it beside the newspaper. The opening scene of the picture was the murder of the story's first victim. Jeanne ran her finger down the cues, making sure her memory wasn't playing tricks.

In the script the killer was seen without definition other than his naked back glistening with the sweat of passion. Over his shoulder the camera caught the rapturous expression on the woman's face as the man's hands moved up her naked body, caressing her thighs, hips, waist, breasts, and shoulders. His fingers lingered sensuously, playing an intimate tune in the hollows of her collarbone. The girl smiled languorously as his hands slid across her silken skin, still caressing. As they closed around her throat, her eyes flew open. Surprise flitted momentarily on her features before it became terror as the hands tightened.

As Jeanne read, the dailies flashed through her mind.

The scene had cut with the killer still astride the woman's limp body, his rigid back defining his ecstasy.

She turned a page. The scene that followed showed uniformed police and plainclothes detectives clustered near a female corpse sprawled on a bloody bed in an unkempt apartment. She switched back to the newspaper article and ran her finger down the story. *Lily White, whose body was found in her Los Feliz apartment* . . .

Jeanne paged through the script to the second murder scene. Again the villain was seen only in silhouette in almost a repeat of the earlier scene except that the couple were lying on a blanket spread on the floor in front of a cold, pristine fireplace. The scene cut back to the main action of the story then, but a few pages later it went to an outdoor shot of the police investigating a body found in a dumpster. Hands shaking, Jeanne went back to the newspaper story. . . . *Vicki Ewing, whose body was found in a dumpster* . . .

She shoved her chair away from the desk as if to distance herself from the possibility that it was more than coincidence. Was she imagining things—nervous because of Glenn's harping about the murders? She reached for the phone, then let her hand fall. What could she tell the police? That someone was using the script of *Dead Past* for a real-life murder scenario? It sounded ridiculous put that way. She wondered if Terry or Brad had noticed the similarities. Terry would have said something when they left the alley.

She looked again at the dates of the first two murders, then flipped through her file of shooting schedules to see when the scenes had been filmed. Lily White's murder had been discovered two weeks after the *Dead Past* facsimile. Vicki Ewing's had taken place two days after that scene was shot. The latest victim had been found *before* they shot the scene. There was no time pattern, but that didn't change the similarity in detail. And now the same location . . .

She jumped when the phone rang. "Yes?"

Terry's voice had a quiet but snappy cadence. "You're holding up things, Jeanne. Better get in here before Brad blows a gasket."

"Oh, Lord." She glanced at her watch. "I'm on my way." She grabbed her script and clipboard and rushed to the studio.

Brad Raven was standing by the door, his expression dark. He glanced pointedly at his watch, like an irate parent. Jeanne murmured an apology, but he turned and strode to the edge of the shooting set, gesturing to Terry, and stood with his arms folded. The set lights came on, and the cameraman began to dolly into position. An electrician backed off the set feeding out cable as a prop man adjusted a shiny board.

"Okay, everybody, let's quiet down and get this shot off," Terry called, materializing out of the confusion. He glanced at Jeanne.

"Slate in," she called, hoping the rest of the crew wouldn't suffer because she had ticked off Raven. She saw Wray Jarvis glance in the producer's direction.

"Scene forty-one K, take one."

"Lock it up, please. Turnover. Action."

Wray Jarvis lifted his head almost imperceptibly as he brushed back his dark curls. He had the face of an Irish choirboy from an old Bing Crosby movie, yet when he immersed himself in the role of the psychopath, Dave Rudolo, Jarvis portrayed good and evil so convincingly, Jeanne wondered if it was more than a role to him. She studied his dark good looks. Remembering the chill that had gripped her when she was watching his performance in the murder scene, she shuddered. Was he convincing as a mad killer because— She pushed away the thought and brought her attention back as the camera rolled on the action.

The scene was a continuation of one that took place in

Rudolo's apartment where he'd stood at the kitchen sink, whistling softly. Terry had the camera zoom on his face and soft-focused the background of the sink and the running water. Rudolo's whistling created a deceptive sense of serenity. Jeanne remembered the breathless tension when the camera focused on the carving knife in his hands, then on the water trailing across the white porcelain sink that was tinted with blood being washed from the blade. Everyone on the set had been mesmerized as Rudolo set the knife on the drainboard, pulled a towel from the handle of the refrigerator door, and walked off camera.

In this shot he was easing open the front door of the apartment. Muffled voices could be heard, followed by a woman's soft laughter. Over his shoulder the camera picked up on a long shot of a woman and a man entering an apartment across the hall. Rudolo closed the door, his body rigid and his expression blank. His breath quickened and his expression altered with the subtlety of a reflection in rippled water. Madness glinted in his eyes as his hands twisted the towel and snapped it like a garrote.

"Cut!"

Raven's voice made Jeanne jump. Terry turned in surprise. "You're giving away too much, Jarvis," Raven said. "You haven't decided to kill her yet. You adore her, and you're jealous because she's with another man."

Jarvis nodded, concentrating.

Raven's voice was hypnotic. "The audience isn't sure what's happening. Until now you've barely spoken to her. They're just beginning to recognize your obsession. In this shot we want to emphasize the contrast between how you look at her and how you see the women you kill. The two parts of your life are still separate. Here we want only a glimpse of them coming together."

Jarvis nodded, his lips moving as he mouthed his lines silently, his face testing expressions.

Sotto voce, Terry said to Jeanne, "Damn it, Brad hit it exactly. I couldn't have said it better. Look at Jarvis. He's soaking it up like a sponge."

"He's fantastic," Jeanne murmured absently. Raven's analysis had unleashed an aura of menace far beyond what the scene evoked. She glanced where he was standing beside a light that cast long shadows across his face. His expression was as intent as Jarvis's. For a moment she experienced the strange sensation that she had seen that expression before, as if he were changing, chameleon like, before her eyes.

Terry was watching Jarvis. "Brad's trying to sign him for another feature before one of the studios grabs him. The kid is Jack the Ripper and the boy next door." He glanced at his watch. "You don't have to worry about tomorrow's permit. I told Brad about the alley thing, and he called someone he knows at LAPD. They're done with the crime scene, so there's no problem about our using the location tomorrow."

"Good." Should she tell him about the similarities she'd found between the script and the other murders? She was relieved when he walked back to the number one camera and she didn't have to decide.

"Okay, let's start with Dave at the door," Terry said.

Jeanne got through the retake, her mind still grappling with the crossover of fantasy and reality. She couldn't forget the newspaper story and the episode in the alley, or Glenn and Pearl's moody warnings . . . the real and the make-believe . . . a script and a murder. . . . What did she really know about these people she was working with?

Ridiculous, she chided herself. No one, absolutely no one here at Harvest was anything more than he seemed.

CHAPTER 23
✝

"DIDN'T I TELL you he'd form a special unit," Pach said as they left the lieutenant's office. "If only you'd taken the bet, Nasty, I'd have your paycheck. Next time I'll sell lottery tickets. You Chicanos are suckers for lotteries."

"I'm too smart to bet against a sure thing," Lopez said.

Nasty had just been appointed to head a special team investigating the Los Feliz murders. At a meeting called this morning, the police commissioner made it clear that the Northeast Division was under pressure to find this killer fast, before he decided to expand his territory and plunge the entire city into panic. The newspapers were running splashy stories on page one, and one tabloid speculated in print whether or not the city had another Hillside Strangler on its hands. The mayor's office was getting calls from Los Feliz citizens demanding the killer be caught. Panic was building rapidly in the hot, dry wind of the Santa Ana. The mayor called the commissioner directly. The commissioner called the meeting. Nobody mentioned it was an election year. Nobody had to.

The media had already nicknamed the killer the Los

Feliz Stabber, and the department was shorthanding it to the Stabber. Three men, including Parch, had been assigned to work under Nasty, to follow up any leads that came in and to correlate results of ongoing inquiries, such as the flyer on the weapon and the investigations of the victims' backgrounds. Additional men would be assigned as needed. It was in essence a mini-task force.

So far, they had damned little to keep four men busy. The flyer distributed to machine shops hadn't produced any results. Nasty was beginning to think Haslett was right about the weapon's being homemade, and if it had been sent out for case-hardening, no one had reported it so far.

Charlie O had sunk back into the slime, and only one other person had come forward with anything even resembling information. Negative information to be more precise. It didn't lead them anywhere and it closed off a faint avenue of hope.

The kid's name was Tim Wilcox. Jamming his hands in the pockets of his faded jeans because he was shaking so badly, Wilcox had nervously shifted as he admitted he'd been with Vicki Ewing the night she was killed. He was a short, skinny twenty-year-old with a bad complexion and thick, horn-rimmed glasses who said he and Vicki had met in a local bar and gone out together a few times. That night they'd eaten at the House of Pies on Vermont and Franklin, then returned to Vicki's ground-floor apartment in the fourplex to have sex and spend the rest of the evening watching a video movie. Wilcox claimed he fell asleep before it was over and didn't know Vicki had gone out. When he woke in the morning, he assumed she'd taken off for work, so he left. He didn't know about the murder until he'd read the story in the paper. The video cassette in Vicki Ewing's machine checked with his story. Lopez was pretty sure Wilcox was a casual bed partner rather than Vicki's steady boyfriend, but he assigned someone to trace his movements.

No tips had been phoned in anonymously or otherwise. Twenty-four hours after the special unit was formed, it had run out of leads.

Despite the extra headaches, secretly Lopez was pleased he had been put in charge of the investigation. The Stabber intrigued him. Often months or years went by before a pattern could be established for a serial killer. This guy made his clear with his second victim, using the same blade, distinctive and unmistakable, as if he were proud of it. Then a third killing right on the heels of the second. And all within the irregular boundaries of Los Feliz. Never once had his bloody trail spilled outside the neighborhood. The guy was sure of himself.

Even though there was a pattern, there was no guarantee it would lead them to the killer any faster than if he varied his MO for each murder. All it did was tell them they were dealing with a man who could and probably would strike again soon. Most serial killers spread out their killings over weeks, months, even years. Once sated, their murderous impulses had to rebuild strength. This guy zapped back fast. Too fast.

The Stabber's file still had holes you could drive a patrol car through. Lopez had pushed one question around in his mind until it was worn-out. He tried it now on Parch.

"Why did the killer take Vicki Ewing's body from the shack where she was killed out to the dumpster?"

"Maybe he thought he could hide the body or delay its discovery," Parch said. It was a system they used often, playing possibilities like a handball against a court.

"Why? He wasn't leaving town."

"Covering his tracks. Creating an alibi."

"If he killed her between midnight and two, he had at least five or six hours before anyone showed up for work. Why risk moving the corpse? That dumpster was twenty feet from the shack. He had to drag her out, heave her up into the damn thing. It doesn't make sense. It gave him another ten or fifteen minutes to alibi, assuming he had clear sailing all the way and didn't have to wait for passing cars or stray dogs."

"In the movies they do it all the time, you know, roll the body in a rug, take it out and dump it somewhere to confuse the issue."

"You and your damned movies."

"Okay, you tell me why he moved her," Parch countered.

"I wish I knew. When you look at the overall picture, everything about this guy's MO is a little out of whack. We're sure it's the same guy. The chance of duplicate weapons or two people taking turns with the same weapon and making the same pattern of wounds is too far out. Even if they rehearsed the scenario until they had it down perfect, I can't buy it. When it comes right down to it, all three murders were pretty sloppy. This killer is dodging potholes every step of the way. He could have tripped himself up a dozen times."

"Maybe he's learning from his mistakes and plans to go on to bigger and better things?" Parch's eyebrows arched with inquisitive awareness.

"You got a better idea?"

Parch scowled. "So he's playing a game, like you said?"

"It fits. Let's say he's out on the street for whatever reason. Maybe he's on his way home from work, or maybe he just wants to escape the heat. He meets Lily White and they wind up in her apartment. They have sex and he kills her, maybe intentionally, maybe not. When he sees what he's done, he panics and bolts. Luck plays into his hand and it's a couple of days before she's found. By then he's had plenty of time to think about what happened."

Parch cracked his knuckles. "He realizes he got away

with murder and decides to do it again? Or maybe he hears voices tell him to keep killing?"

They both knew that serial killers followed weird patterns of behavior, justified by even weirder motivations. The Hillside Strangler killed for thrills. Son of Sam heard God talking to him and got signs in dog shit. Once a killer got away with murder the first time, it was easier to kill again. In cases where torture-murders were linked to sexual pleasure, it wasn't unusual for the pattern to escalate more rapidly. Even so, the Los Feliz Stabber was definitely in a hurry. He waited only two days between the last killings. This bugged Lopez.

"Okay, what's his hurry all of a sudden?"

"Maybe he's on some kind of schedule. He's going out of town next week or next month. He thinks he has some kind of quota to fill before the second coming."

"Or a neighborhood to clean up?"

Parch was quiet a minute, then said, "I like that. That section of Los Feliz isn't exactly hooker heaven, but it has gone downhill. The neighborhood's always been pretty clean because of the hospital and the private patrols, but he got two hookers within eight blocks of each other. He knows his turf. If he doesn't change his pattern, it'll make it easier for us."

"Both prostitutes had the same pimp. Charlie O. At least we know where his girls work. It gives us a place to start." He went to the map tacked on the wall. Parch came to look over his shoulder as Nasty used a red pen to draw a circle around the six-way intersection. "This is where he picked up Miller." He stabbed the red felt tip at the center. "Charlie's girls stay in their own territory, so we can be reasonably sure he met White in the same general vicinity."

"Her apartment's over here." Parch pointed. "That's

five, no, six blocks away. That's a lot of walking time for a hooker."

"Maybe she moved up the avenue away from the adult theater. She could have been wandering or on her way home. If she met him anywhere along the way, they could have been walking to her place, but I doubt it. Time is money to a hooker. She'd take him to a hot-sheet motel. So the only other answer is the guy has a car and they drove."

Parch sighed. "And maybe they sprouted wings and flew. Hell, I don't know, Nasty. I've got the lousy gut feeling that this guy's going to kill again before we even get a handle on this case."

CHAPTER 24
†

GLENN WAS SPRAWLED uncomfortably on the couch when Jeanne got home, his face drawn in tired lines. When she started to scold him about being up too long, he pounded his fist on the cushion and rattled a newspaper at her.

"Did you see this?" he demanded.

"What?"

"The murder. The Los Feliz Stabber." The morning paper had elaborated on the details, and Glenn could no longer pretend he wasn't worried.

"I read it." Jeanne had managed to put it out of her mind during the busy afternoon, but now renewed uneasiness stung her conscience.

"That's what Pearl Gannon was talking about, isn't it?"

"I don't know. I guess so."

"Jesus, Jeanne, do you realize there's a maniac out there killing women in this neighborhood?" His voice rose to a hysterical pitch. "I don't want you out alone, you hear?"

Jeanne kicked off her sandals and collapsed on the chair across from him. "I'm not wandering the streets, Glenn. I leave,

I drive to work, maybe I stop at the grocery store before I come home. I'm not hanging out at Le Sexe Shoppe."

His eyes narrowed suspiciously. "Le Sexe Shoppe?"

"That alley where the woman was found."

He sat up, wincing as pain stabbed his leg. "How'd you know the name of the place?"

Confused, she glanced at the paper he was rattling. Hadn't the name been in the article? Oh, Lord—

"How, Jeanne?"

"If you calm down, I'll tell you." She waited until he settled back.

"So?"

She took a deep breath. "I was there today."

"What?" He started to push himself up again, and Jeanne made an impatient gesture.

She told him about her lunch with Terry and their visit to the alley where the chalk marks were still visible. Glenn raked his fingers through his tousled hair.

"Is Faust going to change the location?"

She shook her head. "We can't. It's too late. We shoot there tomorrow. Anyhow, Terry talked to Brad Raven, and he checked with the police. There isn't any problem about the permit because they're finished with the crime scene. So there's absolutely no reason to cancel the shoot."

"I still don't like it. What's the scene you're shooting there?"

"A murder, but before you get excited, don't think it didn't occur to me, but when I considered the fact that all our location shots are in this area, it's easy to accept the coincidence. It's the old thing about truth being stranger than fiction." She decided not to tell him about the other parallels that could be drawn with the script. She had confided in Terry when she caught him alone for a few minutes on one of their breaks. He listened, then addressed her concerns one by one, and Jeanne realized she was reading too much into vague similarities and ignoring vast differences. Now she was ready to forget the whole thing. "Besides," she assured Glenn, "when we're shooting, there's a mob of people around, including police. The least likely place for the Stabber to be is in that alley. It's probably the safest place in town."

"You said you'd be working late. I'm worried about you coming and going at night."

"I'll have Terry walk me to my car."

"What about when you park out front? Getting home the hours you'll be coming in, you may have to park on the next block. You keep saying how much of a problem parking is."

"I'll have Terry follow me home and wait until I get inside. We've been friends long enough I can ask that kind of favor," she said in total exasperation. "Now, get yourself into bed before you collapse. You've been up too long, I can tell." She got to her feet and thrust her thumb toward the bedroom. "Get going. That's an order. We'll have a late dinner."

"You go ahead and eat without me."

"I need to relax so I can enjoy my food. And you need a decent meal." She waited, arms akimbo, until he struggled onto the crutches, then followed him into the bedroom. He waved her off when she tried to help him into bed. Jeanne turned on the fan and drew the the door shut partway as she went out.

In the kitchen she stood staring out the window at the dust blowing through the walkway between the buildings. She wished she'd never told Glenn about Pearl Gannon's ridiculous babbling. She wished she'd never gone into Pearl Gannon's apartment and heard it herself. She turned away from the window and took a wine glass from the cupboard. She was worse than Glenn, worrying and being frightened. Filling the glass from the chilled bottle in the refrigerator, she remembered the sweet-and-sour coleslaw she'd picked up at the market on her way home. She retrieved the bag from the living room and put the container in the refrigerator. The cold supper would be easy to fix in a few minutes: shrimp she'd bought already cooked, potato salad, slaw, iced tea, and shortbread cookies.

She turned on the radio and the soft strains of a Brandenburg Concerto filled the room. Humming, she was carrying her wine to the living room when she heard a soft knock on the door. She detoured to close the bedroom door all the way before she answered it.

Mark Bonner whispered as if he knew Glenn was sleeping. "How's it going?"

"Okay, thanks." Seeing him reminded Jeanne with a guilty start that she hadn't done anything about settling the matter of the car. She opened the door. "Come on in." She put her finger to her lips and pointed toward the bedroom. Mark nodded and followed her into the kitchen. "Would you like a glass of wine?"

"You're sure I'm not interrupting?"

"Of course not."

"Well, okay then." He smiled.

Jeanne poured wine for him and retrieved her own glass before they sat at the small table. "I didn't have time to go to the bank for a cashier's check for the car. I'll do it tomorrow, I promise. Your friend will think I'm taking advantage."

"It's no problem."

He seemed ready to dismiss the subject, but Jeanne didn't trust herself to postpone it again. "When does he want to sign over the registration?"

His gaze slipped short of hers, and he studied the pattern of the pebbled-glass tabletop. He reached into his pocket and held out the pink slip.

She took it, astonished when she saw Mark's name as the registered owner. "It's *your* car?"

He turned the stem of his wineglass and looked at her apologetically. "I figured you'd think I was trying to unload it if you knew it was mine. I knew how tired you must be of dragging around on buses when you already had your hands full with your job and going to the hospital every day."

She didn't know what to say. He'd done her a favor and she was grateful. What difference did it make if he lied? It didn't change anything, except that she felt awkward offering him less than two thousand dollars. Maybe she should let Glenn handle it.

"Hey," Mark said, looking at her again, his expression reassuring. "I really need to sell the car. I've got the Buick, and I've got a lead on a beaut of a Firebird I can pick up cheap." He grinned sheepishly. "I'm a car nut. My old man used to say I had more cars than brains."

Jeanne felt better. "Don't worry, we're not going to change our minds about buying it."

He smiled as though she'd done him a favor. "That's great. I've taken good care of it. Be sure to check the oil regularly and you won't have any trouble. It's going to need a valve job before long, so I've decided I can only take eighteen for it, okay?" Before she had a chance to recover, he said, "How would it be if I come by the studio tomorrow about one? I'll take you over to the DMV, then maybe we can have a sandwich."

"You've done too much already," Jeanne protested. "Anyhow, we start location shooting tomorrow. I'll be tied up all day." He looked disappointed. Jeanne said, "I really don't know how to thank you, Mark. You've been great about everything, and now I don't think I can get away until Friday at the earliest. I realize I'm taking advantage, but can it wait until then? I can give you a personal check as a deposit."

"You don't have to do that, it's okay. We'll take care of it Friday."

"You're sure?"

"No sweat."

"You've really gone out of your way to be helpful," she said with honesty and appreciation.

He let the grin creep back. "Just my Boy Scout training."

She laughed. "Helping little old ladies across the street?"

His face flushed. "Hey, I didn't mean——" When he realized she was kidding, he laughed too. "It's tough moving and getting used to a new place and having to do everything on your own. I'm glad to help."

"Jeanne?" Glenn's muffled call came from the bedroom.

Mark got to his feet. "I'd better go. I know you're busy. Is there anything I can do——?" When she shook her head, he said, "Thanks for the wine." He hurried ahead of her and closed the front door softly as she went to the bedroom.

Burrowed in the pillows, his eyes heavy, Glenn asked churlishly, "Who were you talking to?"

She ignored his sharp tone. "Mark Bonner came to ask about the car." She didn't tell him that Mark owned the car. In Glenn's present mood it might precipitate another hassle. "I was having a glass of wine. Would you like one?"

He shook his head. "I need one of those pain pills and some water."

She got the water and the pill and sat on the edge of the bed while he swallowed it. When he handed back the glass, his fingers touched hers and lingered.

"Christ, hon, I'm sorry. I got on your case again, didn't I? I don't know what gets into me."

Jeanne wanted to fall into his arms and be held tight, but she was still wounded from his sharp words. "I know it's hard, Glenn. You have to give yourself time. Dr. Ingerman says it will take a couple of weeks to get your strength back."

Glenn lay back against the pillows. "I keep telling myself that, but the next thing I know, I'm snapping and snarling. I'm ashamed to ask you to forgive me again."

He closed his fingers around her hand and she returned the pressure. "I worry about you," she told him. "I don't want you to overdo and have a setback. I feel terrible about my hours this week. It's bad enough that location shooting runs so late, but Brad has laid down the law about screening the dailies every night when we finish up. God only knows what time I'll be getting home."

The tight lines furrowing Glenn's brow deepened before he made an effort to smile. "Hey, I'll manage. I've got to stop acting like a spoiled kid who has to be amused all the time. You've got your job, and I've got to keep myself busy enough so I don't go crazy."

"Without overdoing," she prompted.

"Right. No more heroics, no more whining. My body may be out of kilter, but there's nothing wrong with my head—at least nothing too serious." He tried to grin and squeezed her hand. "I had two great ideas today. First, I want to read the copy of the script you gave me so I know what you're talking about when you come home. I'm ashamed I haven't done it before this. Second, you remember that idea I had for the article on the history of sound recording in movies? I'm going to get to work on it. It'll keep me busy and it will be fun. I can handle interviews by phone and get a messenger service to pick up research stuff. Jim Newell says I can use anything I need from his library. Hearing about Pearl Gannon being our neighbor made me think of it. One of her husbands was head soundman at RKO back in the early days. It'll give me a good excuse to meet her."

"That's wonderful!" Jeanne caught his enthusiasm and felt her spirits lighten. During his university years and their early marriage, Glenn had published dozens of articles in various sound-recording trade magazines. It gave him a chance to use his knowledge and at times, such as the article he was proposing now, to combine that knowledge with his love of cinema history. Writing was one thing that would keep his mind busy without overtiring his healing body.

He lifted her hand and pressed it to his cheek. "Maybe

it'll keep me from wallowing in self-pity and make me better company."

She bent to him, the last traces of her irritation gone now as she stroked his temple and let her fingers cup his chin as she kissed him. His eyes were heavy-lidded and beginning to drift out of focus. "Sleep," she whispered.

"Wake me when supper's ready," he said. The words slurred as the pill began to take hold. He abandoned the effort to keep his eyes open.

Jeanne tiptoed from the room, closing the door behind her. She wondered if they had reached a turning point. Was everything going to be all right from now on? Oh, she hoped so.

She stopped abruptly in the kitchen doorway and a startled sound escaped her lips. Sonny Crenshaw was at the sink holding two small sprigs of deep-purple bougainvillea in a wineglass.

"Gosh, I'm sorry, Mrs. Donovan, I didn't mean to scare you." He looked guilty as he shifted the glass carefully from one hand to the other in order to wipe his wet hands on his jeans.

The knot in Jeanne's throat wouldn't dislodge. "How did you get in?"

"The door was open."

She hadn't taken time to lock the door or set the chain after Mark left. Good Lord, did she have to risk an intrusion whenever she forgot to bar the door? Was Sonny Crenshaw lying in wait for any opportunity to walk in? Anger pushed aside her fear. "You're not supposed to come into people's apartments without being invited. You should know that."

His eyes glazed like a child trying to ignore a scolding. He held out the glass. "I brought you flowers."

"You brought the rose when I first moved in, didn't you?" she accused.

He looked at his feet and his face reddened. Finally he nodded without looking up.

She wanted to be angry, but he was pathetic, and she felt sorry for him. "Why?" she asked in a gentler tone.

"It was a present," he said, "but it fell apart when I took it out of my pocket."

"What about the dowels? The sticks?" Jeanne was trying hard to understand.

"I saw it in a movie." His voice was so low she barely heard the words. "To keep away evil." He stared at the glass holding the flowers. "I—I was glad you moved in."

She wasn't getting anywhere. She sighed. "Well, thank you for the flowers, but you have to go now. Sonny, look at me." When he raised his head, she said, "You must never come in again unless I invite you, do you understand?"

He bobbed his head and put the makeshift vase on the drainboard. "I suppose you're going to tell my mother like he always does." He looked apprehensive.

"I—" It would be like beating a puppy. Jeanne said reluctantly, "If you promise to knock from now on and wait to be invited, I won't say anything."

He regarded her suspiciously. "Not even to him?"

"I won't tell either your mother or father," she promised. He was more like a slow-witted child than a mentally ill adult.

He shook his head. "No. *Him*. 102. Bonner."

Surprised, she said, "Well, no, I won't mention it to him either if that's what you want."

Sonny nodded and backed toward the hall. A moment later the front door opened and closed, and he was gone. She hurried to set both locks and the chain. No matter how childlike Sonny Crenshaw was, there was something frightening about him. She was almost sorry she had promised not to tell anyone about what he'd done.

CHAPTER 25
†

DONOVAN SOUNDED GRUMPIER than hell, but he was still adjusting to being home from the hospital, Mark supposed. How was the guy going to make out when Jeanne went back to work? Maybe Mark should offer to look in on him once in a while. He might appreciate some company, and it would relieve Jeanne's mind to know there was someone around.

He heard the sound of running water in the Donovan apartment. The kitchen of 204 was right behind his bedroom, and the ancient plumbing was noisy. When the pipes quit clanking, everything was quiet for a minute, then he heard a deep, muffled voice. Donovan? Jeanne's voice rose in answer.

"How did you get in?"

When he heard the other voice again, Bonner recognized Sonny Crenshaw. He realized suddenly that because Jeanne had been hurrying to answer her husband's call, she hadn't stopped to lock and bolt the door after Mark when he left. Sonny must have walked in again. Mark strained to listen as Sonny's voice rose and fell in mumbles. He couldn't make out what the kid was saying, but the whine was distinct. Something about his mother . . . Probably pleading with Jeanne not to snitch on him. She wouldn't, either. She was too kindhearted. But somebody had to——the kid just never learned. Mark had caught him snooping around and checking apartment doors more than once. Matter of fact, he was pretty sure Sonny sometimes "borrowed" the building keys from his folks and prowled apartments while people weren't home. He'd never caught him in here, but if he ever did, Mark would do more than tell Lucille and Harry. He'd pick up the phone and dial the landlord right in front of them. Or the police. Maybe then they'd realize they'd better keep Sonny from snooping on people that way. If the cops talked to them, maybe it would sink in that they had to keep Sonny out of people's hair.

When the voices beyond the wall stopped, Mark sprinted through the bedroom and the living room. He opened his front door in time to see Sonny come out of Jeanne's apartment. Mark ran down the hall. When Sonny saw him, he raced for the basement door and was out of sight in seconds. By the time Mark reached it, there was no sign of him. The basement was dark. Mark listened for some sound to betray Sonny's whereabouts, but everything was quiet. He was down there, and there was no other way out. He had him trapped. Mark eased onto the top step and felt for the light switch and snapped it on before he started down slowly. On every other step he stopped to listen. Where was Sonny hiding?

At the bottom Mark turned like a mime in slow motion to peer under the stairs. The space was murky with shadows, but as Mark studied them, there was a faint stir in their depths. Grinning, he spread his arms like the open jaws of a trap and eased around the staircase with his gaze riveted on the spot. He had the little bastard now. As soon as there was enough headroom Mark sprang under the steps. His foot caught in the kickstand of Sonny's bicycle and it clattered over with Mark sprawled across it. A handlebar punched his chest and one foot tangled in a wheel. Cursing, he freed himself and hobbled back to the pale puddle of light at the foot of the stairs, breathing through his mouth as he listened.

"Sonny? Where are you? Come on out. I'm not going to hurt you. I want to talk to you."

Angry now, Mark turned slowly and studied the darkness. Nothing. Wherever Sonny was, he wasn't letting on. Mark reached for the switch at the foot of the stairs. When light flooded the basement, he swiveled rapidly to search the shadowy corners. Still nothing. Sonny hadn't gone past him, so he was there somewhere.

"C'mon out, Sonny. I got something for you."

Sidling so he could watch the stairs, Mark moved down the narrow aisle between the outside wall and the wire-enclosed storage bins. There were ceiling bulbs inside the individual spaces, but without them there was barely enough light to see. As he passed each padlock he tugged it to make sure it was fastened. Satisfied, he turned and went back to the beginning of the row and leaned against the cool concrete as he studied the rest of the basement. The door at the top of the stairs was still closed. He'd have heard Sonny if he made a run for it. So he was still hiding. The little creep knew he was in trouble for pestering a tenant. He'd been pushing his luck, and this time he'd gone too far. No wonder he was scared. It was nothing compared to what he'd be when Mark got done with him.

I should have beat the crap out of him when he scared Jeanne with the dowels. Sonny is completely bonkers. He should be locked up. Sometimes Mark wondered what went on inside Sonny's head and how much he really understood. Well, he'd teach him a lesson this time, before Jeanne could exact any more promises.

Mark was tempted to turn off the lights and wait for Sonny to make a move, but that could take forever. It was nothing for Sonny to hunker in the dark for hours. Well, not this time.

Walking softly, he moved through the basement. The laundry and furnace rooms took up the front half. The laundry room lights were on, and Mark glanced at the open lids of the washer and the dryer. The only possible hiding place in there was a small, padlocked storage closet. From the doorway the padlock looked fastened, but Mark knew a good yank would pull it free. Glancing at the dark maw of the furnace room, Mark ducked into the laundry room, but instead of crossing to the closet, he stopped abruptly. Sure enough, there was a scuffling sound in the furnace room as Sonny tried to dart from his hiding place.

Mark dived at the moving shadow and caught Sonny before he could slip back behind the monstrous, outdated furnace. The force of Mark's hurtling body knocked Sonny from his feet and they crashed to the grimy floor.

Sonny was already blubbering. "Don't hurt me, don't hurt me—"

Mark dragged him up and pushed him against the wall. Holding him under the chin, Mark forced Sonny's head up so his gaze swept the cobweb-infested rafters. "What were you doing in Mrs. Donovan's apartment?" he demanded in a fierce whisper.

Sonny's mouth worked soundlessly as he tried to pull words from his confusion and terror. Mark slammed him against the wall.

"I asked, what you were doing in there, creep?" His fingers poked into the soft underside of Sonny's chin.

Sonny raised his hands like a surrendering soldier. "Nothing—"

Mark grabbed his shoulders and shook him, banging his head against the concrete, then slapped him hard enough to make his head snap. "Don't lie to me, you moron. What were you doing in there? How'd you get in?"

"Don't hurt me, don't hurt me," Sonny begged. Tears began to roll over his eyelids as he raised his arms to ward off any more blows. Mark moved like a street fighter, slamming

Sonny's arms out of the way and lashing a palm across Sonny's face before he knew what happened.

"How did you get in?" Mark demanded. His voice was barely audible but it rang coldly.

Sonny licked his lips and moved his hands pathetically. "The door wasn't locked."

Mark looked at him suspiciously. "How'd you know that?"

Sonny's gaze darted.

Mark shook him again. "How'd you know?" He raised a fist.

"I—I saw you come out—"

Mark punched him in the midsection. Air whooshed from Sonny's lungs as he doubled over. Mark grabbed his hair and yanked him upright, slamming his head against the concrete. "You were spying on me again, you rotten little creep! I warned you about that."

"No, honest—no—" Tears ran down Sonny's cheeks and he hunched his shoulders to wipe them on his T-shirt.

"Don't lie to me, Sonny. I swear, I'll kill you." Mark slid his hand back to Sonny's throat.

"I ain't lying, honest. I come in the back way, and I had these flowers, and they were so pretty, and I felt so bad about what I'd done—you know, with the sticks and scaring her when I didn't mean to—"

"So it *was* you with the dowels and the flower. What the hell did you think you were doing?"

"War—warding off evil spirits—"

"You used your mother's keys, didn't you!"

Sonny tried to nod but gagged as Mark's fingers pressed his throat.

"This time you didn't need them. You just opened the door and walked in?" The ridicule and sarcasm were lost on Sonny.

"I went into the kitchen to put the flowers in water so they wouldn't fall apart like the other time."

Mark's hand rang against Sonny's cheek again. Sonny tried to swallow the sounds erupting from his throat. His face contorted as Mark leaned close. "I'm telling you to stay away from her, understand?"

Sonny's head moved in terrified agreement, jerking back each time it pressed into Mark's gripping fingers on his throat. Mark held him against the wall, almost lifting him from his feet. His free hand punctuated each command with a slap.

"Stay away from Mrs. Donovan, you hear?

"Stay out of her apartment.

"And I'm not going to warn you again about spying on me." He used both hands to grip Sonny's throat hard enough to make the boy's eyes bulge. "I catch you doing it again, I'm going to squeeze your skinny neck so hard you'll stop breathing. You got that?"

Sonny made a gurgling sound. Mark let go with a shove that bounced Sonny against the wall, where he cowered like a frightened animal.

"And you'd better not tell your folks about this either," Mark warned as he started to turn away then looked back. "If you do, I guess I'll have to find you so we can have another talk."

Sonny's head bobbed. "I won't say nothing."

Smiling, Mark patted Sonny's cheek gently. "That's a good kid, Sonny." Then without warning he pulled back a fist and drove it into Sonny's midsection. Air exploded from Sonny's lungs and he doubled in agony. Before he could fall, Mark's knee caught him hard in the crotch. Sonny collapsed to the concrete gasping and crying and choking on his own vomit.

Mark turned away and walked through the basement, turning off the lights as he went upstairs.

CHAPTER 26

✝

THE PARCHING WIND gusted down from the mountains, funneling dust along the street where the trailers and honey wagons were parked. The first afternoon of location shooting was off to a bad start. The scene, which should have been completed an hour ago, was in its fifth take. Crew and cast alike were showing the effects of the heat and the strain, and they still had the night murder scene to shoot after the dinner break.

"Cut!" Brad Raven shouted.

Jeanne riveted her gaze on the dumpster in the background of the scene so Raven wouldn't see her anger. *Go away,* she thought. *Go back to the studio or home or anyplace, just get out of here.* Tension had become palpable because Brad was asserting his presence, demanding a change of wardrobe here, a lighting board moved there, preempting everyone's duties. Genius or not, he was making a general nuisance of himself. What now, she wondered as she saw him accost Wray Jarvis.

"For crissake, Jarvis, what the hell are you doing? Rudolo is a psycho, not a simpering moron."

"Mr. Faust said to downplay it," Jarvis said sulkily.

"Downplay, not kill. Give us what you had yesterday. Pathos, not fucking trite whining." Brad walked away, expelling his breath in exasperation. Terry stopped him and engaged him in low conversation.

Jeanne left her chair, over which a sun umbrella had been attached, and went to Jarvis. She had taken on the role of peacemaker by necessity. While Terry placated Raven, she tried to bind the young actor's wounds. "It was a lot closer that time, Wray. I think beginning your move away from the building as you start your lines may be what's throwing you off. How about not moving away from the wall until you say, 'I've been watching you'? That defines your intention a little better, and it adds menace to your expression. I think it may be what Raven is looking for." She was giving the actor lots of room for interpretation and neither chastising or defending the producer. A way out.

Mollified by her tone and at having a practical suggestion to follow, Jarvis nodded. Jeanne gave him an encouraging smile. "Want Sally to bring you a Coke?"

"No, I'm okay. Whenever you're ready," he said, glancing past her to where Terry was still conferring with Raven, who looked irritated and digruntled.

Jeanne touched Jarvis's arm encouragingly before she went over to the two men. Brad glanced up as she approached, his dark brows drawn together to a cloven hoof on his forehead.

"He's ready when you are, Terry," Jeanne said, ignoring Raven. She had given up trying to assess his moods or cater to them.

"I hope to Christ he gets it right this time," Brad fumed. "At the rate we're going, we'll be into golden time by the end of the week."

"Riding him isn't going to help," Jeanne said bluntly. Brad Raven had thrown everything out of synch today. Blame should rest where it belonged.

Terry shot her a surprised glance. Meeting Raven's cold stare, Jeanne said, "Tempers won't be improved by having to work overtime in this heat. I suggest we get on with it."

Raven's face darkened, and the clefts between his brows became canyons betraying his fury. His mouth twitched as if he were choosing precise words, then he turned abruptly and motioned to Terry, who lost no time in calling for places.

As Jeanne walked away, a gust of wind spewed dust in a wild adagio. She covered her eyes too late to avoid a speck of stinging grit. Blinded, she wiped at the tears that surged as someone sheltered her from the wind.

"You okay?"

She blinked until the speck washed out in the teary flow. Terry produced a tissue and dabbed her eye. "Out?"

"Yes, thanks." She found another tissue in the pocket of her cotton slacks.

Terry smiled. "Thanks for bearding the lion. I should have said something hours ago. He's been in a foul mood all day. He must have had a lousy weekend." He gave her arm a friendly squeeze as he moved away.

She wasn't the least bit sorry she had sounded off. Raven had been blaming Terry or her, anyone but himself, for everything that went wrong or even slightly out of whack. His ego refused to make any concessions for heat or exhaustion or human error. It was a miracle that Terry kept his good-natured composure when he had to deal with Raven on such a close level, yet their friendship had survived. She was glad she only had to work with the man.

She brushed a few stray hairs back into her damp ponytail. If only the heat would break.

When Jeanne left for work, Glenn tried to begin planning the article he wanted to write. What had seemed like such a terrific idea the day before was a chore now. The weeks of inactivity had dulled his brain as well as his body, and he felt the familiar signs of restlessness growing. His leg under the cast itched miserably, and he continually caught himself scratching at it unconsciously. The apartment wasn't unbearably hot because the fan kept the air circulating, but he was sweating. The wind whistling through the trees outside grated on his nerves like sandpaper. Finally he threw aside the legal pad and pencil and heaved himself out of bed.

He had promised Jeanne he wouldn't get overly tired, but he was going crazy lying in bed. He made his way to the kitchen for a glass of cold juice and drank it standing by the window, looking out at the brick wall of the building across the walkway. What a hell of a way to live. He felt like a caged animal. Los Angeles was a zoo. He and Jeanne didn't belong here. No job was worth being cooped up in a dump like this.

The doorbell startled him, and he glanced at his watch. It was too early for the therapist. Setting down the glass, he hobbled to the front door. He was surprised to see Mark Bonner.

"I hope I didn't make you get up," Bonner said.

Glenn supposed he meant well, but how the hell did he think anyone would answer the bell without getting up? "Naw. I was getting a drink."

"Hey, good timing. I thought you might like to read the morning paper. I know Jeanne doesn't always have time to get one."

Glenn felt a tic of irritation at his being so familiar with Jeanne's habits. She hadn't gotten a paper this morning. But he supposed Bonner was trying to be nice. Glenn took the paper he was holding out.

"Thanks. I like a morning paper. I'd better call and start having it delivered." He hesitated, wondering if he should invite Bonner in and not really wanting to.

Bonner didn't seem to expect it. He shoved his hand in a pocket and pulled out a slip of paper. "Here's my phone number. If you need help or think of anything you want from the store, give me a call. I'm in and out all day, so it isn't any trouble."

Glenn glanced at the slip and put it in the pocket of his pajama top. "That's damned nice of you. Thanks."

Bonner passed off the compliment with a shrug.

"Jeanne said you work nights."

"Yeah. I'm a night security guard in an office building. It's a crummy job, but it gives me plenty of time to study, and it keeps my days free for auditions and acting classes."

"You been in anything I might have seen?"

Bonner shook his head. "You never would have noticed me."

"I'm a movie buff. Let me know if any of your pictures turn up on the late show. I'll spot you."

"Okay, I'll do that." Bonner started down the hall, but Glenn called him back.

"I hear that Pearl Gannon lives in the building. Do you think she'd talk to me?"

Mark looked puzzled. "What do you want to talk to her for? She's a crazy old lady."

"I told you, I'm a film buff. I have all her old ones in my collection."

"Yeah?" He looked surprised.

"I'd like to meet her."

Mark laughed. "I guarantee she'll talk to you. She used to grab people in the hall to have an audience for her stories."

"Used to? She's not an invalid or anything?"

"Healthy as a horse except for up here." Mark tapped his temple. "People got tired of it and started avoiding her. You know how it is."

Glenn shifted on the crutches, and Bonner looked alarmed. "Hey, you're tired. Don't let me keep you standing. Be sure to give me a call if you need anything——or even if you just want someone to watch the baseball game with. Okay?"

"Sure. Thanks for the paper. And oh, yeah, thanks for going to so much trouble about the car. Did Jeanne get the check to your friend?"

"We got it all straightened out." Bonner backed away. "Don't forget, call if you need anything. I don't go to work until eleven. So long."

"So long."

Back in the bedroom Glenn straightened the bed before he lay down to red the paper. The first thing that caught his eye was another front-page story about the Los Feliz Stabber. It was a recap, but he read it through twice. Damn, it made him nervous. He wished the nut would pick some other part of the city to do his dirty work.

He read the rest of the paper desultorily and finally tossed it aside and picked up the script of *Dead Past* Jeanne had put on the nightstand. He had to show more interest in her work. In Minneapolis they had shared everything. The least he could do was drum up some interest now. He settled down to read, and in minutes he was completely engrossed in the script.

When he finished, he lay staring at the ceiling, his brow furrowed. It was as if he'd been pulled slowly into a cold ocean. The frustrated concern for Jeanne's safety he'd been yapping about was taking on a new dimension. There had been three murders in the neighborhood, and there were three murders in the script of *Dead Past*. Not identical, but too close for comfort, especially that last one. The script was about a serial killer, and even though the police hadn't made an official statement, that's exactly what they had. Jeanne said Brad Raven had talked to the police. Glenn wondered if he'd mentioned any of this.

He wiped a trickle of sweat from his temple. How would some weirdo get his hands on the script Harvest was shooting? Or was someone at Harvest. . . ? Maybe Jeanne could brush it off, but he wouldn't. He picked up the newspaper and scanned the article for the name of the cop in charge, his hand already on the phone.

Detective Lopez was politely interested. "You say three murders in the script parallel the Stabber's?"

"Close enough to worry me. My wife is the first assistant director on the film, and they're shooting in that alley today."

Lopez asked for the name of the film company and promised someone would look into it. He thanked Glenn for calling.

Glenn disconnected and started to dial Harvest but hung up without completing the call. They were on location. There was no point in alarming the receptionist. No one at Harvest would thank him for putting the police on them, assuming Lopez did anything. Glenn wondered if his would be treated like a crank call. When the phone rang suddenly, he snatched it up. It was the therapist on his way. Glenn heaved himself out of bed and went to unlock the front door.

After the therapy session Glenn slept for an hour before he showered and dressed. He called Detective Lopez back to see if he'd come up with anything but was told he was out. Glenn forced himself to get to work on his article so he wouldn't go crazy. He spent an hour on the phone trying to line up information and interviews. He lucked upon a connection to one of the inventors of an early microphone used in some of the first talkies. Elated by success, he made half a dozen more calls and managed to arrange a phone interview later in the week with the retired old man. Then exhausted, he lay down and slept again. He felt better when he woke and decided to check the mail and knock on Pearl Gannon's door.

He picked up the crutches and pulled himself to his

feet, then stood a moment getting his balance. He wouldn't stay up longer than half an hour. The least he could do to help Jeanne was be a model patient. He found the extra set of keys she'd left on the bookcase and let himself out of the apartment.

When he knocked on the door of 101, a tiny woman with snow-white hair and deep, amethyst eyes opened the door on the chain and peered out. Glenn wasn't prepared for how little she had changed. Older, but the same perfect oval face, with wide-set eyes and delicate, almost fragile features that had made her a close runner-up to Jean Harlow in beauty. Glenn gave her a friendly smile.

"Miss Gannon? I'm Glenn Donovan from 104."

"Oh, my." She closed the door so she could slip off the chain, then opened it wide. "Do come in, dear boy, please. Is something the matter? Do you need something. Can I—?"

"Everything's fine, Miss Gannon, just fine. I really shouldn't be bothering you like this, but I wanted to thank you for the delicious coffee cake."

Pearl's birdlike hands fluttered, making the marquise diamond on her finger flash like a strobe light. "How very sweet." She smiled as she reset the safety chain. Her hand fluttered again.

Glenn recalled the gesture from her silver screen days. It was a Pearl Gannon trademark, and it was still as appealing as it had been then. He grinned. "I'm one of your greatest fans."

She blushed to a delicate rose pink, another Gannon trademark that had not been lost over the years. Her wrinkled face glowed and her violet eyes sparkled. It was a shame that she'd faded into obscurity before Technicolor became commonplace.

"You're much too young," she insisted.

He grinned again. "The late show. I have them all on tape."

"Oh, my." She was obviously pleased. "Do sit down. I'll put the kettle on. I have some lovely jasmine tea that is perfect for a warm afternoon."

"If you're sure I'm not interrupting . . ."

"Oh, my, dear me, no. I go out so seldom these days. An occasional bit part. I did a commercial a few months back. Perhaps you've seen it? Century Airlines? No? It will be picked up for another thirteen weeks. You must watch it then. In any case, I am delighted to have company, especially a handsome young man. Do sit down. I'll only be a minute fixing the tea." She walked in the direction of the kitchen, her back straight and her chin high.

Glenn marveled at the eloquent presence that still commanded attention. He was looking forward to talking to her. He maneuvered himself into an overstuffed chair with antimacassars on the arms and headrest, glancing around the cluttered room as he shoved his crutches out of the way. The profusion of plants and furniture were perfect props for the faded movie star's waning years. A framed studio publicity picture on the wall had to be Pearl and a youthful John Barrymore; in another, she was standing with Douglas Fairbanks. A frame above the mantel held an award of some kind, and Glenn wished he'd read it before he sat down. Well, with any luck, he'd be invited back and would have a chance to look around all he wanted.

Pearl returned with a bamboo tray holding a cozied teapot, cups, and saucers. She put it on the table in front of the Queen Anne sofa. As precisely as if she were entertaining Barrymore himself, she set the cups on the fragile saucers and placed them on the table to await filling. Then, reviewing the tray, she fluttered her hand.

"I should have asked. Do you take cream or lemon?"

"No, just plain."

She smiled. "I like a man who appreciates a good cup of tea." She folded her hands in her lap and studied him.

"You're very pale. You should get out in the sun a bit. You have that lovely little patio. Use it, my dear."

"I intended to," he assured her. "Did my wife tell you about the article I'm doing for *REP*?" He knew she hadn't, but it was a good opening.

Pearl's brow knit—there was no other word for it—in concentration. "R . . . E . . . P?"

"*Recording Engineer Producer*. It's one of the top publications in the sound industry."

"Gerod was a sound engineer. Gerod Haliman, my fourth husband. No, oh, dear me, *third*. He was before Stanley." She smiled, pleased that her past fell into proper sequence.

"I remember that from the biography Keller did on you."

"You read it?" She seemed genuinely flattered.

"I've read everything that's ever been written on you. I told you, you're one of my all-time favorites."

Pearl's face suffused to a pink that made Glenn think of wild roses. She busied herself pouring the tea, which she deemed ready.

Accepting the fragile porcelain cup, Glenn told her about the article and the kind of background he was after. Pearl was delighted to help. Of course she had saved Gerod's papers, and Glenn was welcome to use whatever he wanted. She no longer recalled what the old box contained, but she would have Harry Crenshaw bring it up from the basement. She never went downstairs. The steps were treacherous for one whose eyesight was not what it used to be, and it was much too steep for a man on crutches. She would not allow Glenn to go after the box himself, she warned him before he could suggest the idea.

Impatient to get started, Glenn said Mark Bonner had offered to run errands.

Pearl's fine brows drew together, and she shook her

head. "I do not want Mr. Bonner touching my things." There was a chill in her voice when she spoke his name.

"It sounds like Bonner isn't one of your favorite people," Glenn said curiously.

"I do not trust him. He is a brash upstart who will never make it in motion pictures. He lies about the productions he's been in. I suppose he thinks I am too feebleminded to keep up with the industry, but he would be surprised at the things I know. I read *Variety* and *The Hollywood Reporter* every day, and I have a very good memory." Her mouth set in a moue.

Interested, Glenn wondered if she'd say more if he probed, but before he could formulate any questions, Pearl changed the subject. As if playing a game of silver screen trivia, she shot rapid-fire questions about roles she'd played, who had directed her pictures, which year she'd been nominated for an Oscar as best supporting actress. Glenn's third cup of jasmine tea had gone cold in the cup when he realized the half hour he'd allowed himself was gone, and he was feeling the prickling sensation of pressure in the nerves of his leg.

"Miss Gannon, may I ask you something?"

It took her a moment to switch her thought tracks. Her violet gaze found him. "Of course, dear boy."

"My wife mentioned something you said the other day. Would you mind telling me what you meant?" Pearl gazed inquisitively until he went on. "About the murders in the neighborhood, and good and evil?"

He wondered if it was his imagination, but she seemed to space out slightly. When she spoke, her voice lacked the timbre it had earlier.

"Evil," she pronounced like the tolling of a bell. "Much too much evil hidden behind smiling masks. The difference between fantasy and truth cannot be discarded at whim."

"I don't understand."

Pearl let out a long breath that made her shoulders sag. "I'm not sure I understand it myself," she said sadly. "It's more a feeling, you know, something instinctive. I have never been able to tolerate evil, so I am very sensitive to its being close by."

"Here?" He indicated the apartment.

Pearl waved her hand in the famous fluttering gesture and half closed her eyes. "Here, everywhere."

She wasn't making sense. Maybe Mark Bonner was right about her mental state. Glenn reached for his crutches. "I'd better go now," he said.

"Oh, must you? I have a scrapbook of pictures. I'm sure Gerod is in some of them." She reached for a leather-bound volume under the coffee table.

"I'm not supposed to stay up very long at one time, doctor's orders, but I'd love to come back another day."

"I would enjoy that." She hovered as he moved to the door, then watched from the hall until he reached his own apartment. When he turned to wave, she fluttered her hand and disappeared inside.

CHAPTER 27
✝

WHEN NASTY CALLED the studio where Glenn Donovan's wife worked, the receptionist told him that the entire crew was filming on location. She would be happy to messenger him a script as soon as either the producer or director authorized it. Nasty thanked her and hung up. For a long time he sat looking at the indoor-outdoor thermometer fastened to the window of the homicide room. The temperature was near one hundred. Beyond the glass, dust and grit blew in the churning, restless wind. He hated to go outside. He'd hate even more to be working on a film crew that had to sit out in that oven all afternoon.

Film crews on location were always easy to spot. Trailers and trucks lined the streets, and costume and makeup people spilled around them on camp chairs, ever ready for a call to the set to repair an actor's makeup or hairdo. The sidewalk was dotted with cigarette butts, attesting to the amount of time they spent waiting. The doors of dressing room trailers were closed and air-conditioning units hummed. Cameras and lighting equipment were lifelined by black cable to a truck housing a generator that pulsed monotonously.

He parked the unmarked car half a block away and walked toward the intersection. The filming had drawn a crowd. Funny the way an empty street filled the minute a film company set up shop. People who normally wouldn't walk to the grocery store in this kind of heat were willing to risk sunstroke if they thought they'd get a glimpse of a movie star. Nasty wondered who was in this picture. He should have asked the receptionist.

He stood at the edge of the crowd studying faces, then made his way to a script girl in a white skirt and blouse like the ones Mexican women on postcards always wore. Ducking his head under the red-and-white umbrella shading the high chair, he showed her his badge and asked where the producer and the director were. She pointed out a dark-haired, scowling man sitting in the dubious shade of the buildings and a younger, thin-faced, brown-haired man standing next to the camera shooting the scene. Brad Raven and Terry Faust, she told him, producer and director respectively. She also smiled and advised him to wait until the scene was over before he interrupted. She offered him half of the pool of shade under the striped umbrella.

Watching the actors perform, Nasty realized how much of the glamor of movies came from the intimacy of the theater. Here the actors and actresses sweated like human beings, and the action had to break frequently so someone from makeup could pat a face dry and dust on additional makeup. A darkly handsome youth seemed to be the lead actor. Nasty wondered if he was the killer in the script. Killers in films always had that brooding, slightly ominous look.

The producer said something to a youth in a blue T-shirt, who relayed the message to the director, who yelled, "Cut it," before he walked over for a consultation. After a few moments the director walked back to talk to the actor. Nasty glanced at the girl beside him, who smiled and nodded. He made his way to where the producer was sitting.

"Mr. Raven?"

Raven looked up and his scowl deepened. Nasty displayed his shield, which Raven took time to read before he said, "What's this about? We double-checked the permit."

"Is there somewhere we can talk?"

Raven glanced around, got up, and led the way back to the street. He opened the door of a trailer and motioned Nasty ahead of him. The interior was pleasantly dim and delightfully air-conditioned. A dressing trailer. An assortment of clothing hung on a rack across from a table with a well-lighted mirror above it. Bottles, jars, and tubes of makeup littered the top of the dresser, and a man's limp shirt was in a heap on the chair.

Raven faced him. "What is it you want? We're on a tight schedule."

"I'll be as brief as possible, Mr. Raven. We're investigating a series of homicides."

"The Los Feliz Stabber?" Raven scowled. "That has nothing to do with us."

"It's been pointed out that some of the details of the Stabber's killings are similar to your script. I'd appreciate having a copy of the script, if it isn't inconvenient."

Raven's eyes went cold. "Who pointed out these details?" he demanded.

Nasty's expression didn't change. "Does that matter?"

"No, but if it was anyone in this crew, I'll have her goddamned hide."

"Her?"

Raven's eyes narrowed, but he didn't elaborate. "I'll have a copy of the script sent to your office."

"I was hoping you might have one I could take now."

"Every one on the set is in use, Sergeant Lopez. Each crew member has a specific job or part. They mark their personal scripts to cue themselves."

"Then I'd appreciate it if you'd call your office and

instruct the secretary to send one to my office as soon as possible."

Raven wasn't happy about it, but he nodded. "Is there anything else? I have an entire crew waiting out there."

"Yes. I'd also like a list of everyone working on the picture who might have access to the script. Names and addresses."

"Damn it, I told you there's no connection—"

"Three women are dead, Mr. Raven. I'll decide if there's any connection."

Raven's mouth became a thin slash in his tight face. Obviously he was used to giving orders, not taking them, but he also had a lot of self-control. He nodded again and said, "Anything else?"

"Have you shot the murder scene in the alley yet?"

"It's scheduled for tonight."

"What time?"

The lips pulled tight again. "We'll start at twilight."

"Thank you, Mr. Raven."

"You're finished?"

Nasty ignored the sarcasm. "For now."

"Why the hell didn't the Stabber start his spree on the other side of Normandie so he'd belong to Hollywood Division?" Parch groused. "Hell, if he wants to do the city a favor, he should work over on the Strip. The Community Redevelopment Committee would probably give him a medal."

Nasty was convinced that the killer was staying in a small area because he knew the neighborhood. Maybe he lived here or had at some time, but that didn't make him any easier to find. A messenger had brought the script of *Dead Past* to Nasty's office an hour ago. He read through it quickly while he ate a Big Mac washed down with a carton of milk. He wasn't as convinced as Donovan that the fictional and actual murders paralleled each other. The only real similarities were a body in a dumpster and a murder in an alley. The killer in the script wielded an ordinary switchblade, not a sophisticated, custom-made weapon like the Stabber. He strangled and raped his victims, but that wasn't an unusual MO for a killer. Still, they had nothing else to go on. They'd turned up blanks everywhere else.

Parch parked at the end of the lineup of trucks and trailers belonging to the film crew. The alley was brightly lit by floodlights, and Nasty recognized people on the crew he'd seen earlier. He didn't see Raven. When he caught the eye of the undercover man he had assigned to blend with the onlookers, the man worked his way to them.

"Nothing," he said. "'Course, it's pretty hard when I don't know what the hell I'm looking for. The Stabber could be anyone over there and who'd be the wiser? The crowd's thinned out a lot since dark. A few people drift by now and then. No one sticks around very long. That porn movie house on the corner is getting more traffic."

"Which one is Jeanne Donovan?"

The detective craned his neck. "The one in the light blue dress talking to the tall guy."

"Has she been here all the time?"

"Yup."

Donovan didn't have much to worry about while his wife was in plain sight of forty people. Nasty was beginning to think Donovan was imagining monsters under the bed.

"How much longer will they be here?"

"They should be winding up soon."

"Hang around after they pack it in. I want to know if anyone shows a special interest in the alley." The detective nodded and slipped back into the shadows as Nasty and Parch went on toward the intersection.

Nasty had gotten pictures of every known hooker in Charlie O's stable from Vice. The murders weren't keeping the women off the street so far. Nasty recognized one of them in front of the adult theater. She was wearing tight red shorts and a halter, black nylons, and stiletto heels. She had taken a provocative stand in front of a poster announcing the next feature, named appropriately *Come With Me*. The title spread over her head like an invitation. She was better-than-average looking, with dark hair caught on top of her head in the kind of bouffant style that had been popular when Nasty was a kid. She looked about twenty-five, but it could be the makeup and the distance.

When the girl saw them, her posture changed subtly. Parch said, "She's made us."

"Go talk to her." Nasty said. "I'm going over to Vermont." He was looking for his snitch. Ellie Parker had been his snitch for two years. Vice had booked her half a dozen times for soliciting, and unlike the rest of Charlie O's women, her bail wasn't posted. She accepted her time in the tank as if it were a vacation in Hawaii. Nasty approached her one day as she left the jail and bought her a cup of coffee in a nearby cafe. She accepted the fact that a detective wanted to buy her coffee without question. She wasn't the least bit reluctant to talk.

She didn't deny she was a hooker. Her honesty was refreshing after all the bullshit Nasty usually heard. She even admitted she worked for Charlie O, but she grinned and said she'd deny saying it if Nasty quoted her. Any girl who wanted to work in L.A. needed a pimp if she wanted to stay alive and healthy. Charlie O was a piece of slime, but he was the smallest piece of slime around. More important, he didn't push his girls, and Ellie didn't like to be hassled. She was older, tough looking, with straw-colored hair frizzed like Little Orphan Annie's, but she had an appeal that promised a customer his money's worth. She preferred working for a small-timer like Charlie because he was the only one who'd let her work her own hours her own way. In his way, Charlie respected her.

She liked hooking, she told Nasty. She wasn't trained for anything else, and she made a good living. She claimed the oldest profession had a bad name because too many people were greedy. Ellie wasn't greedy, and as long as Charlie O didn't push her to work harder for his greed, Ellie was content.

At the time, Nasty was working on a case where a prostitute had been brutally beaten and killed by one of her tricks. Homicide knew who the perpetrator was, but they didn't have enough evidence to pick him up. They needed someone on the street to help break his alibi. When Nasty asked her point-blank if she'd work with him, she didn't pretend to be shocked or even surprised. She shrugged and asked for time to think about it. When she called him two days later, she said yes. She also refused to take any money.

Nasty smoothed his pink guayabera shirt and walked toward Vermont Avenue. Changing from his suit wasn't in deference to the heat but so he wouldn't look out of place. Estrella had teased him about being a "mucho macho" looking for action. He sighed thinking about how nice it would be to be home in bed with her now.

He hated Santa Anas with a passion, not because of the heat but because long hot spells shot up the crime rate. The brains of every loony in town shriveled in the scorching wind, and the urge to steal, maim, and kill went out of control. Get any bunch of cops together in this kind of weather and the war stories were a game of "Can you top this?"

He followed Hollywood Boulevard where it angled behind the hospital complex and came out at Vermont and spotted Ellie near the strip shopping center across the street. As he started to cross, a car pulled up in front of Ellie and a middle-aged man leaned out to talk to her. Nasty catalogued an automatic mental ID: heavy build, thinning brown hair, eyes probably dark, thick brows, wearing a yellow sportshirt. The man said something to Ellie, then glanced across the street to where Nasty pretended to be intent on waiting for the light to change. The guy put the car in gear and drove away. Nasty pulled out a notebook and wrote down the license number before he crossed the street.

"You look too much like a cop, Lopez," Ellie said. "He made you with one glance."

"So much for my macho image," Nasty said good-naturedly. He knew she had tipped off the trick, but it didn't matter. Maybe she was right, maybe you could spot a cop just like you could a hooker no matter how she was dressed. It was something in the eyes.

Ellie laughed. "You look great. You ought to give lessons to Vice. They all think they have to look like Serpico." She gave Nasty an appreciative once-over. "You did me a favor, Nasty. Did you get a load of that creep? He smelled like garlic and had that 'let's tie you up and play naughty' look in his eyes. He'd have to hold a woman down to get close to her." Her face sobered. "Hell, that sounds like your Stabber."

"I'll check him out."

"I read about your special unit. If anyone can catch that nut, you're the man."

"Aren't you worried with the killer working this area?"

She shrugged. "I can take care of myself."

He wondered if Lily White and Suzie Miller had thought that.

"Have you heard anything?"

"You know I'd get in touch if I did, Nasty. Whoever this guy is, he's a loner who doesn't call attention to himself. I talked to one of the girls who was working over by the theater near Suzie the other night, and so help me, she didn't see a damned thing."

"Working girls don't like to get involved."

"I don't think any of them are going to hold back now. Working this area has become hazard duty. One more score for the Stabber, and Charlie's going to be running ads in Help Wanted."

"Have you seen Charlie tonight?"

She smiled to show a double row of crooked teeth behind carmine lips. "He was by."

"Which way'd he go?"

She pointed up Vermont. "He's cruising. You can't miss his white van."

"Does he usually head up that way?"

Ellie shrugged, pulling her milky-white shoulders high enough so her breasts strained at the pink strapless blouse. "Charlie is a social climber."

"Do any of his girls work up as far as Franklin?"

When she hesitated, Nasty knew it meant yes.

Finally she said, "Charlie's ambitious. He's gotta be to take on this turf. You know how it is."

"Did Lily White work up Vermont?"

Ellie's glance slid in both directions along the street. "Charlie liked her. She had a way with boozers. She could lure a drunk from a bar while he could still walk, then get her money before he passed out, which was invariably before they got to her place. She cut her turnaround time by not having to put out."

"Did any tricks get as far as her apartment?"

Ellie looked at him. "If you're thinking some guy she picked up might have killed her, I don't think so, Nasty. Believe me, she could figure within ten feet how far a drunk could walk once they left the bar. That's why Charlie let her work up there. There are some nice bars."

Nasty had already checked the booking sheets for drunks down on the night of the murder. No one had been picked up near Lily White's apartment.

"Did you know Miller?"

"By sight."

"Were you working the night she was killed?" She hadn't been picked up in the Vice squad sweep.

"I was busy that night."

Nasty accepted the ambiguous answer. He never pushed Ellie the way some detectives rode their snitches. She always managed to answer his questions without committing herself so if Nasty was called to testify, he wouldn't be able to put words in her mouth. It kept their relationship friendly.

"Can you think of anyone you've seen around lately? Someone new, maybe?"

She shrugged. "There are always new faces. I see dozens every night. Do you have any idea what the guy looks like?"

"No, but my guess is he blends into the scenery pretty well."

"That's a great help, but I'll keep my eyes open. My friends aren't the only ones who are nervous."

"We figure the biggest thing the Stabber has going for him is that it's not out of line to walk down a dark street with a lady."

"I'll keep it in mind. If I see Charlie, do you want me to tell him you're looking for him?"

"Let it ride. I'll find him when I want him."

"Sure."

"If it's any consolation, we have plainclothesmen in the neighborhood."

She raised a pencil-thin eyebrow. "How many? Two? Four? And they follow any twosome who walk off?" She grinned. "I hope to hell I'm not the fifth one to score." She opened the silver pouch belted at her waist and pulled out a cigarette. Putting it between her red lips, she snapped a lighter. Inhaling deeply, she blew smoke over Nasty's head. "Nice talking to you, Nasty. See you around." Inhaling again, she walked away.

CHAPTER 28

†

HE SAT THROUGH both features, watching the screen, indifferent to the cavorting naked bodies and the sexual antics designed to titillate. The porn film had ceased to exist. His mind's eye played instead the script of *Dead Past*. He could no longer separate reality from fantasy. *Dead Past* was no longer make-believe. He was living it.

In the gray, flickering gloom of the theater, a touch on his thigh startled him from the dreamlike quality of his thoughts. He glanced at the profile of the figure hunched in the seat beside him, then slammed the man's wrist with a savage blow with the edge of his hand. The pervert smothered a yelp and scurried across the empty row holding his arm.

He smiled, hoping he'd broken a few bones. Serve the bastard right. He leaned back and tried to slip down into his private thoughts again, but the mood had been dispelled. In its place, restlessness bubbled up, swelling to fill him so quickly it took his breath away. He got up and went out the other end of the aisle and left the theater. Blinking in the light, he paused in the suffocating night heat.

A hooker standing by the coming attractions poster let her glance slide over him, and he was just about to walk over to her when he noticed two men across the street watching her. She was aware of them too, but she made no move toward them. Cops. They were cops. They weren't in uniform, but he knew it as surely as he knew his name. One was young and blond, the other small and dark. Mexican. He turned and walked away from the intersection. At the corner he turned and stepped into the deep shadows of a doorway and looked back. The Mex was wearing one of those fancy pleated pansy shirts like a tourist. Who did he think he was kidding? The newspaper story flashed in his mind. The Stabber investigation cop—Lopez. He'd give odds it was Lopez.

The blond cop started across the street, and the hooker turned quickly and walked toward the bus stop. The cop followed her. Lopez headed off in the opposite direction on Sunset.

Smiling, he sauntered from the doorway and followed him.

CHAPTER 29

IT WAS LATE when she got home and Jeanne was exhausted. Glenn's determined cheerfulness brought a weary smile to her face.

"A glass of wine?" he asked. "I'll even get it. I've been behaving myself all day, honest, doc."

Jeanne worked on the smile. "You stay put. I'll get it, and one for you." She bent and kissed the tip of his nose. When she came back with the wine, Glenn had propped extra pillows beside him on the bed, and he patted them. Jeanne kicked off her shoes and sank down. "God, that feels good."

Glenn kissed her. "How does that feel?"

"Very good, but I warn you I'm too tired to move."

He assumed a wounded expression. "Do you think I would take advantage of a helpless female?" Glenn peered at her. "You look exhausted. Did you eat?"

She nodded. "The caterers put on a spread you wouldn't believe. Anyone who went away hungry is certifiable. How about you, did you have lunch and dinner?"

"I did. I told you I behaved myself today." He settled

back on the mound of pillows and turned so he could see her. "I read the script of *Dead Past*."

Jeanne looked pleased. "Did you like it?"

"It's great. I know now why you're excited." He hesitated, then knit his brow. "I called the detective in charge of the Stabber investigation."

"Oh, Glenn——"

"I had to. I can't buy your coincidence theory. It's just too much. Did the detective come out and talk to you and check things out?"

"Yes." She had already resigned herself to the fact that Glenn had called. Brad Raven was livid after Lopez's visit to the set. He confronted her furiously, as if she were the only one capable of such an act of perfidy. She had faced him with equal fury and said she had not called the police. She wasn't sure he believed her. He drove away during the dinner break and didn't come back, even to view the dailies. Jeanne was afraid she had not heard the end of it, especially if he found out it was Glenn who called. The guilt would be hers by association.

Glenn reached for her hand. "Look, I know you didn't want me to call, but I'm scared. I don't think you should——"

"If you're going to ask me to quit the picture, don't. I won't do it. You called the police and they're checking it. Let it go at that. Anyhow, I still say it could be coincidence. Stranger things happen."

"I'm not asking you to leave the picture, but I want you to be careful. Really careful."

"I will. You don't have to worry about that." She sipped her wine. "Now can we talk about something else? If I don't unwind, I'll never get to sleep."

Glenn gave in grudgingly. "Sure. What do you want to talk about?"

"Tell me about your day."

His face brightened. "Actually it was terrific."

She gave him a worried glance. "You didn't overdo?"

"Nope. I spent most of the day right here on the bed." He told her about his successful phone calls and his growing excitement about the article. "And," he said, "I had a great visit with Pearl Gannon." He held up his hand before she could worry aloud. "I didn't get too tired. Start to finish I was up less than an hour."

Jeanne settled back. "Okay, tell me."

He started with Mark's bringing the newspaper and his session with the therapist. The highlight of his day was obviously his chat with Pearl Gannon, and he related it in detail. Harry Crenshaw had not brought up the box of Gerod Haliman's papers yet, but Glenn was looking forward to the treasure trove.

Jeanne couldn't believe the change in him. It was the first time she'd seen him happy since they arrived in Los Angeles.

"Let's ask Caroline to send out my videos. Can we swing a VCR? I want to watch Pearl's pictures again. I swear, she hasn't forgotten a line or a name or a gesture. She's something." Glenn finished his wine. "One thing, though, she doesn't like Mark Bonner."

"Oh? Why not?"

"She doesn't trust him. She says he lies about the pictures he's had parts in. She seems to take it personally. Icicles drip from his name when she mentions it. *Mr.* Bonner. How long has he lived here anyhow?"

Jeanne shrugged. "It's never come up. He seems to know everyone in the building, so I assume he's been here awhile."

"I get the impression from Pearl that he's more a 'would-be' than actor. I'll find out more next time."

"What difference does it make?" Jeanne said. After the exhausting day on location she didn't even want to think about films. Before Glenn could respond, there was a knock at the door, and she set down her wineglass and slid off the bed. "Who can that be at this hour?"

"Maybe it's Crenshaw with the box."

It was. He was carrying a dusty cardboard box tied with blue cord. Jeanne asked him to put it beside the bed where Glenn could reach it.

"How do, Mr. Donovan. I waited until the missus came home. I didn't know how good you could get around."

"Thanks. And thanks for bringing up the box."

"First time I've known Pearl to take anything out of storage. Usually she's got me carting junk down."

"Thank you, Mr. Crenshaw." Jeanne moved toward the hall so he wouldn't be inclined to linger. Harry nodded to Glenn and followed her out. At the door Jeanne said, "I never thanked you for putting on those locks. I really appreciate it."

"Locks?" He looked puzzled.

"On the sliding door in the bedroom."

"Huh? Oh, sure. You're welcome."

Back in the bedroom Jeanne said, "Do you think he has a drinking problem?"

"Crenshaw? Why?"

"He seemed a little vague."

"My guess is he's a couple of bricks shy of a full load, but I'll bet he remembers to collect the rent on time." Glenn leaned over to look at Pearl's box.

"Not before I dust it, buddy," Jeanne warned.

"I'm not planning on opening it tonight. It's late and I don't want to be up all night."

"You have that much willpower?"

He held out his hand and drew her to the bed. "You need your sleep. Finish your wine and come to bed."

CHAPTER 30
†

ESTRELLA SHIFTED THE dark-eyed, gurgling baby on her hip as she leaned over to touch her husband's arm. Nasty's eyes opened instantly, and he reached for her thigh.

"Aquesta niño y vente la cama," he said sleepily.

Her adoring gaze told him she'd like nothing better, but she shook her head without drawing away. She always hated to wake him when he got in late. He hadn't had a full night's sleep since the Stabber investigation had begun.

"Ken is on the phone, Ignacio. He says it's important."

As he sat up, she bent to reconnect the cord on the phone she'd silenced. The baby grabbed his father's hair. Estrella let her husband nuzzle the child before she carried him out of the bedroom.

Yawning, Nasty picked up the phone. "Yeah?"

"Hate to wake you, but we've got another one."

"The Stabber?" Nasty's mouth was stale and his tongue stuck to his teeth, but he was wide-awake.

"Opara called. White female, approximately thirty-five, bruises on the neck and multiple stab wounds, two right over where a hooker's heart would be."

"Damn."

"Opara and Yankton are on the way, but I thought you'd want to have a look."

Rubbing his eyes, Nasty swung his feet from the bed. "Pick me up in twenty minutes."

He hung up and was already on his way to the bathroom. By the time he showered and shaved, the smell of fresh coffee drew him to the kitchen. The baby was in his high chair, happily mashing a cracker into some spilled milk, like a painter mixing oils. Nasty kissed the top of his head. The baby sprayed a handful of wet crumbs in his father's direction.

"Da!"

"Da yourself, champ." He slipped his arms around Estrella and nibbled the back of her neck. "No time for breakfast, *querida*."

She lifted her face for a kiss. She didn't ask about Parch's call. A good cop's wife didn't ask those questions. She eased from his arms and pointed to an insulated plastic coffee mug. "Breakfast to go," she said, holding up a plastic bag containing four warm bran muffins. "Two for Ken, two for you."

Nasty kissed her on the mouth, and his tongue told her how much he hated to leave. Outside, a horn honked. "I'll try to make it for dinner. I'll call." How many times had he promised that? A lot lately.

Parch leaned across to open the door so Nasty didn't have to juggle the coffee cup and the bag. "What do we have today?" he asked eagerly, taking the bag from Nasty's hand. "Smells great. That woman of yours is something else. Much too good for you." Opening the plastic bag, Parch took a muffin and bit off half of it before he put the car in gear.

Nasty sipped hot coffee. "Where was she found?"

"Parking lot behind the bank on Vermont and Melbourne."

Coffee sloshed over the rim of the cup and Nasty moved quickly so it didn't get on his pale gray trousers. "What's that, four blocks from the last one?"

Parch wiped muffin crumbs from his mouth. "Five, and only two from Vicki Ewing's apartment. Looks like you're right about him playing in his own backyard. According to the first uniform on the scene, it happened right there."

Nasty sipped coffee. The Stabber was killing out in the open and leaving the bodies practically under the noses of the police assigned to catch him.

They were silent for the rest of the drive. Parch polished off a second muffin. Nasty finished his coffee and stared out the window, brooding. Who the hell was this guy? Where did he go when he wasn't prowling the streets in search of a victim? They had interviewed witnesses, neighbors, known sex offenders, and had come up with nothing so far.

Parch double-parked beside a black-and-white blocking an alley. A uniformed officer let them through the crime-scene markers that were keeping the inevitable gathering of curious onlookers at a distance. A television remote crew was jockeying for position. A reporter tried to follow Nasty and Parch past the barrier, but the uniformed man barred his way.

The coroner's van was angled into one of the white-lined slots of the parking lot. Kroeger was squatting beside a body sprawled next to a low wall that separated the parking lot from the alley cutting behind the commercial establishments on Vermont Avenue. He glanced up as Nasty approached, and the corners of his mouth twitched without quite making it to a smile.

"Our boy?" Nasty asked.

Kroeger nodded. "Two in the heart. She died around midnight, give or take, and her skirt's gone."

Nasty glanced at the corpse and the coffee he'd drunk

churned dangerously in his stomach. Her face and torso were streaked with blood, but the face was recognizable despite the blue tinge of the skin and a red slash down one cheek. Ellie's pink strapless blouse had been slit up the middle, and her full, round breasts lay exposed amid a random pattern of wounds crusted with blood. Close to her left breast were two wounds, one a small hole stained with congealed blood, the other painting a trail down her ribs. The waistband of her black, G-string underpants had been cut away, leaving a few tatters of lace.

"Shit," Nasty said savagely as he turned away. He walked to where Parch was talking to Opara, Yankton, and a uniformed officer. Opara and Yankton nodded.

Parch said, "This is Jim Talika. He was first on the scene."

"Tell me about it," Nasty said.

"This kid runs out into the street and flags me down. Says there's a dead woman behind the bank. I figured it was probably some drunk sleeping it off. We get them around here once in a while. I took a look and called it in right away."

"The kid, where is he?"

Talika looked sheepish. "She. Little dark-haired, skinny thing, couldn't have been more than seventeen. She took off like a rabbit while I was checking the body. I'm sorry, but how the hell did I know——"

Nasty waved off the excuse. The chance of a slim, female teenager being connected to the killing was pretty remote. "How'd she happen to find it?" He pointed vaguely toward the corpse.

"Said she was cutting through the parking lot on her way to the bus stop."

"That means she lives around here." Nasty glanced at the assortment of people beyond the barriers. They were talking in hushed tones and craning their necks to see past the coroner's van. "Start with them," he told Talika and Yankton. "Someone's bound to recognize the description. Opara, tell the crime boys to check every inch of concrete around the body. I want to know how he retracts that damned blade." As they left, Nasty glanced at Parch. "Her name's Ellie Parker. She's the snitch I talked to last night."

"Your snitch? Aw, shit . . ."

"I want this bastard." There was something in his voice that made Parch look up. "Put out the word we're looking for Charlie O. I want to talk to him again. And have Vice round up every one of Charlie's girls."

"They'll have gone to ground by now, Nasty. Three of their sisters in the morgue? Hell—"

"Find them."

Parch started to argue but broke off when Nasty glared at him. Ken walked back to the car and picked up the radio mike. Nasty watched Kroeger's men lift the corpse into a body bag. On the sidewalk the remote video camera whirred softly, lens focused on the macabre scene. Nasty spotted a crime reporter from the *Herald* and swore silently. The media were going to have a picnic with the story, and they'd be serving roast pig.

CHAPTER 31

✝

THE LUXURY OF sleeping in was offset by the heat the fan stirred to a warm flow over their bodies. Dull pain pressed behind Jeanne's eyes as she glanced at the clock. She wasn't due in Griffith Park until ten. It would take her only a few minutes to drive up. It was going to be miserable in the hot sun all day. There was precious little shade in the area. According to Terry, the location was a popular spot for filming. On any given night you could tune in at least one TV show or find a movie that had been shot there. The park setting was a chameleon: rural middle-America, a rolling English countryside, or the hinterlands of any place a script required.

Reluctant to stir, she closed her eyes and tried to envision the tangy bite of a Minnesota October. The picture wouldn't focus. She rolled over, trying not to disturb Glenn. Normally she looked forward to working outdoors, but yesterday had exhausted her. The unrelenting Santa Ana had baked the city so thoroughly, heat radiated like microwaves from the pavement, and the temperature had dropped only slightly after the sun went down. Listening to the sibilance of leaves outside, she knew the Santa Ana hadn't broken. She'd dress comfortably and be sure she was protected from the sun.

So up and at 'em, girl, she told herself. As she slid from the bed, Glenn's hand found her naked hip. She rolled back and smiled.

"I was trying not to disturb you."

"I've been awake awhile. My leg feels like it's in a sauna. The rest of me, too."

Jeanne raised herself on an elbow and kissed him. "Retribution. We left Minnesota after one of the coldest winters on record, so we get Los Angeles with one of the hottest Octobers. At least we don't have to shovel the heat."

"You may have to scoop me up pretty soon," he said. "I feel like a puddle of butter."

"Soon as I finish in the bathroom, I'll change the sheets while you have a cool shower. It'll help."

"That's too much work."

"No, it isn't." She kissed him again and rolled off the bed.

When she emerged from the shower, a towel wrapped loosely around her, and went into the den to dress, Glenn labored out of bed and hobbled to the bathroom. Over breakfast he asked her which scenes they were shooting.

"First Rudolo following the girl while she's with the other guy in the park. We wind up with the night picnic scene."

"Baby, I'm still not crazy about the idea of you being up there with that killer running around loose."

"Glenn, please. I promised I'd be careful. What more do you want? I'll stay close to the rest of the crew. Real killers aren't exactly my thing, you know."

"Yeah? Suppose *one of the crew* is the killer? Did you ever think of that? Who would have better access to the script and know where you were going to be next?" He toyed with his coffee mug.

She looked at him helplessly. "What kind of an answer can I give to that?"

"Okay, so I'm a little paranoid—"

"No?" Her eyebrows shot up as she pretended to hide a smile.

He scowled, then grinned sheepishly. "Just a touch, but I can't get it out of my head that there's a connection." He reached to take her hand. "I wish you wouldn't go up there today."

"I have to—"

"No, you don't. Let the cops check it out first."

"You're not going to call them again?" She studied the expression on his face.

"If I don't hear something from Lopez, I'm going to rattle his cage. What the hell is he doing anyway?"

"Brad Raven will blow his cork—"

"The hell with him. Just suppose someone on the crew is the Los Feliz Stabber?"

She tried not to show her irritation. "It's the age-old question of whether art imitates life or the other way around. This script was written more than a year ago. The writer probably did twelve versions of it, and his idea probably grew out of something he read or saw. You know there's no such thing as a new plot."

"That's exactly what I'm saying. Some real-life loony is following the script!"

Jeanne threw down her napkin and carried her dishes to the sink. "Well, I can't stay home. Raven is already madder than hell. He sees everything in dollar signs. Delayed shooting means going over budget, and that spells trouble no matter how you look at it. Besides, we had to sign up weeks in advance to get this location in the park. If we don't finish up in the two days we've got booked, we're out. Another company is shooting there on Friday. If Brad can point a finger at me for any delay, he's just lovable enough to make sure I never work in this town again."

"The hell with Hollywood, and the hell with Brad Raven. He sounds crazy enough to be the Stabber!"

"Glenn!" She whirled and glared at him.

"Okay, I'm sorry." He expelled a long breath. "I know you have to go. I guess I'd do the same. Maybe I'll feel better after I talk to Lopez."

Knowing it was useless to argue, Jeanne finished clearing the table. Glenn picked up his crutches and hobbled into the bedroom. Sitting on the edge of the bed, he dialed the police division. The desk man said Lopez was out. When Glenn asked to talk to someone on the special Stabber unit, the deskman hesitated, then asked for Glenn's name and number. After a delay and a series of clicks, Glenn was connected to an officer whose name slid by too quickly to settle in Glenn's troubled thoughts.

"What can I do for you?" the man asked.

Glenn said he'd talked to Lopez the day before and wanted to know if there'd been any follow-up on their discussion.

"What was it you talked about?" the officer asked.

Glenn shouted, "The goddamned Los Feliz Stabber, that's what! Look, have Lopez get back to me, will you? It's important."

"Yes, sir, I'll see that he gets the message."

Glenn hung up more irritated than ever. For all he knew, Lopez was writing him off as a crank. Well, he wasn't going to let it drop. He snapped on the radio, twisting the dial until he found a news station. He fidgeted through the weather report detailing the unusual length and severity of the Santa Ana, and resultant brush fires that were raging out of control. Finally the local news was recapped. Glenn turned up the volume.

"This morning another body believed to be a victim of

the Los Feliz Stabber was found in a bank parking lot on Vermont Avenue. No information has been released concerning the identity of the victim. We'll have an update on the story at noon."

Glenn realized Jeanne was standing in the doorway. "The script doesn't have a single body in a bank parking lot," she said, looking at him evenly.

Robbed of valid argument for the moment, he said, "Vermont Avenue's only a couple of blocks from here, isn't it? That's too close for comfort." When she didn't reply, he looked away. "Make sure Terry follows you home tonight, okay? Don't trust anyone else."

"Okay. Our last scene calls for twilight. Maybe we'll wrap early." She smiled hopefully.

Jeanne drove across Feliz Boulevard on Vermont and wound her way up through a pleasant residential section and between stone pillars where a sign read: GRIFFITH PARK. CLOSED 10:30 P.M.–5:30 A.M. NO LOITERING. The iron gates were open, and a large padlock hung from a chain. Reassuring. She'd have to tell Glenn.

She put the Toyota in second gear for the steep climb. When she saw the honey wagons, caterer's mobile unit, equipment trucks and assorted vehicles for makeup, wardrobe, special effects and props, she parked in the first spot she came to. As she got out, Terry hailed her, holding aloft a canned soft drink he'd pulled from an ice chest.

"Want one?" he asked as she approached.

"Not right now, thanks." She glanced around the hillside picnic area. A park ranger, a uniformed policeman, and two fire marshals in white shirts and dark ties stood in the shade of a clump of twisted oaks. "Everything okay?"

"Yeah, except for the weather. Of all the times for a Santa Ana to fry the city. Next week they'll probably need jackets here every morning, but we get Hell's Canyon."

Still trying to dispel the gloom Glenn had spread, Jeanne grinned. "Could be worse if it rained."

"It never rains in October, love. This is Southern California. Hot and dry."

"I heard about some fires on the news."

"Yeah, there's one up in La Cañada. The other is in Agoura. Thank God neither is close enough for the smoke to louse up the light." He indicated the fire marshals. "They've banned any kind of open flame. The whole set is no smoking for as long as we're here."

"What about the candlelight picnic?"

Faust shook his head. "It's a moonlight picnic now. Minor script changes. The writer's working on them. We'll have them before we're ready to shoot."

"Does Brad know?"

"He's not here yet." Terry grinned. "Don't worry, kid, it's my job to break the news. You're in a neutral corner."

"Neutral corners have been hard to find around here the past few days."

"Brad can be an asshole, but you have to remember he's a perfectionist. When the picture's in the can, you'll realize all this was a small price to pay. This one's a winner, Jeanne. I feel it in my gut."

She smiled. "Don't pay any attention to me. I think the heat is getting me, not to mention the Los Feliz Stabber roaming around. Glenn's paranoid about my being in danger."

Terry's face puckered and he squinted in the bright light. "Not even a crazy killer would mistake you for a woman of the streets. I think you're pretty safe, kiddo."

"Do me a favor and tell Glenn that. He's the one who called Lopez yesterday. I never should have mentioned that damned alley thing. He won't let it go."

He whistled softly. "Let's not say anything to Brad, okay? The sooner he forgets it happened, the better. Now, let's get to work." He gave her hand a friendly squeeze and glanced at a truck where props were being unloaded. "Do me a favor and check the equipment for the picnic scene. The caterer will fill the basket later, but everything else should be on the truck." He surveyed her cotton slacks, long-sleeved, loose-fitting blouse, and sturdy shoes approvingly. "Did you bring a hat?"

"It's in the car."

"Get it. We're going to be sitting in a blast furnace today. I'm glad we've only got two days up here or we'd be burned Harvest."

As he walked away, Jeanne headed back to her car.

A hundred yards away, on top of a sharp rocky hill that formed a natural wall for the picnic area, Mark Bonner raised a pair of binoculars to follow Jeanne's trek back to the Toyota.

CHAPTER 32
†

"THE LIEUTENANT WANTS to see you, Nasty."

"Thanks."

The secretary was the third person to deliver the message since Nasty entered the building. Several detectives glanced up as Nasty passed, looking sympathetic as they would at a man going to the gallows.

"Lieutenant?" He waited for Hansen to look up. "You want to see me?"

"Yeah. What the hell are you doing on this Stabber? Christ, I got the commissioner breathing hotter than the Santa Ana down my neck. I gotta give him something, for crissake."

"You want me to level with you?"

"You're goddamned right I do."

"We haven't got shit, Lieutenant. We're running down everything that comes in. Nothing on the weapon. If the guy used a machine shop or tool and die maker, we haven't found the place yet. I've requested other divisions to have their beat men check out places personally.

"We did a house-to-house from the bank to Ellie Parker's apartment and a three-block radius around it. We came up with one little old lady who says Parker was a prostitute for the Mafia and had men going in and out of her apartment at all hours. She also says the church on the next block is headquarters for Columbian drug traffic, and the Ladies' Aid Society is stitching the shit into flak jackets for the police department."

Hansen stabbed a pencil so hard on the desk blotter the point snapped off. "What about the other cases? Haven't your snitches come up with anything? *Someone's* seen this guy. He can't just disappear."

"Ellie Parker was my snitch, Lieutenant. I talked to her last night," Nasty said, feeling again the raw pain that hit him when he saw her mutilated body behind the bank.

"Ah, hell, Nasty. I didn't know." Hansen tossed the pencil into a plastic tray on his desk. "What'd she say?"

"Whores are scared because our man's invisible, especially Charlie O's girls."

"No one's invisible, goddamn it! He's walking these streets and somebody's seen him!"

"Two things bother me, Lieutenant. The Stabber picking Ellie Parker as his victim less than an hour after I talked to her, and why the hell were they up on Melbourne? Ellie had a room on Hollywood Boulevard. Her apartment is over on the other side of Western. She kept her personal life separate from her work." Nasty concentrated on a corner of the lieutenant's desk, letting the thoughts that had been buzzing inside his skull all morning form a pattern. More coincidences. They bothered him almost as much as Ellie's death itself. The Stabber case had too many of them.

Hansen tilted his head and waited.

"Why her? Why that spot?" Nasty wanted to know. "Two blocks east by the adult movie house, he could have his pick. Charlie O's women like the action around the theater so they hang out there. But this guy goes over to Vermont where Ellie is. Did he know she'd be there? Did he luck on to her or was he someone she knew? I haven't figured that one out yet, but one thing I do know: Ellie didn't walk with him up to Melbourne. The guy's got a car. He got Ellie into it for a quick one. I figure she was unconscious when he dragged her into that alley and finished her off. Ellie would have screamed bloody murder otherwise. If I'm right, it means the Stabber wanted us to find the body right where it was."

"I'm not going to argue with you, Nasty, but I've got the mayor screaming because the press is slapping blame onto every public office in the city. I need something to hold them off, you hear? Give me a bone to toss them until you've got this guy. The commissioner is talking about turning this over to the Major Crimes Unit downtown, and you can bet he'll find a way to do it so we come out on the short end of the stick."

"I'll do my best, Lieutenant." He'd do his damnedest. He wanted the Stabber worse than the mayor or the commissioner or anyone else.

Parch glanced up as Nasty sank into his chair. "I can tell by your happy face you've seen Hansen."

Nasty grunted. "The mayor wants to turn the case over to downtown."

Parch shrugged. "Hell, let them have it. Good riddance."

Nasty reached for the collection of papers in his basket and leafed through them. Twenty-four hours ago he would have agreed with his partner, but now he kept remembering Ellie Parker's body in the alley. "What did we get on that license plate number of that guy I saw with Ellie?"

"Car belongs to a salesman from Santa Barbara. Your description fits. He hasn't got any priors. Yankton is running him down."

Nasty held up a message slip. "Donovan called again, the guy who says the killer is following that movie script."

"I think he's imagining things."

"Did you read the script?"

"Yeah," Parch said. "The first murder happens in an apartment, and Lily White was murdered in an apartment. The second script victim and Vicki Ewing were found in dumpsters. Hell, do you know how many corpses we get in apartments or dumpsters? The scriptwriter probably got the idea from *us*. The Miller killing in the alley is the only one that lines up with the script so it's noticeable."

Nasty fanned the pages of the script. "Ellie wasn't in the script."

"See what I mean?" Parch leaned back in his swivel chair and propped his feet on an open drawer.

Nasty looked at his partner. "If the killer is playing a game, right now he's got to think he's winning. Not only winning but far enough ahead so he's cocky. He wants to make the whole thing more exciting, so he does something daring, risky. He picks up a woman right under our noses. Not just any woman, but one he's watched me talk to. He wants me to know he's got a line on me. The Stabber was following me last night."

Parch looked skeptical. "How'd he know you'd be over there?"

"He killed Miller in that alley two nights ago. Now there's a film company shooting in the exact spot. Don't you think he'd figure there was a damned good chance of someone from this unit being on hand?"

Parch was still dubious. "Yeah, maybe, but he couldn't know you'd go looking for Ellie. Hell, I didn't know you were looking for her."

Nasty popped the tab on a soft drink can. Ken was right. The killer couldn't have known, which meant he'd decided to kill Ellie after Nasty talked to her. Because Nasty had talked to her. It wasn't a pleasant thought to carry around. "He was on the prowl for a victim and took advantage of the opportunity when it cropped up. One thing, if this scenario holds together, it means he knows Harvest's shooting schedule. And if he's got that, he's probably got the script, too. Maybe Donovan isn't as crazy as he sounds."

"The Stabber's been picking his victims off the street. Why would Donovan's wife be in any danger?"

"Maybe he doesn't care who the victim is now." Like Ellie, Nasty thought. "I'm going to release pictues of all the victims to the media. Maybe we'll jog someone's memory." Another slim hope, but they didn't have much else. "What do we know about Harvest Films?"

Parch shrugged. "They're legit. They did a low-budget film last year that took off like a brush fire. It was called *Death Pact*. You must have heard of it. Hell of a flick."

Nasty didn't remember the last movie he'd seen. When he and Estrella had the luxury of an evening to themselves, they went to a quiet restaurant for dinner, then drove up into the Hollywood Hills where they could park and watch the lights of the city.

"Was it about a serial killer?"

"No. It was about this guy who hangs out in singles bars to meet women."

Nasty thumbed through the papers in his basket. Paperwork. Tons of it. Even beat cops had to fill out reports on every damned thing that happened. The Stabber file was already two inches thick: original reports, follow-up investigations, lab results, coroner's reports . . . The entire department had orders to forward anything with even the remotest possibility of being connected to the case to Nasty's office.

A carbon copy of a memo caught his eye. Dated two days ago, it was a notation that Brad Raven of Harvest Films had called to make sure the company's filming permit wasn't going to be rescinded or postponed because of the murder of Suzette Miller.

"How long in advance would Harvest Films get the permit to use that alley?"

Parch shrugged. "I can call the city clerk's office, but my guess is the paperwork takes a little time. I'd say a company would apply a couple of weeks ahead of time. Some locations like Griffith Park are lined up months ahead because so many outfits want the same spot."

"Isn't there a park scene in the new Harvest script?"

"Yeah."

"Where are they shooting it?"

"Griffith, probably."

"Find out, and I want to know when."

"You think the killer will show up there?"

"It won't hurt to check. And while we're at it, let's check out Donovan and his wife. Who's available?"

"Yankton's over at the restaurant talking to the girl who found Ellie Parker's body. Opara's following up on the list of whores who were working the vicinity of Le Sexe Shoppe last night. I can do it."

Nasty nodded. "Get on it."

As Parch left, Nasty picked up the memo he'd put back in the basket. A permit two weeks in advance. He could squeeze that one until it squeaked, but it wouldn't get him anywhere. Any given week, ten film outfits were on location somewhere in the city. The man assigned to the crowd watching the Harvest shoot last night reported nothing out of the ordinary. He hadn't seen anything because the killer was two blocks away picking up Ellie Parker. But there were too many coincidences piling up again. As soon as Yankton and Opara got back, he'd put them to work on Harvest Films. He wanted to know everything there was to know about the outfit.

* * *

Parch dialed the number Donovan had left but got no answer, so he drove over to the Harvest Films studio on Western Avenue. He flashed his badge for the security guard and told him not to bother calling upstairs to say he was on the way. When he stepped off the elevator on the third floor, Parch looked around appreciatively. The black-and-white color scheme was so dramatic, he wondered who had dreamed up the idea.

The beautiful black woman behind the reception desk smiled. "Can I help you?"

Parch showed her his badge, and she looked at it closely enough to get his number.

"I sent the script and list Detective Lopez asked for. Is there something else?" Her smooth brow crinkled.

"Is Mrs. Donovan in?"

"No. The whole crew is on location today."

"How long has Mrs. Donovan worked here?" Parch wondered if he should sit down. He felt as if he were on a movie set.

"She came in September."

"Where did she work before?"

"In Minneapolis. She's a friend of the director, and he asked her to come out. She interviewed last spring."

"So she started working here as soon as she got to town?"

"Yes, well, almost. She and her husband had an accident on the freeway. Her husband was hurt pretty badly, and she waited until he was out of danger before she came to work."

"How long was that?"

"Two weeks."

"What about the husband? Is he okay now?"

"He went home from the hospital last weekend. He's on crutches and can't get around much."

"Tell me about Mr. Donovan. Glenn, isn't it?" He'd check with traffic and the hospital.

"Yes. I really can't tell you much. I've never met him. Jeanne's been very worried about him. She's been under a lot of pressure working and trying to get settled at the same time."

"Do they get along?"

She hesitated slightly. "Yes, of course. As I said, it's been a strain—on both of them actually. They came out with such enthusiasm and high hopes, it was a real downer to have everything thrown into confusion so suddenly like that."

"Her husband telephoned us. He's got the idea there may be a connection between the script you're shooting and a case we're investigating."

"Whatever made him . . ."

Parch noticed the change in her expression as she let the question wither. He'd bet Donovan was being a miserable bastard. Miserable enough to try to cause trouble for his wife? Parch asked for a rundown on Jeanne's job and the film. Callie Minette didn't know anything about Brad Raven's call regarding the permit.

"Do you usually place his outside calls?" The phone system on the desk was one of the push-button, mini-switchboard arrangements popular with small businesses.

"Not always. Anyone can get a direct line."

"Well, I guess that covers it, Ms. Minette. Thanks for your cooperation."

Her gaze met his directly. "Is there any reason I shouldn't tell Jeanne or the producer about this visit, Detective Parch?"

"I thought they were all on location."

"They are, but they'll be in tonight to view the dailies. I usually tell Mr. Raven about any visitors."

"No reason you shouldn't tell about this one, then. Good day, Ms. Minette. Thanks again."

227

* * *

Parch cruised the block before he parked. After the air-conditioned car, the heat swirled around him like a dust devil. He loosened the collar of his sport shirt and pushed his tie up to cover the gap. If the Santa Ana didn't break soon, he was tempted to call in sick.

The entrance to the apartment building was locked. He studied the bells and took out a notebook to copy the names before he rang Donovan's apartment. After thirty seconds he pushed it again, holding his finger down hard. A crackly voice finally came over the intercom.

"Yeah?"

"Glenn Donovan?"

"Yes."

"Detective Parch, LAPD."

"Hey—sure, come in. Down the hall on the right." A buzzer squealed in the quiet afternoon.

Donovan, on crutches, was standing in the hall waiting for him. As Parch flashed his credentials, Donovan asked, "You work with Lopez?"

"That's right."

"Come on in." He hobbled awkwardly on the crutches. Parch closed the door and waited until Donovan settled himself on the sofa before he sat across from him. He held out his ID again. Donovan glanced at it and waved it off.

"There was another murder this morning. It was the Stabber, wasn't it?"

"About your call yesterday and the one this morning?" Parch said.

"Lopez didn't call back."

"He's busy. I called about an hour ago and didn't get any answer. Is it hard to get around on those things?" He pointed to the crutches.

"It's a pain in the ass, but I can't get around without

them, if that's what you're driving at. As it is, I go only as far as the front door."

"Not outside?"

"Except for the patio, I haven't been out since I came home from the hospital Saturday. I bet you want to know where I was that I didn't answer the phone, right? I could have been in the can or in the kitchen and not been able to get to it in time, but since I didn't hear it, you must have called when I went down the hall to talk to a neighbor."

"You do that a lot?"

"No. I was disappointed she wasn't home. She's something." At the detective's studied glance Glenn shook his head. "Not that kind of something. She's in her eighties. Her name's Pearl Gannon. She was a starlet back in the thirties. I've got this thing for old movies."

"I like 'em too." He pointed to Glenn's cast. "*Rear Window,* Jimmy Stewart, 1954."

"Do you remember Pearl Gannon?"

"*Sam's Girl,* 1939."

"1938." Glenn grinned as if he'd met an old friend, but before he could say more, Parch pulled out a notebook.

"Now, Mr. Donovan, would you mind going over what you told Sergeant Lopez?"

Glenn explained how he thought the killings in the script paralleled three murders on the street. He was convinced the serial killer prowling Los Feliz was following the script, and he was worried about his wife. When Parch asked why Jeanne as opposed to anyone else connected with the production, Glenn admitted he had nothing concrete to go on.

Parch asked a few more questions, but Donovan had nothing to add. Parch thanked him, telling him not to get up, he'd let himself out.

CHAPTER 33

✝

WAVES OF HEAT covered him, and the sun and the wind burned through his shirt like a blowtorch. Gritty puffs of dust driven by the Santa Ana stung his neck and face as he watched the film crew at work below him. From time to time voices drifted up the hill, but the fickle wind distorted them so they were hard to distinguish. Jeanne had come back from the car with a wide-brimmed sun hat, and now it obstructed his view of her face. She was wearing a long-sleeved shirt of some thin material, slacks, and comfortable-looking walking shoes. Smart. The sun would burn her fair skin to a crisp. A few stupid broads had come in shorts and halters, for crissake. One even had on high heels. He hoped she broke an ankle.

Several times Mark recognized Jeanne's voice when she called out. There weren't many women first assistant directors in the business. They tended to sound shrill when they raised their voices, and show business men were a pretty macho lot who didn't like taking orders from a woman, especially if she sounded like an angry wife or girlfriend.

A sudden flash of light blinded him, and he pressed his

face into the dust, cursing. When he raised it, he realized it was only a shiny board being moved that had caught the sun and flashed it across the top of the hill. He relaxed again on the hot stone. He'd scouted the location this morning before the sun came up, long before the honey wagons or any of the crew arrived. Dressed in jogging clothes, he'd loped along the road until he came to the picnic area. He saw half a dozen joggers on Vermont Canyon Road, but he had the hill to himself. The well-tracked and trampled area sprawled in the clearing below was dotted with picnic tables, stone fireplaces, and refuse barrels. He'd walked around visualizing the scenes that would be shot. The cast, crew, and caterers would stake out a claim on the shady grove of trees. By afternoon a strip of shade would form along the base of the hill.

It had taken him ten minutes to find a way up the rocky hill, another ten to climb it and pick his spot. Easier going down, and he slowed to a walk on the road. When he was almost back to where he'd left the car, a ranger in a park truck passed him, and he waved. The dumb kid waved back.

Studying the people below him now, he saw three grips leveling track for a dolly. They were going to shoot the scene where the girl tried to get away from Rudolo. Mark knew the lines by heart. He knew the whole damned script.

That jerk Jarvis couldn't act for shit. A nobody. A nothing. What did he know about how a killer felt? He could tell him, but that would be a stupid move in the game. A pro knew when to play it cool and when to strike out. Like last night. It had been almost too easy going back for the car and picking up the whore twenty minutes after the cop left her. A master move. He'd have given anything to see Lopez's face when he recognized the whore's body this morning. He wondered if the dumb Mex had caught on yet. Probably didn't know which end was up. He didn't have the brains to win the game.

The wind died abruptly, and voices drifted up from the canyon.

"Okay, everybody, we're about ready. Jeanne, check on the status of talent. Where's makeup? We need to dirty her face some."

"Larry, you may want to bring that prop truck up."

"It's on the way."

"Who's doubling for Chris on the fall?"

Jeanne was out of sight below him, probably in the narrow strip of shade cast by the hill. He wished he had a more direct line of vision, but the rock sloped outward at an angle that hid the base unless he stood up. She'd be out in the clearing when the scene was ready to shoot. Patience was part of the game.

Parch drove away from the parking spot in front of the apartment house and made the sharp turn onto the next street so he could circle the block and come down again. He parked a hundred yards up from the building and turned off the ignition.

The somnolent street was lined with ancient eucalyptuses and oaks that dappled shade along its length, giving an illusion of coolness. The block was an oddity. Apartments claimed the lower half of both sides, lined up like old soldiers on review. Some of them were relatively new, but most had the nostalgic pretense of early Hollywood. The upper half of the block was Los Feliz at its best: stately homes, iron gates, and Japanese gardeners.

So Pearl Gannon lived in Donovan's building. Parch was tempted to knock on her door, just so he could say he'd seen the old star, but he had something more important on his mind right now. Would the guy come out? Parch decided to wait ten minutes. If no one showed by then, his hunch was all wet.

He only had to wait five minutes. The guy surprised

him by not coming out the front door but from a walkway between the building and the one next door. Parch had glimpsed the darting figure vanish down the hall as he came out of Donovan's apartment. He didn't get a good look at him in the dim light but knew instinctively that the guy had been listening outside Donovan's door.

There was no mistaking him now. Tall, rangy enough to be called skinny, with a mop of red hair that could house a family of five. He looked young, maybe early twenties. And nervous. He glancd up and down the street, then darted back into the passageway between the buildings. He emerged again with a bicycle. Straddling it, he pedaled toward Franklin and turned east.

Parch mentally reviewed the roster of tenants he'd copied from the bells. He didn't know anything about them except for Donovan and Pearl Gannon. Could be any of the rest. This one didn't seem to be gainfully employed, at least not in a day job. Parch started the car and followed. It wasn't hard to keep him in sight. The kid didn't try any tricky maneuvers like doubling back at the corner or ducking into an alley. He swung around parked cars and pulled back close to the curb as soon as he could. A careful cyclist. Christ, he didn't do a damned thing but pedal. On wheels, he seemed to lose the awkwardness and hesitancy that had drawn Parch's attention to him in the first place. Maybe the whole thing was a wild-goose chase, but Parch paid attention to his gut feelings. Every cop did. The last time Parch had ignored one, he took a bullet in the leg from a hophead holding up a Thrifty Drug. One thing sure, the kid on the bike wasn't armed. The cutoffs and T-shirt he was wearing wouldn't hide a nail file.

The biker stopped for a red light on Vermont, then hung a right. Parch turned on the tail end of the red. The kid was half a block ahead, pedaling carefully through the heavier traffic on the busy street, riding with it, staying close to parked cars, looking both ways at each corner before he crossed. Two blocks down at Melbourne, he stopped and waited for the light to change. Then he pedaled furiously across the intersection and down the side street. Parch barely had time to switch lanes and make the turn in time to see the bike swing into the parking lot behind the bank.

Parch parked at a red curb. What the hell was the kid up to? He was off the bike and walking it through the lot. He seemed to be looking for something. He circled two rows of cars, then started back. Parch got his first good look at him then, and another gut feeling assailed him. The kid didn't have all his marbles. Something in his eyes, an empty look, as if making a decision taxed his brain. The kid hesitated a minute on the sidewalk, then wheeled the bike into the alley and stopped. The Crime Unit had finished with the scene and the ribbons were gone, but Parch knew it was the spot where the Stabber's last victim had been found.

Parch got out and let the car door close softly. He walked up behind the kid, who was staring at the fragments of the chalked body outline that hadn't been worn off by tires and feet going through the alley. Parch had an angled view of the kid's face, and it was definitely scared.

"Hi."

The kid spun around as if a cannon had gone off behind him. He almost lost his grip on the handlebars of the bike but grabbed them in time to keep it from toppling. He bobbed his head, his jaw slack. There was a mean-looking bruise on his cheek.

"You live around here?" Parch asked.

The head bobbed again.

Parch reached into his pocket and took out his ID. He opened the leather folder and held it out. For a moment the kid kept staring at Parch, but finally he glanced down and back up instantly. He hadn't read a word, but he'd seen the badge. It made him go a shade paler under his freckles, and his head bobbed like a rock musician's keeping time.

"What's your name?"

"S—S—Sonny."

"Sonny what?"

"Sonny Crenshaw."

"What are you doing here?"

"Riding." The head jerked up and down again. "Bike riding. I ride a lot."

Parch pointed to the blurred marks on the asphalt. "Did you come to see that?"

It didn't seem possible that the kid could look more scared, but he did. His eyes blinked and his lips worked over his teeth like a nervous squirrel. This time his head jerked from side to side, and he didn't answer.

Parch broke down the question into simple components. "Do you ride over here a lot?"

Up and down.

"Were you here this morning?"

Scared. Side to side.

"Last night?"

Wary. Hesitant, then up and down.

"Do you know about the murder?"

Terrified. Up and down, and a furtive glance at the marks near his feet.

"Did you see it?"

Instantaneous side to side. His freckles looked like daubs of rusty paint on a white wall, and he raised his hand to the bruise on his cheek, then lowered it quickly.

What the hell was he thinking, Parch wondered. He wasn't getting anywhere. He toyed with the idea of taking the kid in but decided against it. He knew where to find him if he could think up any more questions that could be answered by a shake of the head. The kid wasn't bright enough to lie, but somehow Parch had the feeling something was muddling around behind those vacant eyes, something the kid wasn't saying, or maybe couldn't even figure out.

"Nice talking to you, Sonny," Parch said, smiling. "You be careful riding that bike in traffic now, you hear?"

The expression on Sonny's face changed as though a shade had been pulled up. The dull look disappeared and he smiled, bobbing his head happily. Positively relieved, Parch thought.

Walking back to the car, Parch wondered if Sonny Crenshaw had been told too many stories where the cops were the bad guys, or if the kid had something to hide.

CHAPTER 34
✝

HE WAS FUSED to the rock. He no longer felt the heat; he was part of it. He had turned up the collar of his shirt to cover his neck and had tied a handkerchief over his head. He was beyond sweating. The moisture evaporated before it could work through his skin. He had already consumed most of the water in the canteen and was rationing himself to occasional sips.

They had wrapped the scene after three takes. The girl missed her cue on the first take, then Jarvis blew his line on the second one. One stinking line in the whole scene and he fouled it up. Stupid jerk didn't have a brain in his head. It took more than looks to be an actor. Took more than talent too. It took brains.

Below him, the director called for a break while the next scene was set up. Jeanne pulled off the wide-brimmed sun hat and fanned herself with it. Her face was partly hidden by large sunglasses, and her hair shone like gold in the sun. He tried to imagine what it would be like working with her. He'd seen how earnestly she talked to Jarvis when things went wrong. She was patient . . . gentle. . . . Watching her, he felt a warmth in his loins that had nothing to do with the sun-baked rock beneath him.

Jeanne was walking toward the shady place below the hill when someone called to her. His gaze swept across the clearing to where the uniformed policeman assigned to the set was standing with another man. Squinting behind his sunglasses, Mark studied the small man who started toward Jeanne. There was something familiar about him, but his face was hidden by the angle of the rock. Little guy, and thin.

Mark lifted the binoculars carefully so the sun wouldn't hit the lenses. The little guy showed Jeanne something and began to talk. Jeanne frowned. The clipboard she was holding stayed at her side, so they weren't discussing the script. Why the hell was he bothering Jeanne now when she had a few minutes to rest? The least he could do was let her move into the shade.

Almost as if the suggestion had floated down, the little guy pointed and they moved toward the shade. The guy's movements . . . his body language . . . a momentary glimpse of his Hispanic face. . . .

It was the Mex cop he had followed last night.

Jeanne regarded the detective nervously. "What's this about, Sergeant—?"

"Lopez."

Jeanne recognized the name of the detective Glenn had called.

"Is there somewhere we can talk?" Lopez asked. "I won't take much of your time." He motioned toward the foot of the hill. "It'll be cooler there."

She led him past the equipment clustered near the hill. "Watch the cables," she warned. She stopped a few feet from a group of extras waiting for their call. "Is this about my husband's phone call, Sergeant Lopez?"

"Yes."

"I'm sorry he bothered you."

"It's our job to check out every possibility in a case like this."

"Oh."

"Your husband thinks there may be a connection between the picture you're shooting and the Stabber case. I read the script, and he could have a point. There are a few things that may be coincidence or may not. What do you think, Mrs. Donovan?"

"I don't know. That is, I mean, yes, I see the things Glenn pointed out, but they are only coincidence, although I admit it gave me a start when I found out a woman had been murdered in that alley where we shot last night."

"How many people have copies of the script or have access to it?"

"Lord, I don't know. There are dozens of them floating around. Everyone in production has one, of course. We keep extra copies in the office. And the writer."

"Does he work on the set?"

"No. He's on call if we need any changes, but he's not here all the time. He happens to be here today because we need some changes. The fire marshal has banned any flames and we have a candlelight scene coming up."

"Which one is the writer?"

Jeanne pointed. "That's him over there."

Lopez glanced and nodded. "Your husband says you noticed the possible connection between the Stabber and the script when you saw the alley where Suzette Miller was killed. Why didn't you call us?"

Jeanne said quickly, "I didn't see a connection. As I said, it gave me a start, but when I thought it over, I decided it was only coincidence. Besides, I figured you'd think I was crazy."

Lopez smiled, and Jeanne thought how little like a policeman he looked. A relaxed, pleasantly good-looking man, he could be an actor on the set.

"We're dealing with a serial killer, Mrs. Donovan. He's already killed four times. We want to get him before he does it again. It's our job to check out every possibility, no matter how remote. Most of the tips we get turn out to be dead ends, but we can't afford to pass up anything."

"In that case, I apologize, Sergeant Lopez, even though I don't see how it can possibly mean anything. What about the victim you found this morning?" She shook her head. "There's nothing like that in the script."

"Any chance it could have been cut in a rewrite?"

She worked the brim of her hat like a set of worry beads. "Not since I've been on the picture, but I didn't come in until the start of production. There could have been a dozen rewrites before that. Brad Raven or Terry Faust can tell you. Or the writer himself."

There was no reason Brad Raven would have mentioned earlier scripts last night, nor any reason for Nasty to ask. Ellie hadn't been killed then. "Isn't the producer on the set all the time?" He didn't see Raven anywhere.

"No."

"Will he be here later?"

"I'm sure he will."

He had the feeling she was happier when Raven wasn't around. "Is there someone who can tell me how to reach him?"

Jeanne hesitated, remembering Callie's remark about Brad's answering service and wondering why the detective wanted to talk to him again. "The receptionist at the office. Or ask Terry. He might have it."

"Thank you. I appreciate your help."

Jeanne couldn't resist asking, "Sergeant Lopez, do you really think the Stabber is following our script? Conceding the possibility he got his hands on one, why would he bother? It seems to me he'd be making it harder for himself."

Lopez leaned against the rough rock of the hillside and regarded her seriously. "Mrs. Donovan, serial killers are a breed apart. Once they get away with murder, it's a game to them. They're convinced they're smarter than their victims and the police. They believe they're smarter than anyone else. You've read about the Hillside Strangler, Ted Bundy, John Wayne Gacy? Psychiatrists have a hard time figuring out what makes them kill, but when they get away with it more than once, they're usually masters at living their everyday lives without anyone suspecting what's going on. Give a serial killer four quick victories like the Stabber's, and we're talking about a man who thinks he's invincible.

"We'll get him eventually, and when we do, I'll give you odds someone who knows him will say it can't possibly be true. He's been a model employee, or he led a Boy Scout troop, or he's the kind of neighbor who can always be counted on to help when you need him. And the irony is that in most cases, they're right. The guy is average and ordinary in most other respects except that some crazy quirk in his head makes him kill."

"Jack the Ripper and the boy next door," Jeanne whispered.

Lopez was alert instantly. "Why do you say that?"

"Oh. It was something the director said about the actor playing the killer in this picture."

"The director would be Terry Faust. What's the actor's name?"

Jeanne said, "Wray Jarvis. But Terry meant it as a compliment. Jarvis is a fantastic actor. In this picture he's handling a delicate role that calls for the ability to depict normalcy and madness in the same character."

Lopez looked at her. "It comes naturally to killers like the Stabber, Mrs. Donovan. Believe me, it comes naturally."

What the hell was that cop doing down there all this time? Mark cupped his hand over his wrist so the sun didn't hit the watch crystal. Twenty minutes. Was he still with Jeanne, or was he questioning others? Lopez would talk to everyone now that he was here. How did the stupid Mex get on to the script? He wasn't bright enough to figure it out for himself.

He rolled to his back and closed his eyes against the torrid glare of the sun. So Lopez had the connection. What would he do now? Blunder around asking questions that wouldn't get him anywhere because there was no place to go. He'd wouldn't get anything from anyone down there because they didn't know anything. So, what would the cop do next? Stake out the location hoping the Stabber would show? That sounded dumb enough for Lopez to consider.

Staying low, Mark rolled to his knees and crawled across the scorching rock to the path. His fatigues were covered with dust and bits of dry grass, and he stopped to brush himself off before he got to his feet and began the perilous descent. He had to lean back at almost a forty-five-degree angle to keep his balance, and even then he skidded and slid dangerously a couple of times. He landed with a thump at the end of the path behind a prop trailer.

"What the hell were you doing up there?" A tanned, baby-faced youth with a tripod under his arm blocked the way.

"Looking around." Mark adjusted his cap and sunglasses as he glanced to see if anyone else was around.

"Man, didn't you get the word?" the grip said. "The fire inspector put the rock off limits. This canyon is so dry friction could set it off. Christ, you weren't smoking or anything?"

Mark snorted. "Get off my back, kid. I don't do stupid things."

The tanned youth hesitated. "How come I haven't seen you around before? Who are you anyhow?"

"I'm a stand-in for the stunt man." He grinned. "Quit worrying, kid, I've been in this business too long to not know whose ass to kiss. When the producer tells me to go up and check a camera angle, I check. And I don't ask the fire inspector's permission or anyone else's."

The kid backed down. "Well, why didn't you say so? I'd roll down the friggin' rock if would get me on Raven's good side. If he's got one. He's a bastard."

"See ya." Mark went around the prop trailer and past the park ranger's truck, glancing back toward the set to look for Jeanne. He didn't see her. She must still be with the Mex cop.

No, there was fucking Lopez coming right toward him.

They passed within five feet of each other. Stupid Mex bastard. Mark detoured around the back of another trailer and walked down the hill.

CHAPTER 35
†

WHEN THE DINNER break finally came an hour later than scheduled, Jeanne caught Terry before he could head for the picnic tables where the buffet had been set up.

"I'm going home for a few minutes," she said.

"Hey, if Brad shows up—"

"Because he probably *will* show up," Jeanne said emphatically. "I need the fortification of a cool shower and a few minutes of relaxation before I can take my licks. He chewed me out yesterday for everything from the wind to the numbering of the script pages." It was almost as though Brad Raven's creativity snapped into high gear under pressure, releasing genius that drove others insane but made him the brilliant producer he was. After the fireworks of his genius the previous day, his absence now created an aura of expectancy. "Unless you can't live without me, Terry, I really need a break. Besides, Glenn's worrying himself into a tizzy. We'll both feel better if he can pinch me and make sure I'm okay."

"That cop touched a match to everyone's fuse. Yeah, okay, but remember, dinner break is only an hour."

"I'll be back, don't worry. I won't screw you up, I promise. I'll grab a bite and be back before eight, word of honor."

"Remember my butt is in the fire too if there's any delay."

"I'll be back on time and as eager as a starlet," she promised.

"A word to the wise? Just slip that little car of yours in neutral and coast down the hill. The fewer people who know you're off the set, the better."

Jeanne returned his conspiratorial grin and walked toward the road and her car.

Mark lay on the grass, his head propped on his folded jacket. Behind the wraparound sunglasses, his eyes were heavy-lidded but open. The stupid Mex cop had driven past a couple of hours ago without so much as a glance at the small clearing down the road a little way from the filming location. Mark considered going back, but after his encounter with the grip, he decided it was too risky. It would spoil everything if he ran into Jeanne. Besides, if she left, she had to come down this way. He'd spot the car without any trouble. Lying here was a hell of a lot more comfortable than on that hot rock.

He heard a car engine and shifted his gaze to the road. Maroon car. His Toyota. He was alert instantly without moving a muscle. As the car went by, he flicked a glance to be sure Jeanne was driving. Then he jumped up and sprinted for his car, parked in the shade of a stand of oaks.

He caught sight of the Toyota again a block beyond the park gate.

Glenn was delighted to see Jeanne. The bed around him was covered with papers, and his face was more animated than she'd seen it for months.

"I'm going to have a cool shower," she told him. "There's enough leftovers for a cold supper. You game?"

"Sure, but you didn't come home to work. I, on the other hand, have done nothing but loaf all day. I'll put the food on the table."

"I can do it."

"Just relax, baby. You don't have to be superwoman tonight."

Jeanne kissed him. "Not to worry. It hasn't been a bad day so far because Raven has been blessedly absent. He would have had a bloody fit when your detective came to check us out."

"Did Lopez talk to you?"

"I was first on his list." Jeanne stripped off her slacks and shirt and stood in filmy cotton underwear that clung damply to her body. "He seems to be taking the idea of the killer using the script seriously. At least I got that feeling."

"It's about time. His partner was here today, a big guy named Parch. I know damned well he believed me. I feel a lot better about you up in that park with them keeping an eye on things, but I won't relax until they catch that guy."

Jeanne was glad Lopez had followed up on Glenn's call. Even if it was much ado about nothing, Glenn seemed much less worried, and she felt better too. She stepped out of her briefs and unsnapped her bra. Glenn grinned appreciatively, his preoccupation with the Stabber momentarily broken. When she walked into the bathroom and turned on the shower, he got out of bed and hobbled to the kitchen.

They lingered a few minutes over iced tea before Jeanne put down her napkin. "Don't you dare do the dishes, you hear? I'll take care of them when I get back. Now I know you're dying to get back to Pearl's papers, so go. Are you finding anything good?"

"Unbelievable," he said. "Did you know Haliman

worked with one of the first Foley pits? God, the man was a genius at a dozen things. I'll probably do an article on him when I finish this one. With Pearl's box of memories, I could write a dozen of them."

Jeanne ran water over the dishes as she stacked them in the sink. "I want you safely ensconced in the bedroom before I leave. Go."

He picked up his crutches. "With such high-grade word power as 'ensconced,' maybe you should be writing articles."

She threw the dish towel at him. "On your way. You're getting too frisky."

She circled through the hallway ahead of him and smoothed the bed before he got back into it. Glancing at the clock, she said, "I have to run. I love you."

"Hey, babe— Don't forget your promise. Faust or someone follows you home."

"Scout's honor," she said, blowing another kiss from the doorway. "Hopefully I'll be back around eleven."

"I'll be here."

The starter ground but the engine didn't catch. Had she flooded it? She looked at her watch and forced herself to wait until the second hand swept a full circle before she turned the key again.

"Damn!" Of all the times for the car to act up! She tried the ignition again and listened to the awful grinding noise that meant it wasn't going to start. This time when she glanced at her watch, she realized how close she had called the time. How long would it take the auto club to get there? Too long, she was sure. She'd have to call a cab. Furious, she got out and hurried toward the apartment.

"Hey, Jeanne—" Mark Bonner was striding across the street. "What's the matter?"

"Mark! Am I glad to see you! The car won't start and I'm due back at work in ten minutes."

"Let me have a look. Pull the hood latch."

When she did as he asked, he raised the hood and ducked under it. He told her to try starting it. A moment later his face appeared around the edge of the hood.

"I can fix it, but it'll take a little while. Want me to run you to work?"

She hesitated. "I don't want to put you out."

"Hey, look, I sold you the car. I feel responsible. Come on, my car's over there." He led the way to the Buick and opened the door. The car was miraculously cool. When Mark got behind the wheel, Jeanne told him where they were shooting. The engine hummed to life and they were away from the curb.

"I'll be glad to pick you up later," he offered.

"That's awfully nice of you, really, but I can get someone on the set to drive me home." She glanced at her watch. "Raven is going to be on a rampage if I'm late." She knew, just knew, Brad had arrived on the set.

"Raven sounds like a bastard."

"Unfortunately he's a genius bastard, so I guess he's earned the right."

"I don't think so," Bonner said. His sharp tone made Jeanne glance at him, but his scowl of concentration was directed at the traffic on Vermont Avenue. A car pulled out of a side street and turned in front of them, and Mark swerved expertly to pass it. He moved back into his lane at the first opening.

When they crossed Los Feliz Boulevard, she glanced at her watch again. Three minutes. She prayed that Brad, in one of his bursts of genius enthusiasm, hadn't decided to cut the dinner break short and herd everyone back to work.

Then they were in the park, climbing the long hill past the Observatory Road and taking the one that led to the picnic area. When they reached the turnoff where she could see the trailers and trucks, Mark went on past.

"You passed the road," Jeanne exclaimed, glancing back.

He didn't answer.

"Mark, it's back there—" She looked over her shoulder again as the branch of the road became a gray smudge behind them. "Mark—"

Hunched over the wheel, his gaze was fixed on the winding, climbing road ahead.

CHAPTER 36
✝

YANKTON DROPPED A sheaf of papers on Nasty's desk. "You got any idea how many people come and go in a building that size?" He pointed. "Employee lists of Harvest Films and every other tenant in the building, plus the maintenance and security people. That's for openers. We're still working on delivery companies, messenger services, and fast food places that deliver everything from pizza to kosher deli. People in that building have everything brought in. It wouldn't surprise me if we come up with a call girl service."

Nasty grunted. He'd pin a medal on anyone who could save them the work they faced, but it never happened that way. Any investigation required work, a hell of a lot of it and most of it dull. He'd had four sets of each list copied. Now he gave both Opara and Yankton a set and slid one onto Parch's desk.

"What are we looking for?" Opara asked.

"Any names that are on more than one list. I don't care how remote the connection is."

When Parch came in twenty minutes later, the room

was quiet except for the occasional rustle of paper. Nasty looked up.

"How'd you make out with Donovan?"

"He's on crutches and hasn't been outside since he got home from the hospital last weekend. He's got a lot of time to think, maybe too much. This whole thing could be in his head. He doesn't have any more than the few coincidences we've already seen." He rolled his chair close to the desk and glanced at the stack of papers Nasty had put there.

"You get anything else?" Lopez asked.

Parch took out a notebook and passed it across. "List of the tenants in the building. The Crenshaws manage the place. I caught their kid listening outside Donovan's door. I have a funny feeling about him."

Nasty's brows peaked.

"He's pretty slow mentally, but there's something about him. . . . I waited outside and followed him when he came out. He took off on a bicycle, and guess where he went?"

"No idea."

"The alley behind the bank where Ellie Parker was found."

Nasty demanded, "And?"

Parch scowled. "And nothing. He looked around and spent some time staring at the chalk marks. I tried to question him, but his answers were vague. Like I said, he hasn't got it all upstairs. But one thing I'm sure of—he was scared."

"Of you?"

"Maybe, but I had the feeling it was more than that. I've got nothing concrete to go on, but I'd bet the kid knows something he isn't telling."

Nasty said, "About the murders?"

Parch shrugged. "It was almost like he was checking

out something, and coming right after eavesdropping on my talk with Donovan, it makes me wonder."

Lopez glanced at the list Parch had given him. "What about the rest of the tenants?"

"I went back after I followed the kid, but no one else was home. I checked with Donovan again. He says they all work regular jobs except the Crenshaws, Pearl Gannon, and the guy in the front apartment, Bonner."

Yankton looked up. "Did you say Bonner?"

"Yeah."

Nasty glanced at Ken's list again. "Mark Bonner."

"I just saw that name." Yankton shuffled through the pages on his desk, then ran his finger down a list. "Here it is. Mark Bonner works for AIM Security, the outfit that supplies guards and watchmen for the Harvest building."

"Does it give his home address?"

Yankton read it off. It was the same as Donovan's. Nasty reached for the phone and dialed R&I.

Glenn felt like a kid in an ice cream factory. Gerod Haliman had drawn diagrams, made notes, kept daily logs of his work. Bless Pearl Gannon for being a pack rat and preserving the past.

When the phone rang, he reached for it absently without pausing in his study of the sketch of an early boom mike that set the standard for the industry.

"Hello."

"Glenn?"

"Yeah."

"Terry Faust. Where the hell is Jeanne? We've got everything on hold and Raven is storming around like—"

Glenn dropped the sketch. "What do you mean, where's Jeanne? She left here"—he glanced at the clock—"forty-five minutes ago. She was on her way back."

"You're sure?"

"Of course I'm sure." Panic seeped along Glenn's spine, and he tried to stem it. "Maybe she had car trouble."

"I drove down to Los Feliz Boulevard. That's where I am now. I didn't see her anywhere along the way."

"Maybe she pulled into a station—"

"Listen, if she calls, tell her to grab a cab. I've got to get back."

"Terry—"

"Yeah?"

"When she gets there, send somebody to a phone to call me, will you?"

"Sure." The connection broke.

Glenn fell back against the pillows sweating. Forty-five minutes for a five-minute drive. He wiped his palms on the sheet, then reached for the phone again. When he gave his name, he was put through to Homicide.

"Detective Lopez, Homicide."

"This is Glenn Donovan. Listen, something's happened to my wife. I told the man who was here—"

Nasty motioned for Parch to pick up the phone. "Where is your wife, Mr. Donovan?"

"I don't know. She left here forty-five minutes ago to go back to Griffith Park where they're shooting. She hasn't shown up. I just had a call from the director."

"Are they shooting at the same place they were this afternoon?"

"Yes. Christ, if that maniac—"

"Take it easy, Mr. Donovan," Nasty reassured him automatically. "I'll get back to you as soon as I can." He thought he heard Donovan choke back a sob as he hung up.

"Let's go," Nasty said. "Opara, get some backup and a chopper up there. Tell them to meet me on Tac Two. Ken, you check out Bonner's apartment. If he's not there, find him."

CHAPTER 37
✝

JEANNE PLEADED, "MARK, please, I'm due back on location."

"This is a shortcut."

She glanced at the road canopied by branches in one of the deeply shadowed glens dotting the mountainous terrain. It couldn't be a shortcut. They had passed the only road to the picnic grounds.

"Please take me back!" She glanced at her watch and saw it was already after eight. Terry would be frantic, and Brad would be livid. Worse, he'd blame Terry.

A smile curled the corners of Mark's full lips, and his thin shoulders pulled forward as if he were suppressing laughter. Jeanne's anger exploded.

"Turn around right now!" she ordered. "I don't care about any shortcuts. Take me back this instant!" His jaw twitched, and when he didn't take his gaze from the road, Jeanne grabbed his arm and shook it. "Do you hear me! Turn around!"

One hand slid from the wheel and pushed her hand away. His jaw was tight, his teeth clenched, and stiff cords showed at his neck. His breath hissed as he swung the steering wheel sharply. The car swerved, and Jeanne had to brace herself against the dash when the car slewed, tires screeching and spitting loose gravel as it skidded close to the lip of the steep drop where the canyon fell away. Mark pulled the car out of the skid and gunned it back onto the road and Jeanne pressed her hand over her mouth.

Mark laughed. "That fast enough for you?" His eyes were cold steel.

She swallowed, trying to moisten her mouth. "Why are you doing this?"

Tension drained from his rigid pose and he sat back, staring straight ahead and driving effortlessly, almost casually, on the steep, winding road. "Sorry, I shouldn't have scared you. It was dumb."

The abrupt change baffled her, but she couldn't suppress her fury. She grabbed for the ignition key, but again he was too quick for her. His hand came away from the wheel and chopped at her wrist. She pulled back in agony.

"Don't try that again," he snarled.

Jeanne bit her lip. "I'm sorry," she said, trying desperately to placate him. She was thoroughly frightened now. "Please take me back. We'll forget this ever happened."

He turned his head, staring at her. "Forget . . . ?" His eyes went back to the road. "I don't want to forget."

She made another effort to soothe him. "All right, we won't forget. We'll talk about it later, but right now I have to get back to work. Please, Mark. I thought we were friends."

He stared ahead without answering. Under the overhang of trees, the road wound like a dark ribbon through the gathering twilight.

Too restless and worried to sit still, Glenn hobbled through the apartment on his crutches, cursing himself for letting Jeanne go back to the park. Damn it, no picture or job was worth this. He pivoted and worked his way around the chair and the sofa. Damn California! They should never have come out here. Damn! Where was she? What happened to keep her from getting back to work on time?

He was sweating and cold with fear. His gut terror couldn't be talked away by cursing California. The Los Feliz Stabber. *Dead Past.* Why hadn't he forced Lopez to listen sooner? Why couldn't he do something now? His helplessness infuriated him. He swung a crutch at one of the chairs in the tiny dinette and toppled it with a crash. The noise brought him to his senses.

Whining and crying wasn't going to help. He'd done enough of it these past weeks to know. Okay, hero, what now? He leaned against the doorway. He'd already called Lopez. Who else could help? Who else was there? He didn't know anyone in the city except Jim Newell. The studio would be closed, and he didn't have Jim's home number. Mark Bonner? Glenn didn't like him, but that didn't really matter now.

He hobbled through the living room and out of the apartment. At Bonner's door he banged loudly. When there was no response, he banged harder. Behind him Pearl Gannon's door opened and she peered out.

"He's not home. Why, it's you, Mr. Donovan." The door closed and reopened after she slipped off the chain. Pearl gave her trademark gesture with a long-fingered hand. "Come in. I just made a pot of tea."

"Sorry, Miss Gannon, not now." He ignored the disappointed expression on the old woman's face. "Are you sure Bonner's not home?"

"I saw him drive off with your wife."

For an instant what she said didn't register in Glenn's agitated mind. When it did, his head snapped up. "With Jeanne?"

Pearl's hand fluttered at her breast. "Why, yes. When her car wouldn't start he—"

"Her car wouldn't start?"

"Don't repeat everything I say, young man. I am not a senile babbler." Her amethyst gaze challenged him.

Glenn forced himself to think rationally. "I apologize. I'm upset. This is important. Tell me again." He hobbled across the hall and looked down at the frail figure. "It's important, Miss Gannon. Jeanne's life may be at stake."

"Oh, dear . . ." Her face went chalky under the round spots of rouge on her cheeks, and her fingers toyed restlessly with a cameo brooch at the neckline of her dress. "I warned her about him."

"You mean Mark Bonner?" An ice floe jammed under Glenn's ribs.

"The man's a liar and a sneak. I have known from the start that he was never considered for a part in the Harvest picture."

"Miss Gannon, please—Jeanne and the car?"

She closed her eyes for an instant as though preparing herself to walk on camera. When she spoke, her voice was strong. "He came home at seven-thirty. I noticed because he was so determined to get that big car of his into a tight space across the street. He's not one to give up, you know."

Glenn fumed impatiently, wishing she'd speed up her story.

"When he got out, he went up the block instead of coming in. I didn't think too much of it until he came back down a few moments later and got into his own car again. My word, I thought, all that effort to park so he could drive right off again? I thought it rather odd. Then when he didn't drive away, naturally I was curious."

Glenn had trouble controlling his agitation. He wanted to prompt and coax, but he realized the dramatic pauses were indelibly patterned in the old actress's speech.

"He did absolutely nothing until your wife came out. He just sat there. It was as if he'd been waiting for her. Mrs. Donovan tried to start her car, and when she couldn't and came back toward the apartment, he got out of his car and met her. They spoke for a moment, then returned to her car together. Mr. Bonner looked under the hood. A minute later they got in his car and drove off."

Glenn fell against the wall. The sick feeling in the pit of his stomach pulled and knotted, and painful breaths hissed through his teeth. All along he'd thought Bonner was too friendly, too helpful. And now . . . *God, don't let it be so—don't let Bonner be the killer the police are looking for!*

"Are you all right?" Pearl's voice was filled with concern. "Oh, dear, do you think. . . ?"

"I have to call the police. Can I use your phone?"

"Of course." She stepped back, her hand outstretched, ready to help him if he faltered.

Glenn hobbled to the phone, dialed the police number with total recall. He blurted out the story to the officer on the other end of the line, then looked at Pearl as the man began to question him.

"What kind of car does Bonner have?" Glenn asked her.

"A Buick."

"What year and model?"

"Oh, dear—"

"Color?"

"Dark blue."

"License?" Glenn uttered a silent prayer.

Pearl's lips compressed and she shook her head.

"I know." Sonny Crenshaw's voice from the doorway startled them both.

Glenn yelled into the phone, "Hold on a sec." Then to Sonny he said, "Do you know Bonner's license plate number?"

Sonny nodded. "Five, three, four, R,I,T."

"You sure?"

Pearl said, "He has a knack for numbers." She smiled at Sonny, who beamed.

Glenn repeated the license number into the phone. "If this guy is the Stabber and is following that script, they're in Griffith Park." He listened a moment, then hung up. "He says Lopez is on his way up there. He'll get him on the radio. There's a cop on his way over here now. God, if they don't find Jeanne before——" His voice broke.

Sonny plucked at the tail of his T-shirt and twisted it around a finger. "Is Mrs. Donovan with him?"

Without asking, Glenn knew whom Sonny meant. The pronoun was uttered with the same distaste he detected when Pearl spoke of Bonner. "Yes, do you know anything about it? Do you know where they went?"

Sonny snapped his head in a furious negative as if he were being accused. Pearl gestured and gave Glenn a warning look. When she spoke to Sonny, her tone was gentle.

"Did you see Mark Bonner today?" she asked Sonny. He nodded.

"When did you see him?"

Sonny chewed his lip and looked scared as he darted a glance over his shoulder toward Bonner's apartment. Pearl went to him and took his hand, leading him inside and closing the door.

"Mr. Bonner will not find out. Now then . . ." Pearl tipped her head, birdlike, as she saw the bruise on the boy's cheek. Sonny put his hand up to cover it. Pearl drew the hand away. "Did he do that?"

Sonny's face twitched nervously.

"He did that, didn't he?" Pearl snapped. "The man is positively evil."

Sonny agreed quickly. "Evil. I saw it."

Glenn stared at him. "What did you see?"

Sonny fell into frightened silence again, and Pearl reprimanded Glenn with an impatient glance.

"What did you see, Sonny? You can tell us. We're your friends. I know you like Mrs. Donovan. We want to help her."

Sonny's tongue worked nervously across his lips. "He lifted up the hood of her car and took something out."

Glenn shuddered.

Pearl drew a fluttering breath and said softly, "We must help her, Sonny. Is there anything else?"

Sonny darted a nervous glance toward the closed door. "In his apartment. In the bedroom," he whispered.

"What, Sonny, what's in there?" Pearl coaxed.

His lips moved, forcing out the words. "The lady. The dead lady."

CHAPTER 38
✝

"WHAT DEAD LADY?" Glenn screamed, lurching toward Sonny and almost falling as the frightened boy backed toward the door and raised his hands as if to ward off a blow.

"Don't shout at him," Pearl commanded. She stepped in front of Glenn. In a quiet voice she said to Sonny, "It's all right, dear, he's not angry." She shot another warning glance at Glenn, and he looked away. Pearl obviously knew how to handle the kid. *Dead lady.* Jeez...

"Did you see something in Mr. Bonner's apartment?"

Sonny's head bobbed rapidly.

"Not a real dead lady?"

Sonny's brow furrowed. "No. Make-believe."

"How did you know what it was?"

He frowned. "Pictures. Clothes."

Pearl paused for a breath, then very gently asked, "Will you show us, Sonny? You know I don't like Mr. Bonner. He's an evil man. He tells terrible lies, and he hurts people."

Sonny touched the bruise on his face and his head moved rhythmically, but he made no move toward the door. Impatiently Glenn watched Pearl for a signal.

Pearl was smiling as though she had asked Sonny to accompany her on a stroll. She touched his arm and looked up at his gangly height. "Do you have a key?"

He looked frightened again. "Momma does."

"Is your mother home?"

He nodded, still terrified.

"I will get it," Pearl said, moving past Sonny and opening the door. She marched out stiff-backed but stopped in the hall as the doorbell rang stridently. Looking toward the entrance, she murmured, "Oh, my word."

Glenn hobbled into the hall and saw the blond-haired policeman who visited him earlier rattling the knob and pressing bells. Seeing Pearl and Glenn, he reached into his pocket, then held his police badge against the glass.

"Police. Open up."

Glenn shouted to Pearl. "Let him in!"

Pearl hurried to open the door.

"You've got to do something," Glenn shouted as soon as Parch came in. "Where's Lopez?"

"Take it easy. What's happened?"

"There isn't time! He's got my wife—"

"Who?"

"Bonner. He's the Stabber! Goddamn it—"

"Take it easy, Donovan—"

Pearl's voice cut through Glenn's hysteria. "Officer, Mr. Bonner believes he is playing the killer's role in the movie Mrs. Donovan is directing. He told me three months ago he had been cast in the part. He's quite unstable, and we are very much afraid he has become a killer in real life. We were about to get a key and enter his apartment. There is something in his bedroom that will verify what I am saying. Please, come with me to the manager's apartment."

"Where is it?"

Pearl pointed. "Down the hall. 103."

262

"Stay right here." Parch ran down the hall and banged on Crenshaw's door.

Glenn collapsed against the wall. His face was ashen and he was bathed in cold sweat. Bonner had Jeanne. Did she know what was happening? If Bonner was acting out his fantasy by following the script, he was in love with Jeanne. And he was going to kill her.

Parch came back with Harry Crenshaw puffing red-faced behind him. A key chain dangled from Crenshaw's beefy fist, and his glare pinned his son. Sonny studied his jogging shoes as if the answers to all his problems were hidden in the scuffed leather.

"Open the door, Crenshaw," Parch commanded.

Crenshaw's face mottled with rage as he unlocked Bonner's door and flung it open. Parch went in, and Pearl hurried behind him without waiting for Glenn to catch up. Sonny stayed where he was, casting an occasional furtive glance at his father.

Glenn moved as fast as he could on the crutches, ignoring the angry pull of his muscles. Pearl stopped in the bedroom doorway, her face so pale the rouge spots looked like paint spilled on a white canvas. Parch had snapped on the overhead light, and in its glare Glenn saw a mutilated chair holding an obscene array of lewd photographs torn from magazines and articles of women's apparel. A large hoop gold earring, a black satin miniskirt, lace underpants, a single red shoe, Jeanne's tank top with MINNESOTA scripted across the front—all splashed with red.

Glenn shoved past Pearl. What he thought was hair was the gray stuffing from the slashed chair. What he thought was blood was cut-up cellophane that caught the light and gleamed wetly. He raised a crutch to swing at a photograph of a woman fondling herself. Parch grabbed his arm.

"Don't touch anything!"

Glenn lowered the crutch. "He's crazy. We've got to find them. Do you have a car?"

"You're not going anywhere," Parch said. "Okay, everyone out of this apartment. Move!" He herded them out into the hall, then pulled the door shut and pocketed the keys.

"Hey, gimme those keys," Crenshaw blustered.

"No one goes in there, you hear? Now stay put." Parch was already on his way out the front door.

"My wife——" Glenn tried to follow.

Parch snarled over his shoulder, "I said stay put!" He sprinted across the sidewalk to his car.

Nasty got the call as he was driving through the park gates. He speeded up as Parch repeated what Pearl and Glenn had told him and described what he'd seen inside Bonner's apartment.

"That cinches it," Nasty told him. "Keep Donovan and the others there. If Bonner comes back, I want him, you got that?"

"Got it."

"Get another dozen men up here and check on that chopper. Make sure they've got a Probe Eye aboard." He signed off and found the frequency for the park ranger station. He wanted to be in touch with every vehicle moving inside the park.

Darkness crept across the mountainside, painting deep shadows over the details of the landscape and making the wooded roadside an ominous, black thicket. The sky burned from gray to sooty black, like a pan left too long on a high flame, and the road ahead of the car was swallowed by darkness.

Mark didn't turn on the lights. If the park rangers saw the flash of headlights, they might investigate. They were supposed to make sure everyone was off the mountain roads by nightfall. The bastards were probably too lazy to move their butts, but he wasn't going to take the chance.

He didn't want to be disturbed. Not now. Jeanne would

be missed, but Raven wanted to get the picture in on budget. He'd shoot the scene without her. Faust would distribute her work to the second and third ADs. That's show biz, Mark thought grimly. Anybody was expendable.

He didn't have to worry about the Mex cop either. Lopez had checked out the movie crew this afternoon. He wouldn't go back up there because he hadn't learned anything. What did he expect? Christ, talk about jerks. Lopez was running around in circles waiting for something to fall in his lap. The joke was on him. Nothing was going to fall. Mark was too clever for him. Mark had outwitted the stupid Mex before the cop even caught on to the game. He was so far behind already, he'd never catch up.

He glanced at Jeanne sitting bolt upright on the other side of the car. Her face was a pale blur, but he could see her wide-open eyes as she stared ahead. He turned his attention back to the road. Once they got to the place he'd picked out, she'd be okay. Did she recognize the action sequence from the script? She'd be scared if she thought he was going to follow it all the way. Maybe he should tell her he'd rewritten the ending. All in good time. All in good time.

He concentrated on picking out landmarks. The spot was hard to see from the road, even harder now in the dark. The car topped a rise and he slowed for a sharp curve. Moments later he made out the dim outline of the boulder he was watching for, and he smiled.

As soon as he passed it, he flicked on the headlights for a second so he could guide the car onto the narrow trail circling a grove of pines in a shallow basin. He measured the distance by counting slowly as he inched the car down the slope. When he reached twelve, he braked, turned off the engine, and took the keys out of the ignition. He wasn't going to take a chance on Jeanne's trying to bolt now. He had found the spot two days ago and checked it from every angle. A car parked here was completely hidden from the road, even in daylight. It was the perfect place. The natural slope of land formed a small sheltered clearing surrounded by trees and wild brush, and there was a smooth place to spread a blanket.

Jeanne watched him, her eyes wide in the darkness. He opened the car door and in the splash of light, smiled at her. "Know where we are?"

She shook her head, and her hands twisted the cord of her purse. Humming to himself, he got out. She'd figure it out soon enough.

Jeanne's breath made a choking noise as she let it out. The car door closed and it was dark again. She welcomed it now, preferring it to Mark Bonner's scrutiny, just as she welcomed the pain of the stiff straw cutting into her fingers twined in her purse strap. Her first impulse was to lock the doors and lean on the horn, but she stopped herself. He might use a tire iron to smash the window before she could attract attention. They hadn't passed another car since they entered the park.

Why was he doing this? She had missed something. Something she should know or recognize. What? She knew nothing about Mark Bonner except he'd been nice to her and he lived next door. Next door. *The boy next door* . . . Oh, God— *The boy next door and Jack the Ripper*—

She turned and saw the faint glow from the open trunk. She glanced around desperately. The deepening twilight had become blackness under the trees. She couldn't see the road. There were no sounds except the chirrup of crickets and the low sobbing of the wind as it rushed restlessly over the mountain. She untangled her fingers from the purse cord and reached for the door handle.

Panic engulfed her as she opened the door and flung herself from the car. Stumbling, she fell into the brush and was entangled in thorny branches. She was clawing her way out, ignoring the sting of nettles and tugging her clothes free, when Mark grabbed her from behind. Roughly he dragged her back to the car and pushed her against the fender.

"That was a dumb move, Jeanne." His tone was angry and hurt. Air rasped over his teeth with a hissing noise. Jeanne winced as his fingers bruised her arm. They stood locked in the tableau for what seemed an eternity before his grip relaxed and he took her arm. "C'mon, help me get the stuff."

Shaking, she let herself be pulled around to the trunk. With his free hand he reached into it and took out a blanket. He shoved it into her arms.

Still gripping her tightly, he lifted out a picnic cooler and slammed the trunk shut, then guided her in the darkness. "Careful, the ground's rough. Don't fall." He led her to the clearing.

Jeanne hugged the blanket like a shield, her mind sliding from frantic ideas of escape to complete numbness. The possibility that Mark Bonner was the Los Feliz Stabber had shaken her so badly, she couldn't think. It had been a mistake to bolt. He'd be on his guard now. She'd have to plan her next move carefully. But what? Get away. If Mark was a killer— Oh, God. She bit her lip until pain was all she could feel.

Mark's steps were unerring despite the darkness. When he set down the cooler, he took the blanket from her, then staying close enough to grab her quickly if she tried to run, spread it on the ground. His movements were faint, shifting shadows in the pale glow of lights from the city below. He opened the cooler and began taking things out. Deli cartons, plates, a bottle of champagne—

A picnic. The final scene of *Dead Past*. Oh, God.

CHAPTER 39

✝

MARK HUMMED TUNELESSLY as he anchored the corners of the blanket so they wouldn't snap in the wind. A gust caught a paper plate as he set them out, and he dived to save the rest, then put a jar on top of them.

He looked at Jeanne, standing like a goddess above him, and patted the blanket. "Sit." She sat, edging to a corner as far away from him as possible. He resumed humming and took out the votive candles and cups he'd substituted for the decorative tapers the script called for. The cups would shield the flames from the wind but still give a soft romantic glow that wouldn't be enough to draw attention from cruising park rangers.

He took a lighter from his pocket and cupped it to a candle. It took several tries before the wick caught, and he shielded the flame to make sure it didn't go out while he lowered the candle into the cup. He lit the others from it and arranged them around the picnic things. The flames flickered in the wind but stayed lit. The dancing light on Jeanne's face made Mark smile.

"Do you know now?" he asked.

She nodded very slowly, and her tongue traced her lips. "The script. Scene forty-nine."

Mark laughed. "Right! I knew you'd get it. It's really too bad you didn't cast me in the Rudolo part. I can act circles around Jarvis."

"I—I wasn't there when the movie was cast," she said desperately. Had he tried out for the part?

She sounded scared. Didn't she know he wasn't blaming her? It wasn't her fault, but when she saw how good an actor he was, she'd convince them to cast him in the next picture.

"I watched Jarvis this afternoon. You wouldn't have needed all those retakes if I had the part."

Shadows caressed her face and her blond-red hair glowed like embers in a fireplace. Her throat above the buttons of her blouse looked satiny smooth, and he wanted to touch her skin. He wanted to hold her, feel— He sucked air and tried to make his mind go blank, but it was too late. The voracious hunger began to spill over its bounds and stir the familiar restlessness. He turned away as shadows drew sensuous trials across Jeanne's throat like fingers moving toward the low neck of her blouse.

He concentrated on setting out the cartons of salad and packets of cold lobster and chicken. He'd selected the food carefully, good stuff, not the garbage that slob Dave Rudolo chose in the script. If he was changing the ending, he could change the food as well. He bought the kind of gourmet things Jeanne should have. He had ordered everything this afternoon so all he had to do was pick it up when he was ready.

When everything was arranged to his satisfaction, he took a chilled bottle of champagne from the ice compartment and began to strip the foil and wire. He dropped them in the basket, then held the bottle at a forty-degree angle as he worked the cork. It popped with a small sound that was caught in the keening wind and carried aloft like a plume.

Finding the stemmed plastic glasses, he wished they were crystal, but they'd have to do. He poured one and held it out to Jeanne.

"Come on, take it," he said when she hesitated. When she did, he poured one for himself, then propped the bottle carefully back in the ice before he raised his glass. "A toast to lovers, and to us."

Jeanne's whisper could barely be heard above the soughing wind. "To us."

Bonner's voice cracked nervously. "Always?" The word caressed, begged.

For a moment there was only the adagio of the wind in the oak leaves and palm fronds. Mark watched the candlelight skitter and leap across Jeanne's face. Her eyes glinted, mocking him. When she finally whispered, "Always," he knew she was lying.

"This is Lopez. Where are you, Chopper Two?"

"Coming in over the east gate. Where do you want us to start?"

"I'm heading uphill. The movie crew is over near the Observatory. Fan up from there. Our quarry doesn't have a four-wheel drive, so he'll be on the roads as long as he's moving. If he stops, it won't be out in the open. Check out anything that has possibilities."

"Roger."

Cars were supposed to be off the mountain roads at sunset, but kids frequently tried to evade the rangers so they could party after dark. Nasty had called in orders for his men to pair up with rangers, on the move and stationed at every gate. If Bonner knew the park, he could be anywhere. They'd have to check every heat signal the Probe Eye picked up.

He had men up at the movie location in case Bonner headed back there, although Nasty didn't think he would. Too many people around. But you could never tell with a psycho. When Nasty tried to think one step ahead of Bonner, logic didn't apply. Bonner was playing a game where he made up the rules as he went along. He'd already varied the pattern slightly with each killing, escalating the challenge and his own risk. He was sure of himself, too damned sure. Whatever this new move of his was, Bonner had thought it out carefully. Jeanne Donovan had played into his hands by leaving the movie set tonight, but Bonner would have had an alternate plan if she hadn't.

Where the hell was he now?

Nasty slowed the car as he saw the branching road ahead, wondering which fork to take. He spoke into the radio. "Chopper Two, what have you got?"

"A blip almost dead ahead of you, due north."

He took the right fork.

"Is it moving, Chopper Two?"

"Roger. You're practically on it."

Headlights flashed at the mouth of a tunnel. The radio crackled as the police car's red flasher signaled.

"Car Twenty-eight, Stabber Command. We're reading Chopper Two."

"Where are you coming from, Twenty-eight?"

"Western Canyon."

"Anything?"

"Negative."

"Coordinate your points and stay in touch." The patrol car signed off and Nasty got back to the chopper. "Did you copy, Chopper Two?"

"Roger."

"What else can you find?"

"We're looking. The Probe Eye is going to pick up every hot engine and coyote in the park."

"Let's hope it finds the one we want," Nasty said.

CHAPTER 40
✝

HER HANDS WERE shaking so badly, champagne splashed on her knuckles when Jeanne pretended to sip. The flickering candlelight barely penetrated the darkness, but in it, Mark Bonner's expression was terrifying. He would have been perfectly cast in the Dave Rudolo role. The borderline between his psychopathic killer personality and the helpful neighbor was as finely drawn as any actor could portray. As perfect as Wray Jarvis played . . . more so, because Mark wasn't acting. And she wasn't on the set. This was real. She pressed the cold plastic to her lips to hide their trembling.

"You're not drinking," Mark said.

She forced herself to sip. Stinging bubbles brought tears to her eyes as she tried to remember the script. The girl—oh, god, what was her name?—Lucy—Lucy refused the champagne and told Rudolo to take her home. Her demand turned Rudolo from a hopeful lover to a crazed attacker.

"It's excellent," she said in a desperate ploy to gain time.

"Twenty dollars a bottle, it should be. I got everything

at Jurgensen's. You deserve the best, and I'm going to give it to you. Always."

The words hung momentarily as the wind paused to gain new momentum. When it renewed, it was a blowtorch on Jeanne's clammy skin. His words were almost verbatim from the script, even though she had changed Lucy's dialogue. The sip of champagne churned in her stomach. *Sidetrack him . . . cue him new lines. . . .*

"You've been so nice to me since I moved in, Mark. I can't tell you how much I appreciate it. Helping me with things in the apartment, the car, now this lovely picnic." When she tried to smile, her face was stiff and dry in the searing wind. Strands of hair had worked free from the band holding her ponytail, and they snapped across her cheek like whips. The candles flickered and sputtered, and she glanced at them nervously.

"You're the nicest girl I've ever known," he said.

That wasn't in the script. Was she succeeding? "I—I'm glad you think so."

He smiled as he studied his nearly empty champagne glass. One of the candles snuffed out in a gust of wind, and Mark drained his glass and put it down. He reached for the candle holder and pulled his hand back quickly when it touched the hot glass. He pulled the lighter from his pocket and snapped it on. While he was fighting the wind to relight the candle, Jeanne poured the rest of her champagne onto the dry grass beside the blanket. When Mark looked back, she had the empty glass at her lips. Smiling, he lifted the bottle from the cooler and refilled both glasses. Fingering the narrow stem, he stared into the liquid burnished gold by the candlelight.

"I'm a good actor, Jeanne. All I need is a chance. I don't want to take advantage of your friendship, but it would mean a lot to me if you help me get the lead in Harvest's next film." He looked up earnestly. "I can do it, I really can. Wasn't I better than Jarvis tonight? Huh? Weren't you convinced I could be the serial killer?" He grinned.

Confused, she stared at him, measuring what he had said, trying to balance her thoughts between the terror he'd subjected her to and her anger, which was quickly boiling over again. He had been playing a game with her! He had deliberately spirited her away from her work and terrified her to prove he could play a part! She wanted to fling the champagne at him.

"Yes, I was convinced," she said angrily. "You were more than convincing, but that's no excuse for this—charade! Don't you realize I'm due back on location? I have job. Or I did have. If I lose it because of this, I won't be able to recommend you for anything!"

Too late she realized her mistake. Mark Bonner's expression altered as subtly as Wray Jarvis's did in the role of Dave Rudolo. The friendly warmth ebbed as a murderous glint appeared in his eyes. He wasn't acting. Not now.

He hunched on his hip and jammed his hand in the pocket of his jeans. When he withdrew it, he held up a black object that looked like a bicycle grip. He moved his thumb and the end of it snapped off with a faint click. The candlelight glinted on a tiny, needlelike blade.

"I'm sorry—" Jeanne said desperately. He was watching her like a hunter who'd spotted prey.

"Sorry?" he whispered above the wind. "Sorry? Yeah, I'm sorry, too. I should have known you were like the rest. I'm real sorry, Jeanne." He upended his champagne glass, drained it, then threw it aside. When she tried to slide away, he grabbed her arm. Her champagne spilled and the plastic glass cracked with a sharp snap as he forced her down on the blanket. Her head fell against the paper plates he'd anchored with a jar. When it rolled against her neck, it was as icy as her fear.

He pinned her with his body, his face hovering over her. His lips pulled across his teeth and his eyes were black pools lit by tiny candle flames. The point of the weapon touched her chin. "They're always sorry. I don't know what made me think you were different. You've been playing the game from the start, haven't you? But it's my move now."

Jeanne winced at the sting of pain as the blade nicked her chin, and she felt a warm ooze of blood. Grinning, he moved the weapon across her throat lightly.

"I hate to mess up such a beautiful face, but you're begging for it." The blade nicked her again, then he held it up for her to see. "Do you know what happens when I press this button?" When she didn't answer, he poked her upper arm savagely. The metal needle pierced her flesh like an angry bee. She stifled a whimper and watched him in mounting terror.

"You're going to find out," he said breathlessly. "Oh, yes, you're going to find out. But first we're going to play the game a little longer. You'll enjoy it. Oh, yes, you're going to enjoy it, I promise."

He leaned back, straddling her hips and pinning her to the ground. Grabbing her ponytail to hold her head down, he slid the weapon to the bottom of her blouse and slashed upward. The blouse slit open, and he tore it away. His face was a mask of lust as he caught the elastic of her bra under the sharp blade and cut it with a single stroke. The hot wind scorched across Jeanne's naked breasts, and she shivered.

How could she be so cold? She no longer felt pain where he'd stabbed her, only consuming, stark terror. She knew she was going to die. Her body went into a tight spasm, and the broken plastic champagne glass she was still clutching stung her palm. In desperation she swung at him. The jagged shard of plastic caught his cheek, and he howled in pain. His free hand grabbed his face. Blood, black in the eerie candlelight, ran between his fingers.

"Bitch!" He raised the weapon.

In the gyrating shadows Jeanne saw his thumb move to the button in the hilt of the weapon. In panic she arched her back and reared up, jerking her body so he was tipped off balance. With a furious shove born of desperation, she toppled him backward and scrambled from under him. Struggling to get to her feet, she stumbled onto the dry grass. He lunged and caught her ankle. She rolled and kicked wildly—his hand—his face—and finally wrenched herself free.

"Bitch!" His ragged breathing was louder than the wailing wind.

He dived at her and needle point of the weapon grazed her calf. She kicked again, but he was too fast this time. His hand closed around her ankle and he began to drag her back. Clawing, she realized she had dropped the broken champagne glass. She groped for it, screaming as he rolled her onto her back and tried to pin her arms. Searching for leverage, she grabbed the blanket. One of the hot candles seared her fingertips. Biting back the pain, she grabbed the cup and flung it at him.

Molten wax splashed across his face, and the candle sputtered out. Mark screamed in agony as he let go of her and tried to wipe the scalding wax from his eyes. Gasping for breath, Jeanne scrambled away on her hands and knees.

Which way was the road? It didn't matter. Just get as far from him as possible. She glanced back and saw him yank up the blanket to wipe his eyes. The other candles spilled and tumbled, sputtering out except for one that overturned onto the parched, stiff grass. In moments a ring of spurting flames grew around it. Somersaulted by the wind, a paper plate fell into the ring of fire and flared like a torch. In the macabre light, Jeanne stumbled to her feet and raced for the trees.

CHAPTER 41
†

HE WAS ALMOST to the summit. The lights of the helicopter blinked through the trees. It was like looking for a sand fly on the beach, Nasty thought. Bonner had an hour's head start. By now he and the Donovan woman could be on foot. They might not even be in the park, but Nasty was banking on Bonner's sticking to the scenario. He'd consider it part of the game. This was the final scene of the script. To Bonner's perverted mind, the challenge was here.

"Anything yet?" Nasty radioed the helicopter.

"A couple of fast-moving animals," came the answer. "Coyotes, most likely. They're all over the place. We're coming to the summit. Do you want us to go down the other side?"

"Affirmative."

"Holy shit!"

"What is it, Chopper Two?" Nasty demanded.

"Fire! Spreading fast."

"All cars, read!" Nasty yelled into the mike. "Fire on Mt. Hollywood Drive." Overhead, the helicopter began to circle, and its powerful searchlight came on. There was a scramble of voices on the radio asking for coordinates and dispatching trucks.

"There's a car parked not far from the fire," Chopper Two said. "Hey—I've got someone on foot running from the scene."

"Let's go," Nasty yelled. "All cars!"

He hit the accelerator. The car shot into the path cut by the headlights. The tires screeched around a curve. Almost immediately the road twisted in the opposite direction, and Nasty spun the wheel without slowing. The car rocked but held the pavement. When it spun around another sharp turn, Nasty saw the small bright glow of the fire off to the west.

Jeanne pushed through trees blindly. Her feet tangled in undergrowth, pitching her to her knees and tearing at her flesh. Every breath raked her lungs. She slammed into something and fell back gasping with pain. She couldn't slow down. She couldn't take the chance that she had stopped Mark for very long. If he was following her, she'd never hear him until it was too late.

Suddenly she was out in the open. Glancing around, she searched for something to give her direction, but the night was a collage of grays. She stumbled on, staggering like a drunk through the rough saw grass. Her body was raw with bruises and scratches. When she ran into a stand of castor bean plants, she swatted at them in panic.

She didn't dare stop. If Mark came through the trees behind her, her light-colored clothing would make her easy to see and he'd head straight for her. Her brain was still paralyzed by the realization that Mark was the Los Feliz Stabber. How could she have been taken in so completely? He'd been her friend—pleasant and helpful, when all the while . . .

She set out again, more slowly because her throat was so tight she had trouble getting air into her lungs. The wind, tainted now by the acrid odor of smoke, whipped and tugged at her from every direction. Squinting, she saw a darker spot in the gray ahead of her. Another grove of trees? Or was it the same one? She stopped and looked around, terrified of blundering and heading toward Mark instead of away. To her left the glow of the fire was much brighter now, showing above the trees and through them. Against its spectral glow, something moved.

She whirled and raced for the dark spot ahead. It shifted and changed like a mirage, keeping its distance instead of getting closer. Suddenly her foot plummeted into a hole, and she fell headlong into stinging nettles. The breath knocked out of her, she lay whimpering, her eyes streaming. When she finally sat up, she wiped her face and spat dirt from her mouth. A new pain had been added to the agony of her body. One foot felt as if it had been thrust into the fire. She touched it and winced as she forced herself to move her ankle. It hurt fiercely, but it wasn't broken. Her shoe was gone. She groped, found it, and forced it onto her foot, enduring the pain.

Then she looked around again. Where was the fire? She couldn't see it! There was only a dark line against the slightly lighter sky. It took a minute to realize she'd fallen into a shallow wash. Good luck or bad? If she couldn't see the fire, she was hidden from Mark. But she couldn't see him either. How near was he?

She had to rest. She threw back her head and gulped air greedily.

Ten seconds. No more. I have to keep moving. The road can't be far.

Maybe the road was a mistake. Mark would figure she'd head that way, and he would too. If his sense of direction was better than hers, he might reach it first. And be waiting for her. She sobbed. She had no choice. It was her only chance even though she was miles from the movie location

... miles from help of any kind. She sobbed again at the grim irony of considering the park gates a safety factor.

Taking another gulp of air, she made herself move. She crawled up the incline, praying she was going in the right direction. As she reached the lip of the gully, a light swept across the hillside. Terrified, she threw herself flat and pressed her face into the dusty grass. Her heartbeat sounded loud enough to be heard over the wailing wind, and she strained to listen for any sign of Mark. The night was filled with so many noises, her ears thundered. Finally she lifted her head and peeked over the rim of the gully again. The fire was still to her left. In the distance in the opposite direction she saw a clear, sharp light fan among the trees. Headlights! Suddenly another light poured out of the sky. Its huge circle of illumination missed her as it swept across the distance between the gully and the fire. In its bright glare she saw Mark Bonner racing toward her. Sobbing, she got to her feet and ran.

Nasty slowed almost to a stop, peering along the side of the road for a trail. Smoke was already roiling and swirling over the summit of the hill, and he could feel the heat of the fire when he rolled down the window. How the hell had Bonner gotten down there? The headlights poking through the night detailed sooty brush and a heavy stand of trees.

If there was a road, he'd have to keep it clear for the fire trucks. With this wind the whole hillside would be an inferno in minutes. Coughing, Nasty yelled into the mike as he rolled up the window. "Chopper Two, where's the man on foot?"

"Lost him, Stabber Command. He ducked under some trees."

"Turn off the searchlight and use the Probe Eye."

"He's too close to the fire. All I get it one big hot spot."

"Turn off the light and see if you can flush him out."

"Roger."

The spotlight went out and the eerie orange glow of the fire painted the sky.

CHAPTER 42
✝

HER LUNGS WERE ready to explode. The pain stinging her body was overridden by the searing heat of every breath. Blinded by smoke and tears, she plunged on, struggling back to her feet each time she fell and praying that the helicopter searchlight wouldn't show Mark where she was. The keening wail of fire sirens pierced the night, and she saw smoke-veiled lights blink in the darkness as fire engines labored up the mountain.

The heat of the fire was all around her, pressing like a wall from every direction as the wind carried it. How far was it to the road? Had she become confused again? Her body trembled with exhaustion. She wiped her eyes and blinked as a billow of smoke engulfed her. Coughing and sputtering helplessly, she fell to her knees. It was an eternity before she could finally breathe again and raise her head. The fire was closer. For a moment she felt the blessed relief of clear air as the wind shifted, but almost instantly it gave way to thick, eddying smoke that drew her into its core, singeing her hair and scorching her skin. Staying low, she crawled on.

Without warning she was plunged into darkness when

the floodlight from the sky went out. She was blind until her eyes adjusted. The fire was still behind her, but the wind was dropping burning embers everywhere, and new flames were springing up all around her. The ground under her hands and knees was getting hot. She could no longer distinguish the noise of the fire sirens from the roar of the fire and the helicopter. Overhead, the floodlight came back on and swept in a slow circle behind her. She scrambled out of its reach.

When her hands encountered a hard surface, she stopped in confusion until she realized it was the road. She had reached the road! She fell to it and pressed her face and bare breasts against the pavement, sobbing.

A hand grabbed her roughly and rolled her over. She tried to scream but the sound was lost in the deafening roar of the flames blazing a trail through the brush and the trees a hundred yards behind her. Mark Bonner, his face hideously painted by smoke and soot and bits of wax, grinned evilly. His eyes were red and swollen, and his clothes were filthy. A ragged tear left one side of his shirt hanging over his hip. He was still holding the weapon, and the tip of the needle winked in the light of the fire.

Cursing, he fell atop her and put the steel needle to her breast. His voice rasped, "Smart little bitch throwing the candle like that. Yeah, you really caught me with that one. What are you going to do now, huh? Got any more bright ideas?" His hand moved while he talked, putting the stiletto point of the weapon at her waist and slashing her slacks and underpants and ripping them away. He put the steel tip to her breast again while he worked at the fastening of his jeans.

"No more moves for you. I win." He shifted his thumb to the release button. "Listen for the click, baby. When you hear it, the game is over." He positioned himself over her.

Jeanne closed her eyes, and the noise of the inferno screamed inside her head. No matter how loud it was, she knew she'd hear that final small click when it came.

Mark grunted and drove her legs apart. She steeled herself for the invasion of her body and the horror he promised, but suddenly his weight lifted. Click. The faint sound, audible against the dull roar of the fire because of her terror, made Jeanne's eyes fly open. Outlined against a circle of light and the glow of the raging fire, someone was pulling Bonner off her. The weapon in his hand was no longer a tiny needle but a slashing blade that he tried to bring in contact with the grappling figure. Sobbing, she rolled across the blacktop, out of range, too dazed to wonder who had rescued her, wanting only to escape. From the tangle of figures almost obscured by the rolling smoke, one broke away and raced down the hill. The other one started after him, then backed away as the wind swept the fire forward in a sudden burst.

"Bonner!" The hoarse cry was lost in the roar of the inferno.

Mark plunged from the road, arms outstretched, head thrown back like a football player celebrating the winning touchdown, headlong into the flames. For an instant he was a dark outline against the orange holocaust. Then, as the wind swirled and swept the fire downhill once more, he disappeared. The other man ran to Jeanne and grabbed her.

Still terrified, she screamed, "Don't touch me," but the cry was only a pleading whisper from her cracked lips. He pulled her to her feet and dragged her toward the headlights.

Nasty pushed her into the front seat of the car and pulled off his suit coat to wrap around her as he got behind the wheel. He released the brake and put the car in gear. Squinting through the smoke, he inched past the flames that were licking at the roadside. A fire siren screamed close behind them and lights flashed. Nasty accelerated and started down the twisting mountain road.

Her body ached. There wasn't a patch that wasn't bruised or wounded. The emergency room doctor had treated her burns, cauterized the stab wounds, and bound her sprained ankle. Clad in a hospital robe a nurse had given her to replace her tattered clothing, Jeanne lay on the gurney staring at the white acoustical ceiling of the curtained cubicle.

"Mrs. Donovan?"

She turned her head at the soft sound of her name. Sergeant Lopez let the curtain close behind him and came to her side. Lopez's tan suit was smudged with soot and dirt, and one sleeve hung loose across his bandaged left arm.

"Thank you," Jeanne whispered. The sound scraped through her bruised throat, thick with the sedative she'd been given.

"I don't want to tire you," Lopez said.

Jeanne smiled to show him it was all right. Her tongue was too dry to moisten her lips. "Was Mark the Los Feliz Stabber?"

"Yes. We found the items he took from each of his victims in his apartment and a scrapbook of clippings about the murders from the newspapers. That and the weapon he dropped on the road. Did you know he was a security guard in the building where your studio is?"

When she shook her head, Lopez said, "He had keys to every door in the building."

So that was how he had gotten the script and shooting schedule. She wondered if it accounted for the unexplained memo about the alley scene. Poor Mark— She caught herself before she could pity him.

"Is he. . . ?"

"He's dead. There's no way he could have survived. They'll find his body when the fire's out and the ashes cool. What's left of it anyhow."

She closed her eyes. The nightmare was over. How could she have been fooled so completely by Bonner's friendliness? Sighing, she looked at Lopez again. He had saved her life.

"It's like you said, isn't it?" she whispered.

"What's that, Mrs. Donovan?"

"The neighbor who can always be counted on. The boy next door. Jack the Ripper and the boy next door . . ."

"Yes, I guess it is. Speaking of the boy next door, you can thank Sonny Crenshaw for giving us the lead we needed. He saw Bonner tamper with your car so he'd be able to drive you back to the park. And we wouldn't have known about Bonner's collection of murder souvenirs in the apartment if Sonny wasn't in the habit of borrowing his mother's keys so he could snoop when tenants weren't home."

Jeanne's eyes stung with tears. Poor Sonny. He'd been frightened of Mark all along because in his simplicity, he'd seen through Bonner's mask of sanity. She closed her eyes again, and tears squeezed between the lids. Poor, dear Sonny. The curtain whispered softly, and when Jeanne opened her eyes, Glenn was standing beside her.

Lopez said, "I'll leave you two alone now. We'll need official statements from each of you. No rush. Whenever you're strong enough, Mrs. Donovan."

He smiled and left. Glenn propped the crutches against the gurney and bent to kiss Jeanne. His lips were tender. "Are you okay, honey?"

"Yes."

"When I think how close you came to . . ." Tears filled his eyes, and Jeanne raised a bandaged hand to his cheek.

"It's over, hon."

He kissed her again. "The doctor thinks you should stay overnight in case there are any aftershocks."

"I want to go home."

"You're sure?"

"I'm sure."

* * *

She lay staring at the thin slash of morning sunshine beyond the blinds. The fan whirred like a lazy cricket. The bed beside her was empty, and she had the fleeting thought that she should get up and fix breakfast, but she didn't stir. She was content to let the day slide into existence gradually.

The bedroom door opened, and Glenn hobbled laboriously on his crutches as he tried to balance a tray.

"You shouldn't be doing that," she scolded automatically.

"And you should sleep till noon. But since neither of us always does what we're supposed to, what do you say we celebrate with breakfast in bed?" He set down the tray, spilling only a few drops of coffee in the process. A wrapped foil package and two fresh croissants filled a plate beside the coffee cups. Glenn grinned. "The menu this morning includes your choice of croissants, picked up at the bakery by special messenger Sonny Crenshaw, or today's special: fresh-baked coffee cake, compliments of that renowned star of the silver screen Pearl Gannon."

"I'll try the croissants," she said, laughing.

He put aside the crutches and sat beside her. "A wise choice, madam. Very wise." He kissed a bandaged wound on her chin.

"Are you all right, hon?" she asked. The ordeal had left dark shadows under his eyes.

"Stop worrying about me and concentrate on yourself for a change." He kissed the tip of her nose. "Lopez called. The fire's out. They've found Bonner's body. The case is closed."

"Thank God."

"Thank Sonny Crenshaw, too. He showed them the tools down in the storage bin where Bonner worked on the knife when he thought no one was home. He also saw Bonner pick up that prostitute the other night while he was out riding his bike. He recognized the woman's picture on TV. Lopez says they have enough evidence that would stand up in court if Bonner had ever been brought to trial."

"I'm glad it didn't come to that." They'd never know what had driven Mark Bonner to madness and murder. It was over. Cut and a wrap, Jeanne thought.

"Terry Faust called. Brad Raven says you can have the day off." Glenn grinned and winked. "I got the impression it took a little arguing on Terry's part. It's nice to know you're indispensable."

Jeanne studied his expression. There was no hint of resentment or jealousy in his voice. She took his hand.

"Then we're going to live happily ever after in Movieland?"

He brushed her face with his hand and drew her to his lips. "Everything you ever wanted is within reach, baby. Go for it!" He kissed her gently, then more passionately. When he drew away, he grinned. "Besides, with Pearl Gannon sharing her memorabilia and coffee cake, how could I leave?"

Jeanne swatted him lovingly and they fell back against the pillows entwined in each other's arms.

The SILENCE of the LAMBS

THE ELECTRIFYING BESTSELLER BY
THOMAS HARRIS

"THRILLERS DON'T COME ANY BETTER THAN THIS."
—*CLIVE BARKER*

"HARRIS IS QUITE SIMPLY THE BEST SUSPENSE NOVELIST WORKING TODAY." — *The Washington Post*

THE SILENCE OF THE LAMBS
Thomas Harris
_____ 91543-8 $5.95 U.S. _____ 91544-6 $6.95 Can.

Publishers Book and Audio Mailing Service
P.O. Box 120159, Staten Island, NY 10312-0004

Please send me the book(s) I have checked above. I am enclosing $_____
(please add $1.25 for the first book, and $.25 for each additional book to cover postage and handling. Send check or money order only—no CODs.)

Name _____

Address _____

City _____ State/Zip _____

Please allow six weeks for delivery. Prices subject to change without notice.

SILENCE 10/89

THE MEASURE OF A MAN IS HOW WELL HE SURVIVES LIFE'S MEAN STREETS

BOLD NEW CRIME NOVELS BY TODAY'S HOTTEST TALENTS

BAD GUYS (July 1989)
Eugene Izzi
____ 91493-8 $3.95 U.S. ____ 91494-6 $4.95 Can.

CAJUN NIGHTS (August 1989)
D.J. Donaldson
____ 91610-8 $3.95 U.S. ____ 91611-6 $4.95 Can.

MICHIGAN ROLL (September 1989)
Tom Kakonis
____ 91684-1 $3.95 U.S. ____ 91686-8 $4.95 Can.

SUDDEN ICE (October 1989)
Jim Leeke
____ 91620-5 $3.95 U.S. ____ 91621-3 $4.95 Can.

DROP-OFF (November 1989)
Ken Grissom
____ 91616-7 $3.95 U.S. ____ 91617-5 $4.95 Can.

A CALL FROM L.A. (December 1989)
Arthur Hansl
____ 91618-3 $3.95 U.S. ____ 91619-1 $4.95 Can.

Publishers Book and Audio Mailing Service
P.O. Box 120159, Staten Island, NY 10312-0004

Please send me the book(s) I have checked above. I am enclosing $_____ (please add $1.25 for the first book, and $.25 for each additional book to cover postage and handling. Send check or money order only—no CODs.)

Name _____

Address _____

City _____ State/Zip _____

Please allow six weeks for delivery. Prices subject to change without notice.

MS 9/89